LOGAN SPRINTED ACROSS THE FLOOR OF THE SPARSELY FURNISHED HOUSE, AND SUDDENLY SOMETHING SOUNDED WRONG BENEATH HIS FEET.

He'd run across a throw rug, but it had made a different noise from the rest of the floor. He yanked the rug up and, lo and behold, there was a trap door beneath it, with a small hinged ring set into one side.

Yanking on the ring, Logan hauled it open and dropped straight through. Hunt was down there; he could smell him.

It was only as his feet hit the ground in the darkened, unfinished basement that he realized his mistake as he picked up the telltale aroma of cordite.

He had just enough time, in the dimness of the basement, to see Hunt standing by the far wall. Hunt waggled his fingers mockingly and then stepped backward into the wall. Now the only things left in the basement were Logan and the incendiary device that was ticking down to zero.

Logan knew he had no chance of getting clear. That didn't stop him from leaping straight up toward the trap door. He felt the explosion before he heard it, and it propelled him upward, all heat and flame and then the noise came, a split instant later, and it was deafening. The world   im and then black.

I went red and orange around lunch and then

Pocket Star Books
A Division of Simon & Schuster, Inc.
1230 Avenue of the Americas
New York, NY 10020

First Pocket Star Books paperback edition September 2008

POCKET STAR BOOKS and colophon are registered trademarks of Simon & Schuster, Inc.

For information about special discounts for bulk purchases, please contact Simon & Schuster Special Sales at 1-800-456-6798 or business@simonandschuster.com.

Cover art by John Van Fleet

Manufactured in the United States of America

10 9 8 7 6 5 4 3 2 1

ISBN-13: 978-1-4165-1076-5
ISBN-10:   1-4165-1076-1

WOLVERINE®

ELECTION DAY

a novel by
Peter David

based on the
Marvel Comic Book

POCKET **STAR** BOOKS

NEW YORK   LONDON   TORONTO   SYDNEY

Read these other exciting Marvel novels from Pocket Books!

him would be the most uncool thing that anyone could possibly do. "It would be, like, 'How can you be voting for anybody else, because they're all totally losers?'" Matthew said to himself. "Make it so that people would make fun of you if you voted for anybody but Senator Mazone."

He returned to the DVD and was about to start it up again when he noticed the time. Immediately, all thoughts of politics in general and Senator Mazone in specific fled his mind. One had to have priorities, after all, and in this case, Matthew's priorities had shifted away from the real world of politics and into the unreal world of television adventure.

Kaz was on!

His mother hated *Kaz*, absolutely hated it. She said it was mindless and violent and gave Matthew all sorts of ideas that he didn't need to be carrying around in his young head. In retrospect, Matthew decided that his mistake had been in trying to convince his mom of what a great show it was in the first place.

"He's this bounty hunter, see," Matthew had said as he encouraged her to sit and watch an episode with him. "In fact, the guy on TV, that's not an actor. That's really him, playing himself."

"It's a reality show?"

"Nah. Better. It's stories that are based on his actual cases. And all his cases are cool because he's so cool."

"And what's so cool about him?" his mother had gamely said.

Buoyed by the belief that she had seemed willing to share his favorite program with him, Matthew had warmed to the subject immediately. "He's got super-powers. He got his powers from aliens that—"

His mother had stopped him right there. "Aliens?"

"Sure!"

"From another world."

"Yeah!"

"That's ridiculous."

"Aw, come on, Ma! Everybody knows there's aliens!"

"What everybody knows is not what I know," his mother had said in an annoyed tone. "Just because other people are gullible enough to believe in wild tales derived from mass hysteria . . ."

He hadn't known what she was talking about, and ultimately it hadn't mattered. After giving him a ten-minute lecture on the evils of accepting as gospel the wild beliefs and speculations of others, she had forbidden Matthew to watch *Kaz* when it aired in its time slot of nine P.M. every Wednesday on NBC. Mom even made sure to check that if Matthew was up in his room at that day and time, the television was safely off.

Mom, however, had not realized that the Sci-Fi Channel aired repeats of *Kaz* on Friday at seven P.M., and the magic hour had struck. So, after glancing out his door to make certain his mother was nowhere around, Matthew tuned the cable box to the Sci-Fi Channel, turned the volume down, and plunked himself in front of the TV to watch the adventures of everyone's favorite bounty hunter.

Tonight's episode looked primed to be a good one, something involving a competing bounty hunter who was actually a cyborg from the future. Matthew watched the teaser with barely restrained enthusiasm while musing upon the incredibly exciting life that Kaz had. "Nothing cool like that is ever going to happen to me," he muttered.

A glow—a series of glows, actually—came streaming through his window. At first, he thought it was lightning, and then it came across like swarms of fireflies, although he couldn't begin to guess why they'd be amassing there. Slowly, he climbed down off his bed and padded softly over to the window.

Just as he reached it, the lights shone directly in his face, and he realized they were man-made rather than something conjured by nature. He thought he caught a glimpse of shadowed forms in the trees and on the ground, but the light glaring in his eyes flash-blinded him before he could determine exactly who or what was approaching.

He stepped back from the window, reflexively throwing his arms in front of his face, and instinctually called out to his mother.

The window exploded inward, wood and glass spraying in all directions. Matthew let out an alarmed shriek and tried to run for his closed bedroom door.

He was five steps away from escape when a knife

sliced through the air and thudded into the door just above the knob. Matthew had been reaching for it but automatically yanked his hand back.

If Matthew had ignored the threat, had kept going, grabbed for the door anyway, and yanked it open, he might have gotten out. Chances were that whoever was doing this simply would have pursued him to another part of the house, so he would have bought himself only seconds at most. It was as if he were paralyzed, unsure of what in God's name he should do, and that paralysis was all the intruders needed. Matthew's feet left the ground as he was hauled backward. His screams were quickly muffled as he was dumped unceremoniously into a sack.

"We have him," said a gruff nearby voice with an odd accent.

Matthew was able to make out another voice crackling in a filtered manner, which suggested that the man who had just spoken was having a conversation over some sort of walkie-talkie. The responding voice said briskly, "Get going."

"The mother is coming up the steps. Should we—?"

Matthew's heart stopped within his chest. They were going to wait for his mother to burst into the room, and then they were either going to kidnap her . . . or worse. The notion was so horrific that, as much as he wanted to shout a warning, his throat had closed up with terror. He tried to speak but could manage only a constricted whisper.

In the end, it didn't matter. The voice over the speaker said, "She can't ID you, and she can't stop you. Get out of there now."

The brief feeling of relief that pulsed through him about his mother quickly evaporated as his own predicament loomed large before him. He heard the voice of Kaz the Bounty Hunter talking with confidence about the fact that no one and nothing could get away from him if he came looking for them.

"Save me, Kaz," he managed to whisper. Then he was hauled through the air, and he could sense—although naturally he couldn't see—that he was no longer in his room. The chill air cut through the sack, and he shivered, but not just because of the coldness. His world, previously so safe and secure, suddenly had become a terrifying and uncertain place.

In the distance, he heard his mother screaming his name. Then it was cut off by the abrupt slam of what sounded like a car trunk. He could hear an engine already running; the car had been waiting for him. Seconds later, it hurtled forward, causing Matthew to be slammed up against the inside of the trunk. The top of the bag was drawn too tightly, and his body was far too constricted, to make the slightest move.

Insanely, the last thing that went through his mind before the terror overwhelmed him and shut down his conscious thoughts was, *Mom's gonna see that I had Kaz on. She's going to be so pissed off . . .*

2

WHAT HAD BEGUN AS A FRIENDLY CARD GAME erupted into a potential fight, and Corporal Tony Westlake wanted to remain as far away from it as possible.

Unfortunately, he was pulled right into the middle of it.

Five of his fellow corporals were grouped around a card table in the commons room, and up until a minute ago, everything had been quiet.

Corporal Alex Palmer had just put down his winning hand of a full house, aces over tens, and was reaching forward to scoop up the sizable pile of chips that were in front of him. Across the table from him, however, Corporal Jason Wright—who had just seen his inside straight fail to win yet another hand—scowled fiercely and said, "Wait a minute."

"What?" Palmer looked confused.

"Let me see those cards."

Palmer shrugged and held them up. Wright leaned forward, looked closely, and scowled. "The ace of hearts looks wrong."

"Looks wrong how?"

"Because I was holding the ace of hearts before, and the corner was a little frayed, and the one you're holding isn't."

"You're imagining it."

"The hell I am."

Wright started to reach for the deck, and Palmer put a hand on his, stopping him. "What do you think you're doing?"

"I'm gonna look through the rest of the deck to see if there's another ace of hearts, is what I'm doing."

"You saying I'm cheating?"

"I'm saying I'm going to check. If you think it's because you're cheating, then . . ."

That was the moment when Westlake, who simply wanted to get a candy bar from the vending machine, chose to walk across the room. He was oblivious to the problem that was erupting at the table; all he cared about was getting a Milky Way.

"I'm not cheating!" Palmer said loudly just as Westlake walked past him.

Instantly, Westlake's skin turned red. Not red as in blushing, red as in bright, unmistakable crimson.

It was impossible to miss. Westlake was typically fair-skinned, freckled from his time in the sun, with pale blond hair and blue eyes. He had a round, almost babyish face, so when it glowed bright red as it was doing now, it bore a resemblance to a tomato.

Wright's reaction was immediate. He was on his feet, pointing to Westlake but glaring at Palmer. *"Aha!"*

"What 'aha'? There's no 'aha'!" Palmer was trying to sound as if Westlake's abrupt shift in skin color meant nothing, but everyone in the room knew perfectly well that it, in fact, meant everything.

"Keep me out of this, wouldja?" Westlake said pleadingly.

Instead, Wright grabbed Westlake by the arm and pushed him right up near Palmer as he said, "Say it again! Say that you're not lying again!"

"I'm not saying nothing with this freak standing here!"

"Hey! I'm not a freak!" Westlake said, his voice heating with anger. The redness had subsided from his skin.

"You're just pissed with him because he could tell you're a liar!" said Wright.

"I'm *not* a liar!"

The instant Palmer said that, Westlake's skin promptly crimsoned again. Westlake moaned, looking at his hands and seeing the unwanted change that had come over him yet again.

Furious, Wright—having let go his grip on Westlake—upended the table, clearing the path between Palmer and him. The other soldiers yelped as cards and chips scattered in every direction. "You're a damned cheat!" shouted Wright.

Before Palmer could respond (not that anything he could have said would have done him much good), someone called out, "MPs!"

Sure enough, three military policemen strode into the large room. Instantly, all was silent as the MPs looked around at the disarray. The foremost of them, a barrel-chested sergeant, appeared to consider what he was seeing before slowly hooking his thumbs into his belt and saying in a lazy drawl, "Problem in here, gentlemen?"

"No problem, Sarge," came the responses, echoed by several of the men.

"Appears to be a considerable mess."

"I got up too fast," said Wright, although he cast a venomous glance in Palmer's direction. "My fault."

"Mine, too," Palmer said halfheartedly.

The sergeant slowly nodded and then said quietly, "Well, then, I think you'd best clean this up. Disorder like this isn't acceptable, even in a volunteer army, now, is it, men?" There were muttered responses in the affirmative, and the sergeant lanced the entire room with a single gaze and said, "*Is it*, men?"

"*No, Sergeant!*" they said, in unison this time.

"Good." His voice was barely above a whisper. He swept one final look over them and walked out, the other MPs following.

Having no idea what else to do, Westlake said quietly, "Look, Palmer, I'm sorry about . . ."

"Shut up," Palmer said. "Just shut up."

Westlake immediately did so. As Palmer, Wright, and the others set about picking up the fallen cards and chips, Westlake left the room, no longer feeling the least bit hungry. He felt as if every eye in the place was on him and couldn't help but remember the comments from his mother about how his addiction to candy would be the death of him yet. Somehow, he suspected that this wasn't the sort of situation she'd foreseen, and yet her concerns might well be more valid than he'd have ever credited.

Corporal Westlake suddenly awoke in his bunk to complete darkness.

It wasn't a result of the lateness of the hour, although it was a moonless night over Fort Randolph, North Carolina. Instead, it was a result of a blindfold being wrapped around his eyes at exactly the same moment that a length of electrical tape was being slapped across his mouth.

If it had covered his nose, he would have suffocated within moments. The fact that it didn't, and that he was being allowed to breathe, was small comfort.

He tried to sit up, to fight back against whoever was assaulting him, but his attackers were too quick and too organized. Within seconds, they had his hands tied behind him, and his feet were lashed together as well. Then he was lifted clear of his bunk and quickly transported outside the barracks. There was a brief pause, and then he heard a whispered *"All clear!"* Obviously, whoever was abducting him was making sure that there were no MPs around.

Then he was hustled to the back of a Jeep and tossed roughly into it. There was some concerted, triumphant whooping, and he caught a whiff of alcohol. His assailants—and he could guess the identity of at least one of them—had obviously had too much to drink. He could only hope that they were so hammered that they'd wind up crashing the Jeep rather than driving it to wherever their destination was.

Of course, if they *did* crash the thing, that likewise wouldn't turn out too well for him. So it was pretty much a damned-if-they-did, damned-if-they-didn't situation.

He bounced around in the backseat, and the farther Palmer and his friends (it had to be Palmer—he recognized the voice for starters, and then there was the pesky thing called motive) got from the barracks, the louder and more raucous they sounded. They were becoming more confident of not being caught, or else they were becoming progressively drunker and so cared less.

The Jeep abruptly lurched to a halt, and Westlake was yanked up and out of the back. Seconds later, he hit the ground with a bone-shaking thud. Air wanted to escape from his lungs in response, but because his mouth was covered, all he managed to do was swallow the air right back into his chest.

Then a foot struck deep into his gut, causing him to curl up in a ball. He had no protection, clad only in his general-issue green boxers and T-shirt. He whimpered against the restriction on his mouth and would have muttered a string of profanities if his mouth hadn't been covered.

"Here's the deal, freak," came a rough voice. Still Palmer's, but he was belatedly trying to make an effort to disguise it. "You're gonna go to the base commander tomorrow, and you're gonna get out of the Army. I don't care how you do it. Tell him you murdered somebody. Tell him you're gay. Whatever it takes. But I want you off this base and out of the Army. Or what's happening here"—and he was kicked again—"is going to be like a walk in the park compared to what happens next. And don't think you can just ask for a transfer, because if you don't think this is going to happen again, wherever you go, then you're even more stupid than I gave you credit for. Here's just a sample of what you have to look forward to if you don't do what I'm saying."

That was when the screaming started.

But it wasn't Westlake. Not that he could have screamed even if he wanted to. It was only a few moments before he realized what was happening, and even then he didn't really understand. He heard the sound of metal, a *snikt* noise that sounded like someone popping out a switchblade. No . . . a number of switchblades. Was there truly a squad of men there, armed with switchblades?

Whatever was happening, it was fast. He heard bodies thudding to the ground and more screams, each cut off abruptly. Someone managed to fire a gun, and then came the sound of metal on metal, followed by an astounded *"Oh, my God!"* Then more punching, more bodies falling.

And then nothing.

The silence seemed to stretch on forever, although it was just a few seconds. Then the tape was abruptly torn off Westlake's mouth. He let out a startled, pained yelp.

"You Westlake?" came a gruff voice that Westlake didn't recognize.

"Y-yes. Who are you?"

He felt something sharp and metal being slid up under the blindfold, and it was cut loose. He blinked several times. His vision was still blurred, but there appeared to be a man looking down at him. He had thick black hair spiked on either side and considerable sideburns. His eyes were dark and cold and looked as if they'd seen enough violence for a hundred lifetimes.

Palmer was lying unconscious nearby. So were half a dozen other soldiers, scattered all around.

Westlake tried to see how many friends the dark-haired man had brought with him. He had to have several backing him up, because there was no way one man could have taken down all those guys, even though they'd had too much to drink.

There was no one else around. They were alone on what Westlake now recognized as the obstacle course.

"What the hell?" whispered Westlake.

The dark-haired man was now helping Westlake sit

forward. Something sliced through the bonds around Westlake's wrists, presumably the same knife the man had used on his blindfold. The stranger turned and, his back blocking Westlake's view, cut through the restraints on Westlake's ankles as well. Westlake tried to get a glimpse of the knife so formidable that it sliced through just about anything with one swipe, not even any sawing required. But when the man turned back to face him, Westlake didn't see a knife of any kind—his hands were empty.

"Where'd it go?" said Westlake.

The man gave him an odd look. "Where'd what go?"

"The knife. The knife you just used to cut me free." Westlake was shaking his hands and stretching his feet, trying to restore circulation.

"Oh." That's all the man said. No explanation. "Can you stand?"

Westlake paused and then hoisted himself to his feet. He staggered, and the man caught him. At that point, Westlake realized how short the guy was. It wasn't as if Westlake was a giant, but his rescuer was fully a head shorter.

This was becoming more insane by the moment. An unarmed runt had taken down half a dozen men in less than a minute? What the hell?

"Are you Special Forces?" he said.

The man seemed vaguely amused by the question. "You could say that. Come on. In the Jeep. I'll drive you back to the barracks."

"What about them?" He pointed a thumb at the unconscious forms of Palmer and his associates.

"I'll send MPs to round them up. With any luck, when they wake up, they'll be in custody."

The man hopped behind the wheel, and Westlake, still staggering a bit, eased himself into the passenger seat. The stranger gunned the engine and set the Jeep rolling.

Westlake couldn't take his eyes off the guy. He had a thin cigar clutched between his teeth. The cigar was halfway burned through, and Westlake realized he'd probably been smoking it the entire time he'd been dismantling the soldiers.

Incredible.

He didn't bother to ask his identity, because he'd already done so twice and had received no response. As the man drove, the wind that blew past them didn't so much as ruffle his hair. He had to have some high-powered kind of gel keeping it in place. The man noticed that Westlake was eyeballing him and said, "What?" as the passing wind caused the embers of his cigar to flare.

"I don't know who the hell you are," said Westlake, "or what the hell you do, but whatever it is you do do, I have the feeling you're the best there is at it."

Ever so slightly, the corners of the man's mouth twitched.

"I get that a lot," he said.

3

"**WHAT THE HELL DO YOU MEAN, YOU LOST HIM?**"

General Tiberius Doyle, base commander of Fort Randolph, was striding down the corridor while bellowing at Major Concord, his head of base security. Doyle looked heavyset, but most of it was solid muscle. He was middle-aged and broad-shouldered, his close-cropped black hair only just starting to show flecks of gray. He tended to walk with his chin outthrust to give it a leaner edge and cut down on the slight bit of extra skin he had hanging there.

Major Concord, whip-thin and sloe-eyed, spoke with a faint trace of a New Zealand accent he'd inherited from his parents. "Technically, General, not me personally. My men did. But, of course," he said quickly, "the buck stops with me."

"You're not exactly covering yourself with glory here, Major." He stopped and turned to face Concord, so quickly that Concord overshot him by a few feet. "So let me see if I'm fully grasping this. A civilian comes rolling up in a Jeep with Corporal Westlake and tells you, calm as you please, that he ambushed half a dozen soldiers out on the obstacle course. Your men take the unnamed man into custody, and while Westlake is swearing out a statement that claims the soldiers abducted him, the unnamed civilian *vanishes* out of where he's being held?"

"There were two guards on duty at all times," said Concord. "I have no idea how he did it. I assure you, we're searching the base for him. I have every confidence, General, that we'll find him in short order."

"That's a startling contrast to what I have, Major. You'll understand if my confidence level is substantially diminished. I want full statements from all concerned parties."

"Yes, sir. The soldiers that Westlake claims assaulted him are in the infirmary, and from what I understand, they're just starting to come around. We'll make certain to present you with the entire story so that you can take appropriate action."

"That's damned decent of you, Major. See that you do." Doyle stormed toward his office and, as he threw open the door, said, "And find that damned civilian!"

He took two steps into his office and promptly jumped back.

The man that every MP on the base was searching for was seated in a chair facing Doyle's desk. He had his legs raised and his feet propped on the edge of the desk. He was sporting brown leather cowboy boots. His fingers were interlaced and resting comfortably on his stomach. "Hey, Doyle," he said, tossing off a casual salute.

"Son of a—!"

Hearing the general's startled exclamation, Concord had run up behind him and was staring in, goggle-eyed. Immediately, he reached for his sidearm even as he shouted, "He's here! All available personnel—"

But Doyle put up a hand, silencing the startled Concord for a moment. It was only for a moment, though, because Concord pulled himself together and said, "You are under arrest!"

"No, he's not."

Concord looked quizzically at Doyle. "What? Sir . . ."

"You don't have enough men. Not in the building and not on the base. Trust me on that. Just go. On my authority, just let it go, Major."

"Sir, I don't understand."

"It's not for you to understand, Major, it's for you to obey."

Concord stiffened and said briskly, "Yes, sir."

He saluted, and Doyle almost didn't return it, distracted as he was by the utterly blasé individual in his office. Then he did return the salute in a perfunctory manner, and as Concord spun on his heel and walked away, Doyle closed his office door behind him.

"I'll be damned," he said softly. "You look the same, Logan. Exactly the same."

"Looking good yourself, Doyle."

"I'm looking like an old man. But you . . . it's uncanny."

Logan shrugged as if it were no major accomplishment not to have aged a day despite the passage of several decades since he'd last seen Doyle. "If I had the weight of those stars on my shoulders, I'd look older, too," said Logan.

Doyle came around his desk and sat, still looking in wonderment at Logan. "What the hell are you doing here? Now, after all this time?"

"Should be obvious to a smart guy like you, Doyle."

"Yes, it should be. It's about the mutant, isn't it?"

"The mutant has a name."

"Yes. Corporal Westlake." He shook his head. "Shocking business. Shocking." He shuffled through the files on his desk and pulled the one with Westlake's name on it. "Exemplary soldier. Superb chopper pilot, by all accounts," he said as he flipped through the file. "The only problem is—"

"He's one of us."

Doyle carefully closed the file folder and laid it on the desk. Then he folded his hands on top of it. "I hope you realize, Logan, that it's not a problem with me. You do understand that, do you not? Putting aside the fact that I don't believe there's room for racism of any sort in this man's army, I wouldn't be here today if it weren't for another mutant who saved my life in Nam."

Logan simply nodded.

"You never did tell me what you were doing over there," Doyle said after a moment.

Logan nodded again.

Doyle smiled in spite of himself. "And you're never planning on telling me, are you?"

This time, Logan shook his head, although he did allow a bit of a smile to creep across his face.

"Damnedest thing I ever did see. When that crossfire you took for me tore your chest open, and then you just . . . just healed. Do you still have any scars from it? From any of it?"

"None that you can see," said Logan.

"That's always the way of it, isn't it?" Doyle paused. "You know, back then, I don't even think I had the word *mutant* in my vocabulary. Not relating to *people*, at any rate."

"That's the problem," said Logan. "To a lot of folks, mutants ain't people."

"Including, it would seem, to some of ours. Trust me, Logan, the soldiers responsible will be dealt with, and dealt with harshly. But how did you know? I mean, obviously, your coming here isn't simply coincidence. You must have shown up because of Westlake's specific situation."

"We've been monitoring Westlake."

"We being the X-Men."

"We being we," said Logan judiciously. "Fact is, some of your boys have been making Westlake's life difficult for a while now. Just reached a flashpoint, that's all.

Truth to tell, there was a little luck involved in my showing up when I did."

"Then again, careful preparation makes its own luck. I have to confess, I'm still a bit confused about how the boy does what he does."

"Westlake's a low-level telepath. He can't access it consciously. When he's standing near someone who fibs, it releases endorphins that cause his skin to go bright red. He's a walking lie detector."

"That's amazing. Perhaps a chopper is the wrong place for him. He'd be invaluable in the solicitor general's office . . . military discipline . . ."

"Maybe the kid wants to fly. Beats the hell out of being cast as a rat on his fellow officers 'cause that's what his genetics gave him."

"His desire should be to do what best serves his country."

"I'm not much on telling other people what their desires should be. You?"

Doyle was about to answer when his phone rang. He picked up the phone and said briskly, "Doyle." Then he paused, said, "A moment, please," and pressed the hold button. "I need to take this privately. Would you mind . . . ?"

He gestured toward a door at the far side of the room. Logan inclined his head slightly in acknowledgment and headed toward it.

Before he exited, Doyle said, "Don't go far. There's a good deal more to discuss and catch up with. If nothing else, I should buy the man who saved my life a beer."

"You sure should."

"And Logan, I know you said you've been monitoring Westlake's current situation. But how exactly have you been doing that? This is a government installation. There are security matters to consider. So how . . . ?"

"Don't ask," said Logan.

Doyle gave it a moment's thought and, having reconsidered, said, "Don't tell."

Logan stepped out into the hallway and spotted Westlake waiting for him. Westlake was seated in a chair, stiff-backed, chin outthrust. He looked as if he were standing at attention while sitting down. Fatigues had been provided for him, so he wasn't just in his khaki undergarments.

When Westlake saw him, the corporal reflexively started to get to his feet as if greeting a superior officer. Then he caught not only himself but also the amused look in Logan's eye and slowly seated himself once more. Logan leaned against the wall and faced him, his arms folded across his chest.

"You're Wolverine, aren't you?" said Westlake.

Logan cocked an eyebrow. "Finally figured it out, huh?"

"It just . . . it made sense."

"How much you know about me?"

"Some stuff. Not a lot." Westlake shifted uncomfortably in the chair, as if he were suddenly ill at ease. "When I figured out I was a . . . you know . . ."

"You can say mutant. Your head won't explode." Logan paused and considered. "Leastways, I don't think it will."

Westlake didn't seem to know quite how to take that and apparently decided to continue as if Logan hadn't spoken. "When I figured out what I was, I started doing, y'know, research. The X-Men kept cropping up. And you. A lot about you. All kinds of stuff—most of it rumors, I figure."

"Rumors?"

"Like that you're immortal. That you've lived for centuries."

Logan gave a choked laugh at that. "Hardly."

"That you're unkillable."

"Well, I don't like to brag."

"That you've got claws that pop right out of your hands. I figure that's what I heard on the obstacle course." When Logan didn't respond, Westlake continued, "People all over the world say they've seen you or spotted you in action. Japan. France. England. Russia. One really old guy swears you helped liberate a concentration camp in World War Two. Some people think you're some sort of demon." Westlake had seemed apprehensive about looking directly at Logan, as if doing so would somehow blind him. Having finally worked up his nerve, however, he said, "So . . . what's going to happen with me now?"

"Well, that's more or less up to you. What do you want to have happen?"

"Honestly? I'd like to go back to the barracks and forget about this whole sorry incident."

"And you think that'll be it?"

"I don't know what you mean."

"Yeah, you do." Logan tilted his head, studying West-lake. "Someone'll come after you again. You're a mutant surrounded by humans."

"I'm human, too," Westlake said sharply.

Logan shrugged. "They won't see it that way."

"I don't care how they see it."

"Yeah, you do. And if you don't, they'll make sure that you do. And I'm not making it my life's work to cover your ass."

"I didn't ask you to."

"No, you didn't, but the time'll come—sooner rather than later—when you'll wish you had."

"So what are you saying?"

"I'm saying it doesn't have to be this way."

"What other way would it be?"

"For one thing, you can come with me."

"With you?" Westlake sounded skeptical. "You mean, be one of the X-Men? Run around in uniforms and fight evil mutants?"

"That's not all we do."

"Yeah, I'm sure you have killer bake sales."

"You've got a pretty big mouth for a guy whose neck I saved a few hours ago."

Westlake was about to give a harsh retort but then thought better of it. "I'm sorry. You're right. It's just . . . I don't see how I can be of use to you guys."

"Trust me, we'd find uses. And you'd be safe."

"Until evil mutants show up at your headquarters and try to kill you."

"You're in the Army, kid. Worrying about enemy forces trying to take you out should be SOP for you. At least with us, you won't have to worry about having one of your own guys out to get you."

"That's true," Westlake admitted.

He slumped back in his chair and appeared to be giving it some thought. Logan waited. He had all the time in the world.

"My dad," Westlake said finally, "was in the Army. So were my two brothers. So were my grandfather and my uncle. It's what we do. It's our family history."

"You shouldn't let yourself feel pressured just because—"

"I don't feel pressured. It's what I wanted to do my whole life. And now I'm supposed to turn away from that just because of the genetic hand I was dealt?"

"I suppose it don't seem too fair."

"Exactly."

"Well, it ain't. Fair, I mean. You got that right. But it is what it is, and what it is is that there are guys who are going to make your life a living hell because of what you are. But if you come with me—"

"Tell me," Westlake said quietly, "would you have

advised the first black soldiers that rather than standing up to racists who made their lives a living hell, they should just go live in a ghetto with their own kind?"

"It's not the same thing at all."

"Isn't it?"

Logan opened his mouth but closed it again without replying.

"Someone's going to have to take the heat in order to break down barriers," said Westlake, sounding more confident in his position with each passing moment. "If that's going to be me, then so be it."

Logan didn't say anything for a time, and when he did, it was with reluctant admiration. "You got more balls than brains, kid, I'll give ya that. Okay . . . look. I'm staying down the road at some dump called Len's Motel. I'll stay there two more days. If you change your mind—and considering the reception you're probably gonna get when you head back to your barracks, you just might—talk to General Doyle. I'll tell him about our little chat. You'll have an honorable discharge, and you can come with me and participate in things that'll help benefit mutantkind."

"I like to think that's what I'm doing by staying here," said Westlake.

Logan was about to answer, but then he turned and glanced at the door through which he'd just come, the one that led to the general's office. The door opened, and Doyle was standing there. Logan could tell instantly from the look on Doyle's face that something had changed.

"Logan," he said, "we need to talk."

"I'd say we do, yeah."

"Not about Westlake . . . no offense, Corporal," he said. "Something bigger has just cropped up."

"That what the phone call was about?"

"Yes. I need you to come back in and watch something on television with me."

Logan stared at him, uncomprehending. "On what channel?"

"It doesn't matter," said Doyle grimly. "Put on any channel you want. It's on all of them."

4

THE IMAGE ON THE TELEVISION SCREEN IN DOYLE'S office was designed to create tumult, confusion, anger, outrage, and a sense of helplessness—all this and more—in the viewer.

Logan was far too trained, far too savvy, and far too controlled to allow any of those emotions to roll through him. Instead, he simply studied the image impassively, leaning against the general's desk while it played and replayed.

Doyle, a hardened battle veteran and tough-as-nails Army officer, likewise gave at least an outward appearance of dispassion. Logan noticed, however, that Doyle's knuckles were turning white. He was squeezing his fists.

There was a man on the screen wearing a blank-faced mask that completely covered his head. He also appeared to have some sort of voice distorter underneath the mask that made it impossible to identify him.

The masked man, however, wasn't what was clearly churning Doyle's guts. Instead, it was the young boy directly in front of him. The youngster's face was ashen, and he was holding a piece of paper in front of him from which he read.

"My name is Matthew Hayes, and there are many innocent children like me. And they have died because the policies of your president have brought needless war to other lands. Now this man is asking that you reelect him. If you do, then . . ." The boy choked, unable to say the next words. The masked man behind him prodded him in the back with the barrel of his gun, and the boy took in a steadying breath and let it out slowly. "Then these men will kill me."

The words hung there a moment. Logan was perfectly still, totally focused.

"They will kill me and record it and make the recording available to everybody." His voice was toneless, flat. He sounded as if he were already dead and speaking from beyond the grave. "And if that seems unfair, that some random boy was chosen to die, consider that it's no more unfair than all the random children who have died under the bombs and bullets of . . ."

He couldn't continue. The boy lost his voice; his next attempt at words was little more than a hoarse whisper, and this time, even having a gun shoved in his back couldn't get him to continue speaking. He was trembling, having trouble standing up, and the masked man roughly pushed him aside.

He stepped forward, thrusting his masked face closer toward the camera. "It may seem that *we* have the power here, Americans, but we do not. *You* do. What happens to this child, Matthew Hayes, is entirely in your hands. If you make the right decision and force the murdering scum who currently occupies the White House out of office, then Matthew Hayes shall live to see his mother once more. If you do not—if, with your votes, you endorse the bellicose policies of the president—then your Election Day will forever commemorate yet another innocent child sacrificed on the altar of American politics. We leave it in your hands. Matthew's mother will pray that you make the right decision."

The image froze on the screen, and the voice of a newscaster solemnly intoned the history of how this particular threatening recording had arrived at the doorsteps of CNN, MSNBC, the *New York Times,* and a dozen other media outlets. Picking up the remote control, Logan jumped from one channel to the next. Doyle had spoken truly; it was all over the place.

"Hell of a thing," Logan said.

"That, Logan, is an understatement."

"That call you got was about this?" When Doyle nodded, Logan said, "Why'd they call you specifically?"

"They didn't. At the same time I was being contacted, they were informing the heads of every military base around the country—perhaps around the world, for all I know. We don't know what we're facing yet."

"You're facing some terrorists, is what you're facing," Logan said matter-of-factly. "Home-grown or foreign-born, too early to say. Probably few in number."

"Why do you say that?"

"Because if they had the resources and enough men—and, frankly, the stomach for it—they wouldn't grab just one kid. They'd grab a dozen and then kill a couple in advance just to show they mean business. What this says to me is that they're hoping they don't have to kill him. If that's the case, they're not exactly hardcore. Hardcore terrorists, they'd kill the kid as soon as look at him."

"You're saying you think the boy has a chance."

"Depends how the vote goes, I guess."

"It may well depend on far greater things than that. Obviously, the federal government is mobilizing every-thing we have. Something not dissimilar to this hap-pened in Spain not long ago, and it affected the turnout of the elections. There cannot be a repeat of that here. We can't simply allow a terrorist cell to impede or dis-rupt the democratic process."

"Sounds like you got a problem."

"I was actually hoping"—and Doyle fixed a stare on him—"that *we* had a problem."

"We?" Logan tilted his head slightly. "Not sure how it's my problem. I don't vote."

"I'm surprised you'd care so little about contributing to the way your country is run."

"Ain't a matter of that. I'm not an American citizen."

"You're not? Where are you from?"

"Around," said Logan.

"Yes, I suppose I should have known better than to expect a straight answer." He seemed momentarily amused but then grew serious again. "Frankly, Logan, I was hoping you might pitch in. Every base in this country is on alert status. At any given moment, we're expected to provide resources, troops, whatever's needed. Due to the seriousness of the situation and the threat that it poses to the electoral process, the Bureau of National Emergency has been put in charge of coordinating the investigation."

"You keep saying that. That this poses a threat to the electoral process. Way I see it, the only thing being threatened, aside from the kid's life, is the president's job. Either way, I'm still not sure where I come in. I'm just one guy. The BNE has thousands of agents at its disposal."

"I think we both know you're not just one guy, Logan. You're a hell of a lot more than that. I saw you in action in Nam. I've kept myself in the loop in regard to your subsequent activities, something that was easier to do the higher up I climbed in the military food chain. You're the best tracker, the most resourceful individual . . ."

"You'll make me blush."

"One of you, as far as I'm concerned, is worth all the thousands of agents that the BNE has put on this. You could make the difference."

Logan appeared to consider it for a time but then slowly shook his head. "Sorry, General. This ain't my area."

"Your area?"

"The kid who got grabbed ain't a mutant. Got no reason to assume the guys who grabbed him were, either. I just don't see why I'm needed for this."

"Because there's an innocent child in trouble!"

"There's tons of guys out there whose whole thing is helping innocent people in trouble," Logan said. "Flying guys and shield-throwing guys and android guys and god guys. I'm not one of those guys. I don't need to be sticking my nose into this. Don't get me wrong. If I'm walking along and the bad guys drive past me with the kid screaming for help out the back window, the car ain't gonna go much farther. But I'm not a detective or a bounty hunter or some costumed do-gooder patrolling the city looking for crimes to stop. I'm . . ."

"The best."

"True," said Logan.

"The boy deserves the best."

"You know the kid personally? He any relation to you?"

Doyle shook his head.

"Then 'deserves' don't really enter into it. The kid got caught in some political crossfire. The guys whose policies helped put him there are the ones who are working on pulling him out of it. This simply ain't my problem."

"You're saying you don't care."

" 'Course I care. But there's no rule that says I gotta get involved with everything I care about."

Doyle considered that and then said, "And in Vietnam, when you saved me, was I the equivalent of the screaming kid in the back of the car?"

"Pretty much."

"So it was basically luck of the draw."

"Right."

Doyle looked to the TV screen. "Let's hope that boy gets himself the same sort of luck."

"Yeah," said Logan.

5

THE HAYES HOME WAS ALIVE WITH ACTIVITY, AND in the center of it all—seated immobile in a chair, looking as if she were in shock—was Matthew's mother.

Until the recorded threat had arrived and been made public, Ellen Hayes herself had been a whirlwind of movement. Naturally, she'd summoned the local police, who in turn had contacted the FBI. She'd peppered the agents with questions, supplied them with answers to whatever they wanted to know. She had vented loudly and angrily about "the bastards" who had taken her poor, helpless son and kept talking about how, once they were captured, all she wanted was five minutes with them tied up in a room, with a baseball bat in her hands. When she wasn't ranting, she was desperately fighting back tears as she contemplated how scared her little boy must be and wailing that there must have been some sort of mistake. She wasn't a rich woman; there was no point in kidnapping Matthew, of all people.

Her emotional roller coaster had been, frankly, inconvenient for the agents on the scene, who would have appreciated her being on something approximating an even keel. It was understandable that she was acting this way, and even the most experienced agents couldn't say with any certainty that if it were their kid who had disappeared, they or their own spouses wouldn't be as rattled as Mrs. Hayes. Still, they had enough to deal with, having set up field headquarters in her living room as they investigated every square inch of the house looking for clues.

After the boy's plight became national knowledge, however, the agents found themselves becoming nostalgic for the bipolaresque Ellen Hayes.

Not only had there been no lessening of the activity in her house, but it had been ratcheted up a few notches. Agents from the BNE had shown up, which the FBI had more or less expected. With Election Day less than three weeks away, this was as pure a definition of *national emergency* as could reasonably be expected.

The lead agent for the BNE identified himself as Agent Craig. He was a black man with his head shaved bald, so it was hard to get any feel for how old he was. He spoke in clipped, assured tones and seemed to exude efficiency from every pore. He had a dozen men backing him up.

He had shown Ellen Hayes the video mere minutes

before it had broken nationwide. He had inundated her with a series of questions, realizing only belatedly that showing her the video beforehand was a mistake. Mrs. Hayes had become largely unresponsive upon witnessing the direct threat to her son and the promise of his impending demise if Americans didn't vote the way his captors wanted.

He knew he should have some sympathy for her but was too busy trying to get his job done to feel anything other than inconvenienced.

"It's all my fault," Ellen Hayes said.

They were the first words out of her mouth in more than half an hour and thus caught Craig's attention while he was speaking to an underling back at headquarters. "Call you back," he said brusquely. He snapped shut his cell phone and crouched in front of her. "Mrs. Hayes, how is it your fault? If you know something you're not telling us . . ."

"If I were a better mother, if I'd been watching him closer, then this wouldn't have happened."

Craig sighed loudly. This was pointless. "Ma'am, if you had been with the boy, then either you would be dead or they'd have kidnapped you as well."

"If they kidnapped me, then he wouldn't be alone. And if I were dead, then I'd have gotten what I deserved for—"

"Mrs. Hayes," he said sharply, and the tone of his voice snapped her attention back to him. "This isn't getting us anywhere."

"Where do you expect it to get you?"

A new voice had spoken up, and Craig looked in confusion toward the foyer.

A man stood there, filling the doorframe.

Massively built, with long, dirty-blond hair held back by a strip of red cloth around his forehead, he wore brown cargo pants, combat boots, and a black T-shirt with the sleeves torn off. He removed his mirrored sunglasses, revealing a pair of eyes so dark they were almost black.

"Sir, this is a secured area," Craig said, "and I'm going to have to ask you to leave."

"Way I see it," the man replied lazily, "this is a private household, and whether I stay or go is up to the lady there."

"Then you're seeing it wrong."

Craig nodded toward the newcomer, and several of his men started toward him. The man didn't appear to be the least bit perturbed by their advancing, and Craig realized they were about to have a fight on their hands. Well, good. The moment he fought back, they had him on a charge of interfering with a federal investigation, and they could slap his ass in jail for a few weeks until this was all over.

"Hold it!"

Ellen Hayes, suddenly on her feet, had spoken with such ferocity and strength that it brought everyone to a halt. A bank of phones had been set up in the living room, and assorted agents were busy gathering information from all over the country, but even they halted in mid-conversation at the interruption. "This is *still* my house, and I get to say who comes and who goes."

"Ma'am, this person is—"

She rounded on Agent Craig. "I *know* who this person is, and you will shut the hell up or I *will* throw the lot of you out of here. Or are you really anxious to see this whole thing play out on the national news, with federal agents manhandling a hysterical mother?"

The feds had managed to keep the mass of TV camera crews blocked off at a respectable distance so they weren't breathing down their necks, but they were still way too close for Craig's comfort level. He knew that Mrs. Hayes was right. Any altercation within range of the TV cameras would play out on the national news within seconds.

There were times when Craig absolutely hated the First Amendment.

Ellen Hayes took the brief silence as license to gesture for the newcomer to enter the living room. He strode in, allowing for a brief, disdainful glance toward the agents, who were glaring balefully at him in return.

"You're him," said Mrs. Hayes as she stood facing him. She gestured for him to sit as she sat on the couch. He remained standing. She didn't appear to notice. "You're the man from that TV show. Kaz."

He nodded his head slightly. "Pleased you know me, ma'am." His voice, in conversation with her, was startlingly soft. "Actually, a little surprised as well. No offense, but you're not typical of the folks who watch my show."

"Matthew watches it. I . . ." She paused.

"Told him not to?" When she looked surprised, he grinned. "You're not alone. My show's one of the great forbidden joys of young boys. Like finding Dad's *Playboy* collection stashed under the bed."

"Matthew's dad isn't with us anymore. He passed away a few years ago."

"I'm sorry to hear that. Can't be easy for you, a single mother, raising a son all by herself even under the best of circumstances . . . and this certainly isn't them."

Craig detected a faint Southern drawl to Kaz's voice. Somehow, it didn't seem to match up with the visual. Trying to take control of a situation that was rapidly slipping through his fingers, Craig said briskly, "Sir, this remains a government operation. The BNE is in charge, and—"

"With all respect, Agent . . ."

"Craig."

"Craig," Kaz said, "the way I see it, you and your fine men are in charge of jack. The bad guys have the boy, and his mother here is—no offense, ma'am—clearly holding herself together with spit and baling wire. Am I supposed to be impressed by your attempts to throw your weight around with someone who's just trying to help?"

"Do you think you can? Help, I mean?" said Ellen

Hayes. She sounded as if she were afraid to hear the answer.

"Mrs. Hayes," Craig said, "we don't need some at-large individual mucking up our operation."

"Your operation?" Kaz snorted disdainfully. "Your operation appears to consist of a bunch of men sitting around, pummeling this poor widow for information that she couldn't possibly have."

"We have a massive manhunt under way."

"Which means to me that you have no clue where to look, so you're looking everywhere. Someone like me, I tend to narrow-focus my efforts. Gets results for me where others come up with nothing."

"I'll pay you whatever you want," Ellen Hayes said abruptly. When Kaz looked at her, she continued, "I'll empty out my life savings. Mortgage the house. Whatever it takes."

"Ma'am," Kaz said, "I wasn't thinking about anything like that."

"No," said Craig. "You were simply thinking about the publicity you'd get if you found the boy." Once again, he wished that the TV cameras weren't set up outside so that he could have his agents give this idiot the heave-ho.

But Ellen Hayes gave Craig a frozen glare. "Do you think I give a damn about whether or not he gets publicity? If one of the conditions of his finding my son is that I strip naked and ride cross-country on a horse while shouting his praises, I'll do it. Where the hell are your priorities, Agent Craig?"

"Our priority is finding your son and bringing him back in one piece."

"And the more time that passes, the less chance that'll happen. Isn't that right, Agent?" Kaz said quietly. "Statistically speaking, I mean."

Craig didn't reply, but his silence was enough of an answer.

"Is it true what they say?" Ellen Hayes asked.

Kaz swiveled his gaze back to her. "Ma'am?"

"Matthew told me . . ." She paused, clearly feeling ridiculous even as she said it. "Matthew told me you have some sort of special powers that space aliens gave you."

"I don't like to boast, ma'am. Let's just say that whatever you've heard about me that can help you is true, and anything else can be left by the wayside. Okay?"

She nodded and actually smiled. Craig noticed only then that she was quite attractive. Hell of a circumstance to get to know a woman.

"Okay," she said.

"I'm going to want to look around his room." To Craig's surprise, Kaz turned to him and sounded genuinely deferential. "If I can do so without disturbing the forensic work that I'm quite certain Agent Craig and his men are currently undertaking. Absolutely no reason we should be functioning at cross-purposes, is there, Agent Craig? After all, getting the boy back into his mama's arms is our mutual goal. Correct?"

As it turned out, he wasn't the only one. Sometime during the summer, people started listening to Mazone, and on September 1, in a fiercely contested national convention, Mazone had beaten the odds and been named his party's presidential candidate.

Unfortunately, there were some who believed that Mazone had been offered up as a sacrificial goat. That although the sitting president's policies were unpopular with some, there weren't enough people who were sufficiently dissatisfied with him to vote him out of office, particularly since they were in the middle of a war. They saw the upcoming election as a losing proposition, and it had been decided (some theorized) behind closed doors that it would be best to let Mazone take the political hit of being a failed presidential candidate and instead look toward the next midterms and subsequent presidential election.

Matthew hated that kind of talk, but he was hard-pressed to see the flaw in the logic.

Now he was draped across his bed, watching Senator Mazone deliver a televised speech. Although the sun had not yet set, the skies had already darkened, and there was a fierce wind blowing; a storm was rolling in. The branches of a large tree were whipping about outside Matthew's windows, but they were far enough away that he was certain the windows would remain intact.

The speech wasn't live; rather, it was on a DVD that Mr. Schwartz had given Matthew, which he, in turn, had

Winston Mazone was tall, just over six feet. He had a shock of gray hair and eyes that seemed to burn with not only knowledge but also a thirst for more. Not that Matthew was capable of analyzing them in such a fashion; he just knew that Senator Mazone seemed like a pretty smart guy with a lot on the ball. He had specific opinions about certain topics that he was willing to speak about in plain, no-nonsense terms (unlike some of the other candidates, who appeared determined to talk their way around some of the touchier points). As opposed to other candidates who seemed overrehearsed, their speeches carefully screened, Mazone wasn't afraid to say exactly what was on his mind.

"It's like he's actually thinking about what people are asking him," Matthew had told his teacher, "instead of thinking about what other people told him to say." Mr. Schwartz had been extremely pleased with Matthew's analysis of the candidate and said that Matthew was far more perceptive than many adults, much less other kids.

All through the end of the school year, Matthew had pushed the idea of Senator Mazone to be his party's candidate. When his class had conducted the mock election, Matthew had been so frustrated when Mazone had only finished third in his class's election results that he'd almost burst into tears. Mr. Schwartz had taken him aside and told him that, for what it was worth, Matthew had convinced him that Mazone was the best man for the job and, come the primaries, Mazone would get Mr. Schwartz's vote.

of learning more about it so that he could understand more clearly just what it was that the adults were always going on about.

Mr. Schwartz had challenged the students to "sell" a candidate of their choice. First they were to comb through the field of candidates in any party—Democrat, Republican, independent, whatever. Then they were to zero in on one whose opinions on various topics were in line with their own. After that, they had to develop their own version of a "campaign" in which they would endeavor to convince their classmates that their particular candidate was the best suited for the office of president of the United States.

Some of the kids had snorted derisively at the idea or laughed outright. Quite a few had called it a waste of time, saying that all of the candidates were exactly the same. Their teacher's response had been that that was the cynicism of their parents talking, not the kids themselves, and that if they would only take the time to investigate the candidates' policies themselves, they might well be surprised at what they discovered.

Matthew had taken Mr. Schwartz at his word, and he'd actually been impressed to discover genuine differences among the candidates, if one were willing to look past all the surface similarities.

The candidate Matthew had been most taken with was on television right that very moment. Wisconsin senator Winston Mazone was, as far as Matthew was concerned, extremely presidential.

MATTHEW HAYES HAD COME TO THE CONCLUSION that he hated, despised—no, *loathed*—the concept of democracy.

In his twelve years of existence, he'd never actually had any strong feelings about it before. Back in the days when he'd had two parents, he'd heard them discuss such matters, usually with their voices extremely loud. Then again, anything his parents discussed tended to be at a high volume, so politics had simply blended in with everything else they talked about. When the subject of politics had been broached at his school, however, his social studies teacher, Mr. Schwartz, actually had managed to make it sound kind of interesting.

What helped was that the country was in the throes of an intense and hotly debated campaign for the presidency. As apolitical as Matthew was, even he was aware of such things. He was rather taken with the prospect

"Correct," said Craig, although his tone was non-committal. He glanced toward one of his men and said, "Jenkins, oversee Mr. . . . Kaz's inspection of the kidnapping site."

"Yes, sir," said Jenkins.

He gestured for Kaz to follow him. Kaz paused long enough to place a hand on Ellen Hayes's shoulder and say, "Have faith, ma'am. The good Lord guided my steps to your front door, and he'll bring me to your son as well."

She laid her hand on his and squeezed it.

Craig tried not to groan.

6

Logan liked to live by the axiom "Expect nothing, anticipate everything." In this instance, however, although he anticipated the possibility that Corporal Westlake might come knocking at the door of his room at Len's Motel, he certainly wasn't expecting it. So he was very mildly startled when, as he sat cross-legged on the floor, deep in meditation, a pounding fist at his door disturbed his thoughts.

Instantly, he considered the possibility of an attack but promptly dismissed it. If someone were attacking, they wouldn't take the time to warn him by knocking; they'd just burst in, door shards flying everywhere. He uncurled his legs, stepped toward the door, and detected a familiar scent from the other side. He said, "Hello, Corporal," and opened the door.

Westlake looked slightly startled. "Oh . . . how did you . . . ?" He looked at the door and saw no peephole there. Deciding not to pursue it, he said, "Can I come in?"

Logan gestured for Westlake to enter, glancing outside to see that he wasn't followed before shutting the door. He took a mental note of the Army Jeep parked just outside. Obviously, Westlake wasn't on leave if he was driving an Army vehicle. "Sit down," Logan said.

The only place to sit was the edge of Logan's bed or on the floor. Assessing both, Westlake continued to stand. Logan did as well.

"So. Change your mind?"

"You need to help."

Logan blinked. "Help?"

"That boy. The one who was kidnapped. General Doyle asked if you'd help, and you turned him down."

"Told you that, did he? In hopes that you'd come and bring me around to his way of thinking."

"It's a kid in trouble, Wolverine!"

"Logan. Call me Logan."

Westlake looked surprised. "Really?"

"You got a problem with Logan?"

"Uh . . . no. You just don't seem like a Logan to me."

"Well, I am."

"Okay. Well . . . Logan, it's a kid in trouble."

"I been over all this with the general. There's tons of kids in trouble, all over the world. If I try to help everybody, I wind up helping nobody."

"I'm not asking you to help everybody. Just this kid."

"Oh, *you're* asking now. This ain't Doyle talking through you?"

"No. This is me, here, now, saying that you should pitch in. If anyone can help, you can."

Logan pulled at his whiskers thoughtfully. "I figure there's no point in my telling you all the stuff I already told Doyle, 'cause he probably already told you. So why go back and forth? But you tell me why *you* think I should get involved. And don't parrot whatever Doyle said, 'cause I'll know."

"You should help," said Westlake immediately, as if he'd given the matter some thought and had an answer prepared, "because it'll make mutants look good."

Logan moaned softly. "Awwww, kid, is that the best you can do?"

"What? It's true!"

"Kid, mutants have saved the whole damned planet more times than I can count, and humanity still hates us. What makes you think that saving one kid is going to make the slightest difference?"

"Because people can't wrap themselves around the idea of saving the whole damned planet. It's too big. But this is a tragedy with a single human face on it. Think about it. People get way more worked up about the rescue efforts of, I dunno, one little girl stuck in a well somewhere than they do about Red Cross efforts for thousands of victims of a monsoon in a foreign country."

"Maybe," Logan admitted, "but still . . ."

"There's no maybe about it."

"You got no idea how this stuff can rebound, kid.

The moment people hear a mutant was involved in saving the boy, they'll start thinking that maybe we were involved in his kidnapping in the first place."

"No. That won't happen. I'll tell everybody, and you can bet the general will, too. If you . . . no, not if, when. When you save that boy, everyone's going to know that it was a mutant who stepped up and got the job done when nobody else could."

"You," said Logan, "got a lot of confidence for somebody that just yesterday was getting himself beat up in his skivvies and needed me to save his ass."

"And if I weren't a mutant, you wouldn't have been there to help me, right?"

"Right," Logan said readily.

"But you were there. And I owe you. And if you rescue Matthew Hayes, then everyone else will owe you, including, let's face it, the president of the United States, who's getting freaking hammered over this in the polls." Westlake had a copy of *USA Today* tucked under his arm, and now he pulled it out and handed it to Logan.

Logan scanned the headlines. Westlake was correct. The announcement of the kidnapping had sent the president's polling numbers straight down the toilet. Even though criminals were responsible for the boy's kidnapping, seventy-one percent of Americans polled laid the blame for the crisis at the president's feet.

"You pull this off, save the kid, prevent these bastards from taking over Election Day and spinning it to their own ends, and they'll probably want to stick the Medal of Honor on your chest."

"Never had much use for medals."

"Logan . . ."

"Shut up. Lemme think."

Westlake promptly closed his mouth. Logan appeared to be looking far off into the distance, as though he could perceive future events.

"Let's go," he said finally.

"Where?"

"You're taking me back to the base, and we'll have a chat with Doyle."

"What are you going to say?"

"We'll find out together."

"That's the conditions. Take it or leave it."

Doyle sat back in his desk chair, steepling his fingers. From Westlake's look of surprise, Doyle could tell he hadn't had the slightest clue what Logan was going to say. Part of Doyle wondered if even Logan had known what he was going to say before he said it.

"You want me to provide you with a helicopter," Doyle said slowly, "and Corporal Westlake here to fly it. That's it?"

"That's it. The chopper because it'll make getting around easier and faster. And Westlake because having a guy around who can tell when somebody's lying would be pretty handy."

and Matthew was on to a new school year, he was still thinking along the lines of possible election strategies. He figured that, if nothing else, it might be valuable practice should he ever have the opportunity to work in a real election.

The longer Matthew listened to the speech, the more he started to believe that he preferred the senator in a debate situation. In debates, the senator had to think quickly, respond to questions posed to him. Mazone seemed to enjoy the challenge more, and it showed in the way he conducted himself. Here, delivering a speech, Mazone was certainly interesting and compelling, but he lacked the spontaneity that Matthew had come to enjoy.

Matthew paused the DVD and went to his computer. He sat and started checking the latest opinion polls he could find, praying that the results would be more in line with what he was hoping for than what he had been reading lately. Unfortunately, the news continued to be bleak: Senator Winston Mazone still trailed the president by a considerable margin.

He found it frustrating. How could the majority of voting Americans be so blind as not to see a real leader when he was staring them in the face?

A possible angle to take for the campaign began to form in his mind. Everybody always wanted to be part of the new, cool thing. Nobody ever wanted to be left out or left behind. So maybe, he reasoned, he could find a way to position Senator Mazone so that not voting for recorded off the feed from some cable station or other. It was from way early in Mazone's initial campaign, before he'd been made the nominee. Matthew had seen it before, but he enjoyed watching it, since it had been the first complete, uncut speech from Senator Mazone he'd ever seen, and it was—to use Mr. Schwartz's phrase—a "barn burner" (although Matthew didn't see any barns in the process of being burned, but go figure out what the hell adults were ever talking about).

"The president," Mazone was saying to an appreciative crowd, "has failed the American people on every level. He has failed us as a leader. He has failed us as a voice and a face for this country. He has failed his vow to uphold the Constitution of these United States. His aggressive actions have not only failed to make America safer from those who would threaten our way of life, but they have actually turned our own allies against us. His failed wars and failed policies cannot be allowed to continue, and when I am your president, I assure you that I will not be the one to continue them!"

This prompted a rousing cheer from the audience, and Matthew nodded in agreement. It wasn't as if he was positive that everything Winston Mazone was saying was right, but it certainly *sounded* right. He'd come to understand that the way something came across was often more important than whether or not it was accurate.

Senator Mazone continued to excoriate the president's policies, and Matthew listened and dutifully took notes. Even though the course had ended months ago

Doyle picked up his phone. "I'll requisition a chopper immediately."

"General!" said Westlake. "Wait!"

The general looked at him blandly. "Problem, Corporal?"

Westlake looked as if he wanted to say a dozen different things, but then he looked at Logan and also at the way the general was staring at him. "No, General," he said. "No problem at all."

"Good to hear." He reached into his desk drawer, removed a business card, and slid it across the desk to Logan. "That's a direct line to me. Keep in touch. Anything else you need, you contact me immediately."

"Will do."

"And Logan . . . thank you."

"Wait 'til I've done something before you thank me."

Westlake couldn't believe that he had to run to keep up with Wolverine. He was easily a head taller, with a much longer stride, yet Logan was moving so quickly that he would have left Westlake in the dust if he hadn't been practically sprinting. "Logan! Why're you doing it?"

Logan stopped in his tracks so abruptly that Westlake nearly plowed into him. "You went to all the trouble of telling me I should get involved, and then you ask how come I'm doing it?"

"I just . . ."

"Maybe because I figured if you worked side-by-side with me, you'd see that you had something to contribute to the X-Men. Or maybe I thought I'd prove to you that they're always going to hate us, even if we rescue one of their kids. Or maybe I just felt like it."

"Well, whatever the reason, thank you."

"If Doyle shouldn't be thanking me, neither should you. Especially since he doesn't even have to worry about getting shot at."

Westlake blinked. "I'm going to get shot at?"

"Probably not. You shouldn't worry about it."

Westlake promptly turned bright red.

"Maybe you should worry a little," said Logan.

He remained red.

"Okay, a lot."

7

"WE'RE SCREWED EITHER WAY."

Winston Mazone sat in the cramped office of his campaign headquarters and processed what his campaign director, Caroline O'Shea, had just told him.

He rarely found himself back at home base; his schedule had kept him crisscrossing the country almost constantly, and he'd been battling exhaustion for weeks. His staff knew that every so often, he needed to return to the humble home base in Iola, Wisconsin, where it had all begun, to "detox," as he called it.

O'Shea, as was typical for her, was pacing. When she'd first signed on with Mazone, he'd found her incessant movement disconcerting. He had since grown accustomed to it. If nothing else, it made it almost impossible for anyone to fall asleep during a meeting.

"I don't see how you come to that conclusion, Caroline. If anything, it bears out what I've been saying."

"I'm not following."

"Day after day in this campaign, I've been hammering at the fact that of all the candidates currently running against the president, I'm the only one who stood up in the Senate and told him that this war plan was a mistake. Everyone else was rolling over with their legs waving in the air, and I was one of the only *no* votes. At the time, the pundits tried to crucify me as being un-American. My numbers in Wisconsin were in the toilet. But the years have borne me out, and so has this."

"I still don't get where you're going with this, Senator."

"Don't you see?" When she shook her head, he continued. "I've been saying all along that the president's policies were going to be disastrous here at home. Anyone who's been listening to my speeches would've seen this coming. Months ago, I talked about how our children were at risk from terrorism and that—"

"You said that. In a speech."

"During a Q-and-A with some women's organization."

"Were those words reported?"

"I don't think so, no. You know perfectly well that getting the press to pay any attention to us at all is a problem on our best days. But they're going to pay attention this time," he said with determination. "When I remind everyone that I predicted this—"

"Senator," she said, interrupting him and raising a

finger sternly. "The day you say that is the day I resign from the campaign."

"What?" He was stunned. "Why?"

"Don't you see how that would be spun?" She put her hands out as if framing a headline. "'Mazone May Have Been Inspiration for Terrorist Plot.'"

"Oh, that's ridiculous."

"Here's another one: 'Mazone Uses Tragedy As Basis for Game of I-Told-You-So.'"

"Caroline, that's . . ."

"Don't say ridiculous again, because we both know it isn't. In situations like this, people are always looking for someone to blame. Oftentimes, they don't care if it makes sense or not. They just need to put their anger somewhere. They want a target, and if you go out there and give people the slightest reason to believe that you somehow inspired the kidnapping or are in some way looking to benefit from it, then it's not just this campaign that's dead. It's your political career."

Mazone was about to offer another protest, but it died in his throat. He sat back and considered what she had said. "You really think that's how it'll play out?"

"Absolutely."

"It's insane."

"It's an insane world we live in, Senator."

"So what do I do? Restrict my comments to 'My heart goes out to the boy's family, and I join my fellow Americans in praying for his safe return'?"

"That's exactly right."

"It's hollow. Hollow and canned and—"

"And safe. You're threading a needle here, Senator, and I've no desire to see you get stuck."

"And what do I say when asked how I think Americans should vote? Whether they should let the boy's safety affect their ballots?"

"You say that every American has to vote his or her conscience. It's not going to affect *your* vote, obviously; it's not as if you were going to vote for the president, anyway."

"I suppose." He looked up at her. "It really is a no-win situation, isn't it? If the president wins the election, an innocent young boy dies. If, on the other hand, *I* win, then my presidency is tainted by the concept that I wasn't really the choice of the American people; they were simply pressured into it."

"Perhaps. But you know what? Once you're in office, at the end of your first hundred days, people won't care about any of that. They'll have forgotten. Americans have memories like sieves. All they're going to care about is how you do once you get there, not how you got there."

"You're kidding yourself, Caroline, if you really believe that. If my election seems to be for less than legitimate reasons, it's going to hang around my neck like an albatross for all four years. It'll be brought up every time someone wants to undercut my authority. You know that as well as I do. The more I think about it, the more

I think your first thoughts were right on the money. I'm screwed either way."

She stopped pacing. That, in and of itself, was unusual. It caught his attention, and he looked up at her questioningly.

"What?" he prompted, knowing from the look on her face that she was thinking of saying something and was trying to figure out the best way to say it.

"Not . . . necessarily," she said slowly. "Senator, I need you to go to the men's room."

"I beg your pardon?"

"If you wouldn't mind."

He was about to ask her what in the world was going on and why she was asking him to do this. But then he decided that she'd been with him long enough that she deserved the benefit of the doubt. With a shrug, he said, "You know what? I believe my bladder is full. If you'll excuse me . . ."

She stepped aside and opened the door to his office. He walked through and headed for the restroom. Various workers nodded in acknowledgment as he passed them.

A Secret Service agent was standing outside the men's-room door. They had been assigned to him as soon as he'd gotten the nomination, as was standard operating procedure. Mazone hadn't questioned how they did their job; they were the old hands at this stuff, not he. Still, having someone positioned outside the restroom seemed odd, even for the Secret Service. Had O'Shea informed them that they'd be needed to . . . what? Make sure the senator wasn't interrupted?

He hesitated, considering the idea that perhaps it'd be better if he returned to Caroline and asked her point-blank what the hell was going on. But then he decided it would probably be best just to see this through.

He stepped into the restroom. The door swung shut behind him. The room was empty.

Since he didn't have to do anything in particular, he simply stood there and waited, although he wasn't sure what he was waiting for.

The door to one of the stalls swung open.

That startled Mazone; the squeaking of the door was the first noise he'd heard since he entered.

An oddly dressed man with long, dirty-blond hair and sunglasses swaggered out of the stall as if rendez-vousing with a presidential candidate in a men's room was the most natural thing in the world.

"Nice to meet you, Senator," said the man, extending a hand. Mazone briefly wondered if it was clean, then shook it cautiously. "Name's Kaz."

"I've heard of you," said Mazone. "A television bounty hunter, aren't you?"

"Real-life bounty hunter. Television's just a side-line."

"I see. So . . . why are you here? I take it that Ms. O'Shea has set up this . . . meeting."

"I came to her with a proposition," said Kaz. "She felt

that it'd be best if I spoke to you directly. But she didn't want anyone to see me coming into your office. Not even your own people, workers and such. Very cautious lady."

"Well, of course, because having me meet up in a restroom with a strange man . . . how could that possibly backfire?"

Kaz flashed a smile, and then his face returned to its stoic deadpan.

"So . . . the proposition?"

"I find the boy for you."

"Really." Mazone's eyes narrowed suspiciously. "You didn't have anything to do with his—"

"I would be most obliged," said Kaz, his voice suddenly harsh, a sharp contrast to the soft drawl he'd been using until that point, "if you didn't complete that sentence, sir. I don't assault youngsters. Youngsters are our future and should be protected at all costs, don't you agree?"

"I absolutely do."

Kaz looked Mazone up and down and seemed satisfied with the response. "As I was saying, I'll find the boy for you."

"What do you mean, for me?"

"I mean whatever credit is doled out by the grateful public and media, I'll make sure it's focused on you."

"And how much is this endeavor going to run me?" Money wasn't particularly a problem for Mazone; he asked more out of morbid curiosity.

"Nothing."

"Nothing? Not even expenses?"

"I got plenty of money from my TV show. Money's not an issue."

"So you're doing this out of the goodness of your heart."

"My heart's filled with goodness, all right. But my brain's filled with the broader picture."

"Meaning you're not interested in being a bounty hunter all your life."

Kaz tipped his head slightly in acknowledgment. "You *are* quite a smart fella, Senator. Look, fact of the matter is, I'm not getting any younger. And I don't know that I want to keep tearing around the country-side searching for lowlifes. It's a living as it stands but not necessarily something I'd like to be doing in my old age. And I figure that the gratitude of a president isn't such a bad thing to have."

"Really. Then why not go to the president himself with this offer?"

"Man doesn't like my TV show. Said so in an interview. Don't rightly see why I should give him the bump in the polls that my rescuing the boy is inevitably going to provide. So I'd rather be hitching my star to the up-and-coming president."

Mazone paced slowly, as if Caroline O'Shea's nervous habits were beginning to rub off on him. "Here's my concern," he said after a long moment. "This thing could go wrong."

"Go wrong?"

"You're out there in the field 'on my behalf.' It's uncontrolled circumstances. You can't possibly cover all the angles. You have to admit that even for someone as experienced as you, the unexpected can rear its head."

"It can at that," said Kaz.

"My concern is that, for instance, you track the kidnappers down to a remote cabin somewhere, a shootout ensues, and the boy catches a bullet in the head from the crossfire. Doesn't matter if the bullet was from your gun or one of the bad guys. And what we wind up with is a botched rescue attempt that's going to be attached to me. Remember way back, when that rescue mission for the American hostages that the Iranians were holding went down the crapper? It took Jimmy Carter's presidency along with it. You can't guarantee that things will play out the way you believe they will."

"No," Kaz admitted, "I can't. But I can tilt the odds in my favor. And I can promise you that, God forbid, if the play did go south, no one would ever know about your involvement."

"I don't need or want people keeping secrets about me, because secrets have a way of getting out. Always. No," he said before Kaz could interrupt. "Here's how it plays out. Any hard information you gather about the boy you send on to me. I then inform the authorities. This office, this candidate, is not going to be painted as working around the individuals charged with finding

Matthew Hayes. We have to work together for the common good."

"If you do it that way," said Kaz, "there's every chance that when the boy's recovered thanks to me, they'll try to squeeze you out of the limelight."

"Yes, there is that chance. But I wouldn't be concerned about that. I have a few resources of my own, Mr. Kaz. And among those resources is a reporter for the *New York Times* who will be more than happy to be fed the info on an embargoed basis."

"Embargoed?"

"It means that he'll keep it quiet until the story breaks. If the boy's rescued, then he goes public with 'the untold story' of how Senator Winston Mazone . . . and his special agent," he said with a little salute to Kaz, "were instrumental in providing the information to federal agents that resulted in the rescue."

"And if the poor lad should die in a crossfire . . ."

"Then the botched rescue attempt occurred at the hands of federal agents acting on information that came from me in good faith, as a civilian doing his civic duty. And I assure you that as president, one of the first things I will do is implement an overhaul of FBI and BNE procedures to try to make sure that no hostage will ever suffer the same tragic fate as Matthew Hayes. An overhaul that will be overseen by some of the finest criminal-tracking minds that this country has to offer."

Slowly, Kaz applauded. "You're good," he said.

"I know. Do we have a deal?"

Kaz appeared to consider it, but Mazone was certain that he'd already decided and was simply dragging it out. "I would say so, Mr. President."

They shook hands, and Mazone reminded him, "Let's not be premature. I'm not president yet."

"Maybe not. But when I'm through, you will be. So you might as well get used to it."

"I think I can do that," said Mazone.

8

AGENT CRAIG WAS WATCHING THE SKIES, SQUINTING against the brightness of the sun, when he finally saw the approaching helicopter. It was one of those times when he was lucky to be a law-abiding citizen, because he would dearly have loved to take a rocket launcher and blow the damned thing out of the sky.

Neighbors and news crews, all of them still being held back by police barricades, pointed and babbled as the Army chopper drew nearer. A Black Hawk, from the look of it, with Army markings on the side.

It hovered above the front lawn for a moment and then settled in. Craig watched in disgust as people reflexively ducked their heads, as though they were in danger of being decapitated by the blades, even though they were nowhere near the damned things. Idiots.

As the chopper's motor powered down, the doors

slid open. A corporal stepped out from the passenger side. He also ducked. Idiot.

Another man emerged from the passenger side. He didn't duck. He didn't seem the least bit concerned about the blades or about anything except the scene in front of him. Craig was annoyed with himself, because he immediately admired the shorter man's nerve, even though the guy was being foisted on his investigation courtesy of the armed forces. The last thing he was going to do, however, was let any of that show.

"Agent Craig?" said the corporal as he approached, pitching his voice above the noise of the motor as it powered down. "Corporal Westlake. And this is Logan." He glanced right and left and then said in a lower voice, "He's really Wolverine."

Responding in the exact same *entre nous* tone, Craig said, "I know. Because I'm with national security, and we know these things." He turned to Logan and said in a normal voice, "Heard a lot of things about you, Logan. Guess we'll see now if they're true."

Logan inclined his head slightly. Craig liked that as well. In his experience, the guys with the most to say had the least to offer, and vice versa.

Craig gestured for Logan and Westlake to move past him, which they did. Logan trotted up the front steps so smoothly that he looked as if he were weightless. Craig kept studying this short and unprepossessing individual and tried to see in him the savage fighter and former "Weapon X" of Canadian intelligence that he'd read about. It was hard to discern, and he supposed he'd actually have to see the man in action to reconcile the record with what he was now observing.

In the living room, Ellen Hayes—who had gone back to sitting in that same worn easy chair and staring off into space—looked up at Logan as he entered. A look of puzzlement flashed across her face, as if she'd come to understand why all these other people had to be present but had no clue who this new man was or what he was doing there.

"You the mother?" he said. She nodded. "Okay."

That was all he said. *Okay.*

"Are you another bounty hunter?"

Logan looked to Craig for answers.

"A bounty hunter came through," said Craig. "Name's Kaz. Said he'd find her son."

"Oh. Him." Logan seemed unimpressed. "Well . . . maybe he will."

"Are you?" she said once more, underscoring the fact that Logan hadn't answered her question.

"No."

"Then what are you?"

He paused and then said, "Tell me what you saw that night."

She did so.

Logan sat and listened, never interrupting, nodding now and then. His face was inscrutable; it was impossible for Craig to determine if there was anything Logan was being told that he was finding particularly helpful. As for Craig, he was reflexively listening closely, even though he'd heard it all before. If nothing else, professional pride was making him competitive. He didn't want Logan to perceive some particularly salient piece of information that had eluded the BNE agent.

Ellen Hayes finished describing everything that had happened. Logan was quiet a moment, processing it all.

"The boy's father?" he said.

"Bob died a few years ago. It's . . ." She hesitated. "I know it sounds stupid, but I keep thinking that if Bob were still with us, maybe it would have turned out differently. That because I'm a single mother, they figured Matthew was an easy target. If Bob were here, then maybe they would've gone after someone else, which I know is a terrible thing to say"—she went on in a rush of words—"wishing a disaster like this on someone else. But . . ."

"You're right," said Logan.

"I . . . I am?"

"It sounds stupid. No offense, because I know you're grieving and all, but yeah. Dumb as a box of rocks. Why your son?"

"What?" She looked as if she were still trying to cope with the harshness of what he'd just said to her.

"Why him? Why did they grab your son, of all kids?"

"We've been investigating that," said Craig.

"Yeah? What've ya got?"

"That's classified."

Logan turned to the corporal with him and said,

"That's what they say when they've got nothing." He stood up and said briskly, "I'm going up to the kid's bedroom. See what I can pick up."

He turned and headed for the stairs, and Craig stood partly blocking his way. In a low, angry voice, he said, "You didn't have to be like that with her."

"Yeah, I did. She needs the guilt slapped out of her—not literally, but still—ain't no point in her feeling that way. So I told her so. Any luck, she stops thinkin' along those lines. Guilt just distracts us from doing what needs to be done."

Logan shouldered past him and headed up the stairs. Craig followed on his heels, the corporal right behind him. Logan went straight to the boy's bedroom without having to ask which one it was. Craig wasn't all that surprised. If Logan's olfactory skills were everything they were reputed to be, picking out Matthew Hayes's bedroom should have been effortless.

When Craig entered the bedroom, Logan was already sniffing around. His nostrils flared, and he tilted his head slightly like a bloodhound trying to pick up a scent. "You could've displayed at least a fragment of sensitivity down there," said Craig.

"She don't need sensitivity. She needs her son back in her arms. When I put him there, she's not gonna give a damn what I said to her just now. Besides"—and he sniffed around the edges of the room—"someone has to act like a professional around here. You're treating this like it's some random kidnapping, and I don't buy it."

"Random kidnappings happen."

"I might go for that if they'd grabbed the kid off a sidewalk, chucked him in a van, and sped away. But that ain't what happened, is it?"

"No. It's not at all," Craig admitted. "This boy was targeted."

"Right. And we find out why and who, then it's a short jump to finding the kid. Until we know that, it'll be that much harder. Not impossible. Just harder. That's okay. I can work with harder."

"You have the boy's scent?" said Westlake.

" 'Course I do. I had that within thirty seconds of walking into this dump. I'm trying to get everybody else's scents." Shattered glass still speckled the floor— forensics had taken some but not all—and now Logan was sniffing the remaining shards, one by one. "Okay. Got 'em all. There's four distinct scents, in addition to the kid's."

"You can do that?" Craig, despite his pride, was unable to hide his astonishment. "You can actually distinguish individual scents to that degree of specificity?"

"Sure. Can't you?"

Logan had responded so deadpan that it was difficult to determine if he was serious. "No, I can't," said Craig, not hiding his annoyance. "I don't possess that talent."

"Yeah, well, on the other hand, you can use *specificity* in a sentence, so that's a plus."

With that, and clearly feeling no compulsion to explain what he was doing, Logan turned and headed out of the room. Once again, Westlake and Craig found themselves hurrying to keep up.

Logan strode through the living room without slowing.

"Where are you going?" Ellen Hayes asked.

"To find your son," Logan said, as casually as if he were heading down to the corner store for a pack of cigarettes. "Wish me luck."

With that, he was out the door, Westlake and Craig in his wake.

"Good luck," said Ellen Hayes tonelessly.

Logan moved quickly through the backyard of the house and vaulted a short barrier of bushes that separated the edge of the property from a forest expanse.

"You sure they went this way?" Craig called out.

Logan did not deign to answer; he simply flashed a contemptuous glance and kept moving. Westlake and Craig had no choice except to hurry to keep up. Craig suspected that Logan could have ditched them with no effort if he'd been so inclined. That, in fact, he was slowing himself down so that they could keep up with him.

Ellen Hayes had told Craig that she had always loved the location of their house, right on the edge of a forest preserve. They would regularly see various small animals and even deer wander right up to the edge of their property, although the charm admittedly had been lost a bit when some deer had made short work of her prized tomato patch.

Now, though, it appeared to Craig that the location had proven to be a liability. If the house hadn't been up against a forest—if, instead, Matthew Hayes had lived on a busy suburban street—it was entirely possible that the kidnappers wouldn't have been able to slip close enough without being observed.

Perhaps, Craig reasoned, that was the answer that Logan was looking for. Perhaps that was why Matthew Hayes had been selected. It could be that the explanation was no more sinister than that he was the right age for the kidnapping victim they were looking for, and they liked where the house was situated. What was the old saying? The three most important things in buying and selling real estate were location, location, and location. There might be nothing directly relevant to the boy himself, instead being simply a matter of the oldest reason for misfortune in the world: he was in the wrong place at the wrong time.

Still, it didn't quite smell right to Craig. That being the case, how much worse did it smell to Logan and his hyperacute nose?

They continued to move through the woods. As the sun slowly crawled across the sky, Craig was feeling increasingly out of place. He always took pride in the way he dressed, unlike so many of his fellow agents. His dark suit was pressed with sharply creased pants legs, his tie was knotted in a well-crafted Windsor knot, and his shoes were shined to the kind of gleaming black that the nuns who had taught him in Catholic school had forbidden because they were concerned that if you stood just right, you could catch a reflection up under a girl's pleated skirt.

Of course, that had been the case when Craig had first set out in pursuit of Logan. Now the suit was looking disheveled, covered with brambles and such. He'd loosened the Windsor knot, and the tie was askew; his shoes were covered with a fine film of dust and dirt.

Westlake, by contrast, looked fine. In his digies— the nickname for the gray-patterned fatigues he was wearing—and boots, he was attired correctly for the environment. As for Logan, he seemed so much a part of the environment that Craig suspected the man could have been sporting a tuxedo and still would have made it work. Like James Bond. He was a damned sawed-off James Bond with outsized whiskers and oddly moussed hair.

Craig both envied and hated him.

The forest ahead of them was thinning out and then opened up into a vast clearing. At some point in the distant past, Craig suspected, there likely had been a lake there. It had long ago dried off, leaving a vast, flattened bed. A small private airfield had been erected in its place, with a runway and at one end a little ramshackle building that served as the office. A couple of single-engine planes were parked, undoubtedly belonging to private owners who flew them for leisure or perhaps gave flying lessons.

Logan stood on the edge of the embankment that

led down to it and then turned with a raised eyebrow to Craig. The unspoken question was clear, and Craig promptly answered it.

"We knew about this place."

"Didja, now?"

"Yes." Craig reached into his inside jacket pocket and pulled out a notepad. He flipped through it with brisk efficiency. "Spoke to the manager. Albert Danson. Said the office was closed the night of the kidnapping. He lives there, if you can call it living. Has a cot in the back. Said he was asleep, didn't hear anything. We ran a background check on him; came up clean."

"Uh-huh." Logan considered that. "You wouldn't mind if I spoke to ol' Albert myself, wouldja?"

"It wouldn't make any difference if I did mind, would it?"

"Nope."

"In that case, by all means, go with my blessing."

Logan headed sure-footedly down the embankment. Westlake followed. Craig went after Westlake, but the smooth soles of his designer shoes betrayed him, and his feet went out from under him. Craig tumbled down the embankment, uttering a string of curses as he bumped, thumped, and thudded to the bottom. He lay there for a moment, the world spinning around him, and Logan stepped into view.

"Didn't know we were racing to the bottom," he said laconically, "but for what it's worth, you won."

Logan went on ahead. Westlake extended a hand

down to Craig, and Craig, trying not to let his annoyance show and failing utterly, gripped it and allowed Westlake to haul him to his feet. He was surprised at the strength the young corporal displayed. He looked slender, but he had some genuine muscle.

By the time they caught up with Logan, he was already rapping on the office door. There was a brief sound of shuffling feet from within, and then the door swung open. Standing in the doorway was a man with a hangdog face who wore indifference like a cape of honor. A flicker of recognition surfaced when he saw Craig, and then he looked back at Logan.

"You a fed, too?" he asked.

"Freelance," said Logan. "You Danson?"

"Nah. Got two left feet."

Logan stared at him blankly for a second and then processed it. "Got it. Cute joke."

"Never gets old."

"You say it again, you won't get old, either."

"This is him, Logan," Craig said, feeling that nothing was going to be gained from prolonging the encounter. "Interviewed him myself."

"Thought I recognized you," said Danson. "Your clothes looked sharper last time. Have an accident?"

"Want to ask you about the kidnapping," Logan said, cutting short the pointless exchange, much to Craig's relief.

"Already talked to him." Danson indicated Craig. "Don't see why I need to talk to you." He was remaining firmly in the doorway, his body language indicating that he wasn't about to invite Logan in or give him any excuse to remain longer than necessary.

"If you really didn't see anything and weren't here, then it shouldn't take long, and you can go back to doing whatever it is you were doing."

Danson eyed him in confusion.

"Tell me what you told him," Logan said, indicating Craig. "I just wanna see if the two match up."

"Do I have to talk to this guy?" Danson said to Craig.

"No," said Craig. "But you do have to talk to me, so if you insist, Logan here can ask me questions, then I can ask you, and you tell me, and I tell him. It sounds rather time-consuming, and it'll take you that much longer for us to leave, but I'm willing if you are."

Danson rolled his eyes and blew air impatiently between his chapped lips. "Fine. What do you want to know, short stuff?"

He wasn't all that much taller than Logan, but Logan let it pass. "The bad guys who grabbed the boy came from this field."

"Okay," said Danson. He sounded uncaring, so much so that he didn't even bother to ask how Logan knew that.

"I want to know what kind of craft they came in, who it was registered to, and how much they paid you to lie to Agent Craig here."

Danson chuckled as if the questions were the silliest things he'd ever heard. "You got some imagination there, sonny."

"I'm pretty sure I've got a few years on you, so you can bag the sonny stuff."

"Fine, whatever," said Danson with a shrug. "So I'll tell you the same thing that I told the agent here: I don't know jack. Not what kind of craft they came in, whoever they were, and not who it was registered to, whatever it is, and nobody paid me a dime to lie to anybody. And frankly, shrimp, I resent the hell out of . . ." His voice trailed off as he stared at Westlake.

Craig looked toward Westlake and actually took a step back in confusion. Westlake's skin had gone bright red, as if he were suddenly the most massively embarrassed individual who'd ever walked the planet. Westlake glanced at his own hands as if he were as surprised as anybody. Upon discovering what had happened, he just smiled grimly and exchanged looks with Logan, indicating that the sudden shift in hue was of great significance.

"We have a winner," Logan said.

"I don't understand," said Craig. "What are you talking about?"

"I'm a human lie detector," said Westlake.

Danson begin to quiver in what might have been indignation but could also have been good old-fashioned stinking fear. "Human? Nothing human can do that! You're one of those damned mutants, aren'tcha?"

"Yeah, I am," said Westlake with rising heat. "But better a damned mutant than a damned kidnapper."

"You're going to have to come with us, Mr. Danson," Craig said. He stepped forward, but Danson already had started swinging the door shut. Logan reached out and easily placed his hand against it. Danson, thinking he had sufficient strength to slam it anyway, was visibly astounded when Logan's arm didn't give way as much as an inch.

"I have rights!" Danson bellowed. He pointed at the still-red Westlake. "This is incrimination right here! Entrapment! I got rights!"

Craig was still trying to process the new information about Corporal Westlake. What the hell was this guy doing as a chopper jockey? He should be working for the BNE. A talent such as his would be invaluable. Then he pushed his thoughts aside, deciding that they could be attended to later. Right now, he had this lying cockroach to deal with. He was feeling no end of quiet fury that the bastard had lied to their faces and they'd been made to look like fools, particularly in front of an upstart like Logan. He was determined to take a sizable percentage of his humiliation out of Danson's hide.

"Rights?" Craig said angrily. He stepped past Logan, grabbed Danson by the front of the shirt, and hauled him out. "You may well be a material witness to a federal offense that could easily interfere with a national presidential election. Right now, you sack of crap, you are officially a person of interest. And if I determine that you are a terrorist combatant—and I'm ready to make a ruling on that right now—then you got about as much rights as a rabid Doberman. Am I making myself clear?"

"What are you going to do?" Westlake asked. The tint of his skin had subsided to its normal color.

"We're going to bring him in for questioning."

"It's a waste of time that we don't have," said Logan.

"Look, Logan—"

"I'm not telling you jack!" Danson said to Craig. "I want my lawyer! You can't do anything once I ask for my lawyer!"

"You heard him," said Logan. "He's not telling you jack. But I'm thinking I can be more persuasive."

"We're going to handle this my way, Logan," said Craig. "I appreciate everything you and the corporal have done so far, but this is a BNE matter, and I'm in charge of this operation."

"Sorry you feel that way," said Logan. "And I'm sorry about the other thing."

"What other thing?"

Craig, half turned toward Logan, had barely enough time to see Logan's fist coming straight toward his face. It hit with such bone-jarring fury that Craig was convinced he could feel his brain sloshing around in his skull even as the back of his head slammed into the ground.

"That other thing," he heard Logan's voice say with an actual tinge of regret. Before Craig could respond, the world went black around him, and he heard nothing more.

9

THE MOOD IN THE OVAL OFFICE WAS GRIM.

The president was seated behind the desk that he had picked out personally from the vast assortment of furniture stored at the White House. It was big and broad and still had initials carved in it by a former president's young son who had managed to get his hands on a letter opener. It gave the president a comforting feeling, looking at those initials just above his right leg. It seemed to help humanize the office.

Seated across from him were his chief of staff, his campaign director, and his attorney general. They all appeared sullen. The president, attempting to lighten the mood, flashed the sort of congenial smile for which he was famed. None of them responded, which he frankly found a little bothersome. If nothing else, they at least customarily smiled back at such times, because, well, he was the president, and it was expected.

Taking a more businesslike approach, the president tapped the folders in front of him. "How recent are these intelligence reports?"

"Less than ten minutes old," said the chief of staff.

"And if I were to read them, what would I be forced to conclude?"

"That we're no closer to finding the boy than we were before."

"That's what I was afraid of." He sat back in his chair and stared into space for a moment. "How's this polling?"

"Frankly, Mr. President," said his campaign chief, "it's along the lines of the worst-case scenario that we developed when this all began. Fifty-seven percent of registered voters polled said that if the election were held today, they would vote against you in order to save the boy. Thirty-one percent said they wouldn't allow the threat to affect their vote."

"But how many weren't planning to vote for me anyway?"

"Twenty-eight percent."

The president groaned softly.

"The remaining twelve percent said either they hadn't decided or would feel compelled not to vote so they wouldn't contribute to the situation one way or the other."

"This is a fiasco. An absolute freaking fiasco," said the president, thudding his palm on the desk for emphasis. "What the hell kind of wimps are out there, that they'd allow such a blatant terrorist attempt to manipulate their votes?"

"They're the kind who don't want a boy's death on their consciences."

"Well, they voted for me in the first place, and I took them to war, and now we have dead soldiers! Are those deaths on their consciences, too?"

"With all due respect, Mr. President," said the chief of staff, "that may not be the best angle to take if we're trying to frame this as a national debate."

"Yeah. Yeah, I see your point there. But . . . so what do we do? Be honest. What are our chances of finding the boy alive or in time for the election?"

"I'm being told that we have a very high confidence level."

"And I'm thrilled that that's what we're being told. But right now, it's just us here in the Oval Office, and I don't need some federal bureaucrat in Justice saying what he thinks I want to hear because he's concerned about keeping his job. I want you to tell me now, realistically, what are the chances?"

The chief of staff drew in a deep breath. "I'd rate it as one in five."

This prompted another groan from the president. He sank back, resting his chin in his hand. Then he turned to the attorney general. "What are our options?" he said. "Can we postpone the election?"

"There are circumstances under which an election can be postponed," the attorney general said guardedly. "A national attack, for instance."

The president appeared to perk up on hearing that.

"Well, that's what this is, isn't it? I mean, this is sort of an attack. It's an attack on the electoral process. That's close enough, right?"

"Generally, the law is understood to mean cataclysmic military strikes that would make it impossible to count the votes because a significant number of voting machines have been destroyed."

"Oh. Well, that's obviously not this."

"No, sir."

"Well, then, what else? There has to be something else! I mean, if the election goes against me because of this, that's simply intolerable! I cannot, will not"—and he again thumped the desk for emphasis—"let terrorists get the better of us on my watch."

"Well," said the attorney general, but he didn't immediately continue.

"Well what?"

Responding to the president's prompting, the attorney general said slowly, "There is the possibility—I would have to research it, understand—but there is the possibility that the results of the election could be set aside."

The president and the chief of staff exchanged looks. Previously, this possibility had seemed merely an abstract, long-shot notion. But if the attorney general was bringing it up, that took it to an entirely new level.

"Set aside?" asked the president.

The chief of staff said carefully, "How would that be possible?"

"Essentially, we would be asserting that this scheme, this threat, is tantamount to election tampering. We say that they effectively interfered with the American people having a genuine opportunity to express their true feelings because of this impediment to their consciences."

"Can we prove that?"

"We can point to the polling that had us ahead by a twelve-percent margin."

"But that margin was falling steadily," the chief of staff reminded them. "And you can bet our opposition will make a point of that."

"They can make all the point about it they want," said the attorney general. "It won't change the fact that we were ahead until this happened, and then we were behind. It can easily be argued that it's a case of cause and effect. We shouldn't be penalized for it or have the election stolen from us because of the actions of a band of lunatics. They're making the American public afraid to vote the way they want . . ."

"Because," said the president, "the voters don't want to feel they have Michael Hayes's blood on their hands."

"Matthew," said the chief of staff.

"Pardon?"

"Matthew Hayes. The boy's name is Matthew, not Michael."

"Whatever." The president impatiently waved the trivial detail aside. "The point is, if we can void the election, have another one done at a later date after the crisis has been resolved, that would solve everything."

"And what if the polls are wrong?" said the chief of staff. "What if we win on Election Day and *Winston Mazone* declares that the results should be set aside because his voting pool was tainted?"

"Not the same thing at all," the campaign director said confidently. "Remember, the threat was that people should vote against the president lest Matthew Hayes die."

"Right. But Mazone could argue that people who ordinarily would have voted for him either voted against him or didn't vote at all because they were rebelling against the notion of terrorists telling them what to do."

"It'll never fly," said the campaign director. "Never. No way in hell. He'll just come across as being massively insensitive to a national tragedy."

"Tragedy?"

"Yes, Mr. President," said the campaign director patiently. "The tragedy of the boy dying. If you win, he dies. The terrorists were very clear about that."

"You don't think . . ." He didn't finish the sentence.

He didn't have to. The chief of staff had known him for far too long not to be aware of what he was about to say. "That you should withdraw from the race? Step aside for the vice president?"

The president shrugged.

"Absolutely not," said the chief of staff firmly. "As you said yourself, we can't let the terrorists win."

"Even at the cost of a young boy's life?"

"I'd never say this in front of anyone else, Mr. President, but yes, even at that cost."

"You realize"—the president's tone was hollow—"that if we try to set aside election results and hold on to office, people are going to say it's a coup d'état."

"They'll probably say that because there's an element of truth to the claim," said the chief of staff.

"I don't need that kind of grief. How do I cope with that?"

"You don't," said the chief of staff. "I do. That's my job. That's why you keep me around. People can see things as they wish, but I'll make certain that the people who matter see things the way we want them to."

"God bless you," said the president, smiling.

This time, the chief of staff returned the smile, but it didn't seem sincere. "Somehow, Mr. President, I rather doubt God is going to get around to doing that anytime soon."

"You're probably right," he said. "You find out as much as you can about this setting aside thing. You let me know as soon as you can, okay, Mr. Attorney General?"

"I will, sir."

"You'd better," said the president. "If there's one thing I hate, it's being kept dangling."

10

DANSON SCREAMED AS HE REGAINED CONSCIOUSNESS only to discover that he was being dangled upside down from the edge of a cliff.

Westlake stood several feet away and watched the proceedings with a mixture of revulsion and pleasure. The latter stemmed from the fact that he knew Danson was somehow connected with the kidnapping, and he was pleased to see him getting his comeuppance (or perhaps, he thought morbidly, "falldownance" might be the better way to describe it). The revulsion stemmed from the realization that ultimately, this guy was still a human being, and what Westlake was seeing was tantamount to torture. And it was happening while he stood by and did nothing.

On the other hand, when one looked at it realistically, there wasn't a whole hell of a lot that he could do to prevent it. Honestly, what was he supposed to do? Go toe-to-toe with Wolverine? Try to impose his will on someone with a short temper and long claws? Whatever else Westlake might have been, suicidal he most definitely was not.

The drop-off that they'd managed to find certainly wasn't something on the level of the Grand Canyon. But it was a far enough drop and sufficiently sheer that if Logan had released Danson and allowed him to plunge headfirst into it, he would have snapped his neck, broken his back—in short, sustained any number of fatal injuries.

Plus, it was a truism that any drop looked even farther than it actually was when you were standing at the top of it or, for that matter, hanging over it.

Westlake was amazed at the effortlessness with which Wolverine was supporting Danson. Danson wasn't a lightweight by any means, but Logan was holding him with one hand and didn't seem to be showing any sign of stress. How strong was he, anyway?

Danson twisted, trembling in fear, and when Logan spoke, it was with a relaxed casualness that didn't at all indicate that he was holding a full-grown man by the ankle with one hand. "I wouldn't be doing that. I don't have the world's greatest grip, and I'd hate to lose my hold on you. If that happens, you won't be able to tell me what I want to know, plus there's the whole matter of you winding up dead."

This was enough to cause Danson to stop moving. He hung there, motionless, like a plucked chicken in a butcher shop's window.

"Better," said Logan approvingly. "Now, here's how it's going to work . . ."

"I don't know anything! I swear!"

Logan cast a sidelong glance at Westlake. Westlake was turning red.

He released his hold on Danson.

For half a second, Danson was in free fall. He let out a scream like the damned and fell about a foot before Logan reached out with his other hand and snagged him again. Danson continued to screech; it took him a few moments to realize that he was no longer falling.

"Ever play softball?" Logan asked casually. "Not a serious game. More for fun."

"What? What?" Danson was so terrified that he had no idea how to respond to the seeming non sequitur.

"Sometimes, to keep the game moving along, instead of batters having four balls and three strikes, they get three balls and two strikes. That's what we're gonna do here. Instead of giving you three strikes, you get just two, because I don't have all day, plus I don't know how long I can hold you without getting tired. Two strikes, you're out. And just now, when you said you didn't know anything, that was strike one. Strike two, and you're done. You understand me, sonny? I will end you, right here, right now."

"You . . . you wouldn't dare! That government guy'll

have your hide! You heard him! I'm . . . I'm a person of interest!"

"Bad news: I'm a lot more interesting. As for you, I suspect Craig'll lose interest pretty fast once you're a mass of blood and guts on the canyon floor. Now, listen very carefully, and consider your answer, because whether or not you die in the next five seconds is going to be decided by how you reply. Who hired you?"

Danson hesitated only a second, and then, trying to bring his voice under control and not scream the answer, he said, "A-a couple of guys."

"Ah. Now we're getting somewhere. These guys have names?"

"They never told me. I don't know their names."

Westlake was almost afraid to look at his own skin to see whether it indicated that Danson was lying. He had no doubt that Logan would carry through on his promise, and Westlake wasn't looking forward to being an accessory to murder. But his skin tone remained the same, which was a relief, because Wolverine was looking his way for verification.

Logan nodded approvingly. "Okay. Now we got ourselves a ball game. How much did they pay you?"

"Fifty grand. Fifty grand, they use the airfield, and I don't keep any logs of their coming and going. They didn't tell me what it was for, and the money was so good I didn't ask."

"What'd they look like? These two guys?"

"I dunno . . . regular guys. Wearing baseball caps

and sunglasses, so I never got a good look at their faces. Never saw what they were flying, neither. I just minded my own business. If . . . if I'd known a kid was involved . . ."

"You'd've what? Felt bad about pocketing the money?"

"I'd've told 'em to shove it!"

Westlake turned red again.

Something in Danson's mind obviously warned him. He craned his head around and saw the change in Westlake's skin.

" 'Fraid the ball game's over," Logan said softly.

Westlake was about to cry out to Logan to stop, not to do what he was about to do, but Danson beat him to it.

"Wait! Wait! I remember something else about the guys!"

Logan paused. "And that would be . . . ?"

"One of the guys, he had this big scar across his chin, in a U shape, and his sleeve rolled up when he was reaching for something—scratching the back of his head, something like that—and he had this weird-ass tattoo!"

"A weird-ass tattoo. Specifically . . . ?"

"A dragon with its teeth in a lion's throat! The dragon and the lion, they were regular black and white, not colored in. But there was a single drop of blood from one of the dragon's fangs, and that was red!"

Westlake never looked away from his own hands, which had returned to their normal color. There wasn't the slightest flicker of change. Every word that was spilling out of Danson's mouth like a runaway horse was the truth. And Logan, watching Westlake, knew that as well.

"Anything else you can tell us that would be helpful?" said Logan.

"Nothing! I swear on my mother's grave, that's everything!"

Again, Westlake's skin didn't react.

"That's good to know. Give my regards to your mother."

Logan released him.

Danson's arms flailed as if he thought he could defy gravity and was about as successful as one would have expected. Westlake let out a startled yell, but he was too late to do anything about it as Danson fell out of sight. He heard Danson's terrified scream, and then it came to an abrupt and horrifying stop.

"You son of a bitch!" shouted Westlake, and he charged forward toward Logan. Logan looked at him blandly as Westlake skidded to a halt a foot away from the edge of the drop. "You didn't have to kill him!"

"Yeah, I know," said Logan.

Westlake was about to continue with his tirade, and then he heard gasping and whimpering from below. He peered over the edge and gaped. Danson was dangling from a rope tied to his ankle. The other end was tied off around a small stump at Logan's feet that Westlake was only now seeing. The rope had drawn taut, and Danson, ten feet down, was bumping up against the side of the drop.

"You let him think he was going to die!" Westlake said accusingly.

Logan nodded. He didn't seem particularly put out by the accusation.

"I didn't see you tie that rope around his ankle. For that matter, where the hell did you get that rope in the first place?"

"Out of his office. Grabbed it after I knocked out Craig. And I tied it around him when you weren't looking."

"I never took my eyes off you!"

"Obviously, you did. Like one of the times you flinched and looked away while I was questioning him. You need to grow a stronger stomach, Corporal."

"And you need to remember that we don't torture people."

Logan looked at him with what seemed like pity. "You didn't get the memo, did you?"

He turned and walked away from the dangling Danson. Westlake followed him, pointing behind them. "Wait. You're not just planning to leave him there!"

"Yup."

"But you can't!"

"And yet I am."

"Logan!"

"Calm down," Logan said, his calmness a stark contrast to Westlake's growing agitation. "I left Craig a note telling him which direction we were heading. He'll follow us and find his person of interest right where we left him."

"Craig could be out for hours!"

"He'll come around in less than forty-five minutes."

"How do you know?"

"When you've knocked out as many guys as I have," Logan said, "you get a feel for that kind of thing."

They were heading back in the direction of Matthew Hayes's house. "So what's the next step? We don't know any more than we did before."

"Yeah, we do. You ever heard of Dragon Corps?"

Westlake shook his head.

Logan didn't appear surprised that Westlake was unfamiliar with them. "They were a special Army task force composed entirely of mutants. The kind of group that gives mutants a bad name."

"What do you mean?"

"I mean they went renegade. Took both their special services training and their mutant powers and decided to sell themselves to the highest bidder. They took on whatever scummy job people wanted guys with their special talents to do."

"Are they still operational?"

"They're not supposed to be, what with them being dead and all."

"Dead?"

"Yeah. Supposedly, they all went boom when a job involving swiping a nuclear device went south a few years back. Now I'm startin' to wonder if that was all an elaborate ruse. A big fake-out to make ol' Uncle Sam think that they were off the playing field. Easy to go to ground if people think you're a radioactive cinder."

"So, if this Dragon Corps was involved in the kidnapping, do you know where to find them?"

"I'm working on that," said Logan. "Here's the one upside we can take from all this: Danson's still alive."

"Because you didn't kill him."

"No, chowderhead," Logan said irritably. "I mean, yeah, I didn't do him. Point is, neither did they."

"Yeah," Westlake said, realizing the implication. "They could have just killed him. Tie off that loose end. Why didn't they?"

"Could be that they figured he didn't know anything useful, not realizing he'd seen the tat. Maybe they didn't want something as conspicuous as a dead body lying around or maybe people asking around if Danson disappeared. Corpses and missing people can be real attention getters, and they decided to roll the dice and leave him alive. Hoping he'd keep his mouth shut but figuring that even if he blabbed, they wouldn't be implicated."

"Or," said Westlake, "it could be something as simple as that they don't want to kill people. If that's the case, then Matthew Hayes might have a chance."

"You really are an optimist, aren't you?"

They were drawing within the general vicinity of the Hayes residence. "You know," said Westlake, "the guys from the BNE are gonna wonder where Craig is."

"We tell 'em he's right behind us. By the time they realize he isn't, we'll be long gone."

"What if they don't believe us?"

"Then I cut them to pieces."

Westlake looked distinctly queasy.

"Relax, kid," said Logan. "I was joking."

"Yeah, except if you'd been joking, that's the same as lying, and my skin would have reacted. But it didn't."

"Huh," said Logan. "Fancy that. And here I thought for sure I wasn't serious. Well, I guess you learn something new every day."

General Tiberius Doyle hadn't been expecting Logan and Westlake to return as quickly as they had. Nevertheless, he took in stride both their abrupt arrival and their request for aid in searching through the classified military database.

As Logan and Westlake stood on either side of him, he spread several sheets with head shots of a group of supposedly dead men across his desk. Each sheet had specific bio and contact information. In addition, each one had "Deceased" stamped across it.

"Dragon Corps, huh?" said Doyle. He wasn't especially pleased to hear this particular little tidbit. "I never had any direct dealings with them, but from what I've heard, they were as predictable as a crazed ferret."

"Didn't seem to bother the government much so long as they were working for us."

"True enough," said Doyle.

"Here," said Westlake. He was pointing at one picture toward the end. "This one has a scar that matches the description Danson gave us."

Doyle and Logan leaned in closer. "U-shaped, on the chin," Logan said. "Probably a piece of shrapnel tore it open."

"We can't all heal instantly from wounds," said Doyle.

"Yeah. That's too bad, ain't it?" Logan turned the fact sheet around to read the specifics. "Eli Brohn. Nickname's Brawn, which apparently is how his last name's pronounced. Looks brawny enough."

"Think you can take him?" said Westlake.

"Since he's a dead guy, gotta say I like the odds."

"Except you don't think he's dead."

"Not looking that way." He flipped through the other information they had. The membership of Dragon Corps seemed, to put it mildly, fluid. There were even reported members about whom the government had nothing but code names: Quince. Haze. No full identities, not even details about their powers.

Logan set that material aside and went back to the Brawn file. "See here, there's a list of his old haunts. Former associates besides the other guys in Dragon Corps. That's where we start."

"Sounds like a plan." Doyle looked at him cautiously. "By the way, I've received a few rather angry phone calls from one Agent Craig."

"Oh, yeah?"

"Making some wild accusations. Something about you interfering with the investigation. Assaulting a federal agent. I can't see you doing something like that."

"Meaning . . . ?"

"Meaning if you're doing it, make sure I'm nowhere around."

"So you can't see it."

"Exactly."

Logan nodded. "I think I can live with that."

11

WESTLAKE HAD NEVER FOR A MOMENT THOUGHT it was going to be easy. He never imagined that he would wind up feeling morally unclean as he and Logan chased down leads in the kidnapping of Matthew Hayes.

Eli Brohn's main stomping grounds had been in downtown Chicago. So Logan and Westlake did some stomping of their own, and they did so with the equivalent of jackboots. They crashed through assorted dives, bars, and low-level weapons suppliers. Logan displayed neither finesse nor subtlety. He didn't care whom he had to punch out in order to get answers regarding the "late" Eli Brohn, which was how the assorted scumwads and miscreants kept referring to him. The fact that Westlake's skin didn't react to such protests as "What do you care about some dead guy?" seemed to indicate that if Brohn were indeed alive, the crop of cretins that Logan was busily threshing through didn't know a damned thing about it.

This didn't diminish Logan's enthusiasm or his sense of urgency.

Having landed the chopper at Chicago O'Hare, they were getting around in a rented convertible they'd obtained gratis with the combination of Westlake's military credentials and Logan's remarkable charm . . . or lack thereof. Westlake was driving while Logan sat next to him, unruffled despite the wind blowing past him.

"Why doesn't this bother you?" said Westlake. "The way we're trampling on people's rights."

"People." Logan seemed amused by that. "Have you been paying attention to the guys we've been questioning? Lowlifes and slugs, barely qualifying as human."

"Isn't that what people say about mutants?"

Logan no longer seemed amused. "Difference is, they're wrong."

"But isn't that always the way, Logan? In order for people to oppress others—to treat them like they have no rights at all—they dehumanize them. Think of them not as people but as . . . as things that 'barely qualify' as being human."

"I'm not interested in getting involved in a philosophical debate. I'm interested in finding the kid. If it means I have to kick the asses of a few slimeballs, then consider their asses kicked. And if that bothers you, feel free to pull over and get out. I can drive just as well as you. Maybe better."

"Ohhhh no," said Westlake with determination. "I've gone this far. I'm in it all the way."

"Good."

The next three places they stopped yielded no new information. Nor did the two after that.

The next one, however, resulted in a name—and a place.

The name was simply Hunt, and the place was a small cabin in a farming community called Elk Run.

Hunt, according to the source whose face Logan had cheerfully rearranged, was the best weapons supplier in the Midwest. He had been Brawn's go-to guy, and if there was any chance that Brawn was alive, then Hunt would know about it.

Westlake, consulting the GPS, followed the directions to Hunt's hideaway. Eventually, the path took them off major highways and even paved surface streets. They were trundling along down an unpaved road, the tires kicking up a steady spray of dirt and gravel as they progressed. The road gradually narrowed to a single lane, and several times they had to pull over to make way for the occasional tractor or thresher on its way to wherever.

"You are arriving at your destination," the GPS informed them. Westlake was having trouble believing the place they were heading had any sort of address. He drew the car over to the side of the road, because there was no manner of driveway outside the house at which they'd arrived. It was a ramshackle affair, its perimeter ringed by a barbed-wire fence. A small path ran from the roadside down to the front door of the dilapidated house, one story tall, with a slanted roof and windows that appeared to have been darkened with some sort of pitch. The lawn was overrun with high weeds, and it looked for all the world as if the place was deserted. Westlake said as much.

Logan was standing in the car, sniffing the air. "No," he said finally. "No . . . there's someone here."

"Are you sure? How can you be sure?"

Logan didn't bother to reply, and Westlake figured that, really, he should have known better than to ask. Logan vaulted out of the car, and Westlake took the more conventional means of exit by opening the door and stepping out.

"Stay in the car," Logan said tersely.

"Look, Logan, I've been with you every step of the way."

"This is different. This ain't a bar or a local dive. This could be—"

"Dangerous? I'm a soldier. Believe it or not, the prospect of thrusting myself into dangerous situations has come up every now and then." As he was speaking, Westlake was already walking toward the house. A gate was hanging lopsidedly on a pair of rusty hinges. He pushed it open without thinking.

A second later, he was facedown on the ground, Logan on top of him. "What the hell . . . ?" he started to say, right before gunfire ripped through the air above him. He heard the thud of crunching metal and winced inwardly. The shooter had hit the car.

"You tripped an alarm," Logan said tightly.

"How do you know?"

More shots winged over his head.

"Okay, I'm going to take your word for it," said West-lake.

He started to reach for his sidearm, but Logan clamped his hand around Westlake's wrist. "We don't need a shoot-out," Logan said tightly. "If he winds up with a bullet in his brain, he's not gonna do us any good. Just stay down."

"Where the hell are you going?"

"Where I want."

Then the pressure of Logan's body was off his back. Westlake lifted his head slightly to try to see where Logan had gone.

There was nothing to see. Logan had vanished.

This was what Logan lived for.

There were times when he felt as if the things he spent most of his time doing—talking to other individuals, eating food while using utensils, not killing—weren't truly him. When he was engaged in such activities, it was as if he were watching himself from the outside, marveling at the steps he was taking to fit in with others. That wasn't the "real" Logan; it was a construct, a personality he'd created so that he would be able to interact with others.

Logan wasn't even his real name. It was simply an arbitrary marker used by others to identify him.

This creature now, creeping toward the house, moving through the high weeds that surrounded the domicile without so much as stirring them—this was the real him. A creature of pure hunting instinct, for whom the entire world had telescoped to two things: himself and his prey.

He distantly heard Westlake's confused calling of his name, but he ignored it. Westlake no longer mattered. Even the boy for whom they were searching didn't matter. The only thing that mattered—the only thing—was finding and capturing the shooter, the possible source of information . . .

The prey.

Shots were no longer being fired from the house. Logan didn't entertain the notion that the shooter had simply become bored or was convinced that there was no longer a threat. No, he was waiting to see if anyone or anything moved out there, so he could see it and open fire once more.

Logan was moving, yes. But being seen? No way in hell.

It should have been impossible to move through the weeds unnoticed, but it was simple for Logan. He had popped his claws and was carefully, delicately cutting down any weeds that happened to be in his way. It was easy to spot movement when the overgrowth was moving from side to side, but straight down? Far more problematic.

Logan had drawn within striking distance of the house. It was less than five feet away. Another person's pulse would have been racing, but not Logan's. His heartbeat remained slow and steady. He was far too accomplished a hunter to allow himself to be anything other than cool and calculating. There would be no wasted movement, no sloppiness.

Crouched against the corner of the house, below any view that a window could provide—even if the windows weren't already painted over—Logan assessed the situation. He tried to determine where the shots had originated. It would have been impossible to tell from up on the road, especially since he'd neglected to bring binoculars. This close up, however, he was able to discern a viewing port that had been built into the front door. It was a peephole with a small slat beneath it, and Logan could now see the muzzle of a gun glinting in the sunlight.

Perfect, thought Logan.

He moved quickly, so quickly that even if the shooter had realized that he was coming, he wouldn't have had time to react. Granted, if the door had been armored, Logan might have been faced with a problem, but he didn't think that it was. As it turned out, he was correct. He slammed his shoulder into it, and all it took was one try for the portal to crumble under his assault. He heard a startled outcry from behind him, and then he was in, shattered wood everywhere. A sizable portion of the door was still intact, however, and it was now pinning down a thoroughly startled Hunt. He was still clutching his rifle and trying to bring it to bear on Logan. Not that it would have done him any good; it took more than a few bullets to put paid to Logan. Nevertheless, just on the principle of the thing, Logan sliced down and through it with his claws, and a second later, Hunt was looking goggle-eyed at the remains of his weapon.

And Logan got a good look at his adversary. Hunt's shining pate, shaved bald, was decorated with a series of free-form tattoos. If they symbolized anything besides that Hunt thought he was a total badass, then Logan didn't know what that might be.

The problem was that the entire situation smelled wrong.

Hunt should have been afraid. Here he was, confronted by some lunatic who had just smashed in his door, immobilized him, and—oh, yeah—sliced and diced his popgun with huge razor blades that had popped out the back of his hand. Fear was the proper response to such stimuli, and Logan should have been able to detect it.

Instead, after being initially startled, Hunt just looked bewildered. "Wolverine?"

Logan cocked his head slightly, taking care not to

shift his weight. He didn't want to give Hunt the opportunity to throw him off and prolong the encounter.

"We know each other?" He didn't think it likely. He never forgot a scent, and this guy smelled completely unfamiliar.

"No. But I know of you." Hunt's voice was low and growling. "What the hell is wrong with you, turning on your own kind?"

"Own kind?"

Hunt's follow-up wasn't spoken. Instead, he sank through the floor. One second, he was there, and the next, Logan was standing alone in the room.

He phased! The son of a bitch phased!

Logan spat out a curse, even as he dwelt ever so briefly on the irony of being on the receiving end of a phasing opponent, someone who, like Kitty Pryde of the X-Men, was able to blend his own molecules through another object and pass through it like a phantom. Obviously, Logan had no problem with the power when someone on his own team was displaying it. When it involved someone Logan was pursuing, that was a different story.

He did not think about it overlong, though, and even as he did so, his body was in motion. If Hunt had sunk into the ground, then it was hopeless. The bastard could wind up in China. On the other hand, if Hunt still needed to breathe, his escape would be limited by how far he could get on one breath. The best hope was that there was, in fact, a basement right below them. If that were the case, then Hunt might well have trapped himself.

Logan sprinted across the floor of the sparsely furnished house, and suddenly something sounded wrong beneath his feet. He'd run across a throw rug, but it had made a different noise from the rest of the floor. He yanked the rug up and, lo and behold, there was a trap door beneath it, with a small hinged ring set into one side.

Yanking on the ring, Logan hauled it open and dropped straight through. Hunt was down there; he could smell him.

It was only when his feet hit the ground in the darkened, unfinished basement that he realized his mistake as he picked up the telltale aroma of cordite.

He had just enough time, in the dimness of the basement, to see Hunt standing by the far wall. Hunt waggled his fingers mockingly and then stepped backward into the wall. Now the only things left in the basement were Logan and the incendiary device that was ticking down to zero.

Logan knew he had no chance of getting clear. That didn't stop him from leaping straight up toward the trap door. He felt the explosion before he heard it, and it propelled him upward, all heat and flame and then the noise came, a split instant later, and it was deafening. The world went red and orange around him and then black.

• • •

Hunt emerged from the ground, wraithlike, and gasped for air. He had taken an incredible risk in doing what he'd done. Phasing through the earth was like being buried alive, and it was easy to lose track of which way was up. He could have been wandering around underground, moving sideways, and then suffocated half an inch below safety when he finally rematerialized. So he was relieved when he surfaced with no problem. He had to take care to keep himself incorporeal until he had managed to bring himself completely to the surface; the last thing he wanted was to find his body merged with hard earth.

He still wasn't entirely sure how he managed locomotion when in his phantom form. After all, there was nothing for him to be pushing against. It seemed a matter of willpower more than anything else. His forward motion was governed by his determination to keep moving.

Once he was on the surface, he turned and looked back with satisfaction at the conflagration behind him. He wasn't thrilled with having to blow the place up; it had been his residence for quite some time, and he'd become accustomed to it. It was not, however, his home. A man like Hunt made sure that he didn't have a home, or at least someplace that he thought of in that manner. The fewer ties to any one place, the better.

He saw the car that Wolverine had come in by the side of the road. What he did not see, however, was the guy who had accompanied Wolverine. And there had been another one—that much Hunt was sure of. He'd only gotten a quick glimpse of him before Wolverine had knocked him to the ground. He was positive that the guy hadn't been carrying a rifle, and so he decided that he was reasonably safe. He was far enough away that even if the other guy were armed, it would be impossible for him to make Hunt a target, particularly with the high weeds serving as cover.

Hunt had a getaway vehicle, a motorcycle with a tarp over it, five hundred feet in the other direction. He started toward it and never heard the shot that took him down. The bullet had already thudded into his upper right thigh before the crack of the gunshot echoed through the air.

Hunt cried out and went down, grabbing at his leg, and he looked in fury and horror at the blood seeping between his fingers. He twisted around to try to make out where the shot had come from.

It didn't involve much guesswork on his part. A soldier was coming toward him, a look of intense and—worst of all—carefully controlled anger on his face. His weapon was pointed straight at Hunt, and there was smoke wafting from the barrel.

Hunt considered trying to phase out of there, but there was nowhere for him to go. If he went down, he might well be creating his own grave. He started to pull out his own gun from within his jacket, but the soldier snapped at him.

"Keep your hands where I can see them, or I'll put a bullet in your other leg."

"Son of a bitch."

"Yeah, well, you would know," said the soldier. He was now only a few feet away, and the gun he was holding on Hunt wasn't wavering by so much as a centimeter. "The only reason you're not dead is because of what you can tell me."

"Then that's not much incentive," Hunt said through gritted teeth, "for me to tell you anything at all, now, is it? Because the moment I do—whatever the hell it is you want to know—you'll put a bullet in my brain."

"You don't tell me what I want to know," said the soldier as he cocked the hammer of his gun, "and by the time I get through with you, you'll be begging me to put that bullet in your brain. So . . . about Eli Brohn. Tell me everything about—"

That was as far as he got before he was slammed in the back of the skull.

The soldier's eyes rolled up into the top of his head, his knees buckled, and he crumpled to the ground. Hunt couldn't understand what had just happened and was even more confused when he saw the person standing behind where the soldier had been. He was holding a riot stick so comfortably in one hand that he looked as if he'd been born holding it.

Hunt recognized him immediately. He just had no clue whatsoever what he was doing here.

"Kaz?"

"Yup. Now, then"—and Kaz strolled over, crouched next to him, pulled out a gun from the holster at his side, and tucked it directly under Hunt's chin—"do I have your attention?"

"Undivided."

"Good. Then let's"—he smiled thinly—"chat."

12

"KID. COME ON, KID, SNAP TO. WE DON'T HAVE time for extended naps."

Tony Westlake felt a steady throbbing in his head. He was sitting up, but it wasn't of his own volition. Logan had pulled him upright and was crouched in front of him . . .

Logan?

It took a few moments for reality to seep through his still-jangled brain. He'd seen Logan go into that house. He'd seen the house blown to pieces, transformed into a fireball thanks to some sort of booby trap. He knew that Logan had a healing capacity, but certainly that couldn't begin to cover damage as catastrophic as . . .

His vision focused on Logan, and he gasped.

It would have been generous to say that Logan's clothes looked the worse for wear. There were huge rips and gashes in the fabric, or what was left of it. Much of it was scorched. As for Logan himself . . .

Not a scratch.

"I don't believe it," said Westlake.

"Yeah, well, you should've seen me ten minutes ago," said Logan. "Actually, probably better that you didn't. Now, get up. Gotta go while the trail's still warm."

"Trail? What trail? Where's Hunt?"

"Dead."

Westlake's eyes widened. His brain had been fuzzy until that moment, but when Logan spoke the word *dead* that matter-of-factly, it snapped him out of it. Logan was yanking him by the elbow, getting him moving. They were heading in the opposite direction of the road, but Westlake hadn't realized that yet. "Dead? You killed him?"

"No. Found him that way. Top of his head was blown off. Come on."

"Come on *where?* The car's that way!"

"You got three spare tires in your pocket?"

It took a moment for Logan's words to penetrate. "Somebody slashed our tires?"

"Yeah."

"Then what—"

"Shut up, or I'll leave you behind."

Westlake wanted to reply to that, but he knew Logan wasn't kidding. It was hard enough for him to keep up as it was. Then Logan vanished into the forest of weeds.

Westlake started to call his name, but suddenly, he

heard the sound of a motorcycle engine gunning to life. It roared forward, Logan gripping the handlebars, and slowed only long enough for him to shout, "Get on! Now!"

Westlake did as he'd been ordered, and seconds later, the motorcycle was slicing through the overgrowth. When the brush became too dense, Logan slashed his claws out and hacked a path.

They skidded out onto a dirt road, the wheels spinning for grip and kicking up dust. Logan righted the cycle and tore off down the road.

"Where are we going?" Westlake called out over the engine roar.

"Following the scent."

"Whose scent?"

"That's what we're gonna find out."

Westlake couldn't fathom it. He accepted the notion that Logan's senses were so heightened that he could pick up a single spore from within the field and follow it. Dogs could do that. But that he could perceive it traveling at this speed . . . impossible.

The dirt road smoothed out into paved, but it was still narrow, and, worse, they were heading up the side of a mountain. Westlake expected Logan to slow down; instead, he gunned the engine and picked up speed.

The road blurred beneath the wheels as Logan opened her up. Tearing around the hairpin curves at top speed, Westlake feared that any second, they'd go flying off, crashing through the guardrail and tumbling down into the chasm that lay to their right.

A truck labored along twenty yards ahead, and in one fluid motion, Logan dropped the cycle left, then right, and was back in front seconds later. "There," he said.

Westlake saw it. A blue four-by-four, racing down the road, a hulking, wide-shouldered man at the wheel. Wind-whipped dirty-blond hair swirled and twisted behind him. The man glanced in his side-view mirror, and his head snapped around. Mirrored sunglasses hid his eyes, but his arched eyebrows spoke volumes.

That was when Westlake recognized him. "That's the bounty hunter guy from TV! Kaz!" he shouted into Logan's ear.

Logan nodded.

"Is that our guy?"

Logan nodded again.

Kaz sped up. Knowing he'd been spotted, Logan did likewise. Westlake braced himself for the crash that he was sure was now inevitable.

"Get ready," said Logan.

"Ready for what?"

Logan coaxed more speed from the cycle. Then he darted forward into the oncoming lane. Fortunately, there was no one coming from the other direction; if there had been, Westlake and Logan would have been smeared across the grille of whatever hit them, and Westlake didn't have the benefit of a healing factor.

By moving inside, Logan cut the distance between them and was practically on Kaz's rear fender.

"Grab the handles!" said Logan.

"I've never ridden a cycle!"

"No better time to learn."

He reached around Logan and grabbed the handlebars.

And then Logan jumped.

It seemed impossible to Westlake. Logan had gone from being seated to hurtling through the air in one movement, as if he had a catapult in his ass. The cycle wavered and almost toppled, but Westlake somehow managed to keep it steady.

Logan landed in the back of the four-by-four.

It all went downhill from there. Literally.

Logan had no respect for TV guys, those bounty hunters who ran around on television with camera crews following them or the glory hogs who "played themselves" in dramatizations. Logan did for real the types of things that these guys only pretended to do—with the help of eager producers, clever editors, and credulous television audiences—while Logan did all he could to fly below the radar.

He, in short, was the real deal. They were not.

When Logan hit the backseat of the open-topped four-by-four, he landed in a crouch and popped his claws. Kaz glanced over his shoulder at him and pulled off his sunglasses.

In a heartbeat, just from one look, Logan knew that Kaz was also the real deal.

Kaz slammed the wheel to the right, then to the left. The sudden reversal of direction sent Logan off balance before he'd had a chance to brace himself fully. Logan fell backward out the side of the car, and only a lightning-fast grab of his hand enabled him to catch the wheel well before he landed on the ground.

His legs skidded raw on the asphalt as Kaz drove the car up against the guardrail. Logan smashed into it, grunting. Another man's frame would have been crushed on impact, but Logan's adamantium-laced skeleton suffered no damage, although it did hurt like hell. His grip remained unbreakable.

A bullet ricocheted off Logan's knuckles. Kaz was trying to shoot him loose.

Logan howled in pain. The skin shredded and split, but the bones held tight, and Logan was officially pissed off.

He released the grip of his right hand and jammed his claws into the right front tire. It shredded instantly. He swung around and slashed out the rear one as well, and at this, Kaz lost control of the car. It veered toward the guardrail at full speed.

Logan swung his legs up and landed in the passenger seat just as Kaz was about to leap clear of the car. Logan grabbed him and snarled in his face, "Not so fast."

Kaz looked at him, and to his credit, there was no fear in his eyes, just irritation.

The four-by-four spun out and crashed through the guardrail.

Logan, still holding Kaz by the front of his shirt, leaped from the car. In midair, Kaz punched him hard in the face.

It was a formidable blow, even for Logan. His skull rang, and for just a heartbeat, it was enough to disorient him. The leap fell short of the road, and they hit the side of the incline. Kaz tried to pull free, but Logan didn't permit it. Instead, the two of them, struggling hand to hand, started rolling uncontrollably down the side of the incline. The four-by-four tumbled yards ahead of them, its engine propelling it downward, and then it flopped end over end, ricocheting off several trees before crashing to a halt in the underbrush.

Logan and Kaz, still pounding on each other, skidded and fell farther down the side of the hill. Kaz gave as good as he got. Logan knew that one good slash of his claws would put an end to this, but that would put an end to Kaz as well. And Logan still needed him, needed to find out what he knew.

Suddenly, they jolted to a halt, having crashed up against a thick grove of trees that the car had somehow managed to miss. Logan's head was spinning, but he shook off the dizziness. Kaz was still punching him in the side of the head, but Logan had absorbed as much punishment as Kaz was capable of dishing out, and he was still functioning.

Time to end this.

Logan drove his right fist toward the side of Kaz's head and snapped his claws out. Kaz heard the sound and froze, the points of the claws right up against the side of his head. His fist was cocked, ready to punch Logan again, but this time, it stayed that way.

Silence fell. They remained frozen.

"Good move," said Logan.

"Was I hurting you at all?"

"Stung a little."

"Thanks for saying that."

Still, they remained in the exact same position.

"You gonna put those pig stickers away?" said Kaz. His voice was surprisingly soft-spoken, all things considered.

"Haven't made up my mind yet."

"Kill me, you can't talk to me. Which is ironic, considering I was having this exact conversation a few minutes ago . . . except I was on the other side of it."

"Yeah? Had it with Hunt, right before you killed him?"

"I didn't kill him. Wasn't going to. Sniper did that."

"You expect me to believe that?"

"Haven't really built up any expectations of you one way or t'other."

Logan kept his claws where they were for long seconds, and then he retracted them into the back of his hand.

Kaz observed the action with mild interest. "You have to trigger something physically to make that happen, or just think it?"

Instead of answering, Logan pointed to the top of the road, where Westlake was standing, looking down at them in concern. "Think you can make it back up there on your own?"

"If I don't have you pounding your little fists on me, yeah."

"Don't get cute."

Kaz seemed more amused by Logan than Logan would have liked. Without another word, Kaz began climbing the steep incline back toward the road above. Logan followed. It was slower going for Kaz, since he was seeking out natural handholds such as rock formations or stray roots or limbs. Logan made faster time by the simple expedient of driving his claws into the rocky surface and carving out his own hand grips.

When they got to the top, they faced each other. Logan noticed that Kaz was poised on the balls of his feet. It was a subtle movement but sufficient to indicate to Logan that Kaz was ready for just about anything, including Logan making a sudden attack.

"You owe me a new car," said Kaz.

"Say it again."

"You owe me a—"

"Not that," said Logan. "Your claim that Hunt was snuffed by a sniper."

"Why?"

"Because my associate here is a walking lie detector. You lie, he turns red."

"Mutant, huh?" Kaz gave a small shrug and said,

"Hunt was killed by a sniper. I didn't see who did it. It wasn't me."

Logan turned to Westlake and waited for some change in skin color. Nothing happened. Westlake even looked at his own hands to see if he could spot any shift in hue, but there was nothing.

"Huh," said Logan, unable to keep surprise out of his voice. "Okay. Kind of figured you were lying."

"And now you know I'm not?"

"Yeah. Now I know. And Hunt didn't tell you anything of interest?"

"Nope," said Kaz without hesitation.

This time, Westlake lit up like a Christmas tree.

Logan stepped up to Kaz, grabbed him by the shirt-front, and slammed him to the ground. He drove one knee into Kaz's chest, knocking the air out of him.

"You lied," Logan informed him. "I'm thinking that you lie again, I start cutting pieces off you."

"And I'm thinking I'll be stopping you."

Suddenly, Kaz's feet were dug deep into the pit of Logan's stomach. He thrust up and back, and Logan was sent tumbling off him. He almost skidded off the edge of the road and down the incline once more, but he caught himself at the last moment and instead scrambled to his feet.

Kaz was up as well, and he said grimly, "I could dance like this all day."

There was the warning sound of a round being chambered, and Kaz's gaze shifted toward Westlake.

Westlake had his weapon out and aimed right between Kaz's eyes.

"Move again, and I'll freaking kill you," said Westlake.

Annoyingly, Kaz smiled. "Got spunk, son. I like that. And I'm a big supporter of our armed forces. If I weren't, you'd be dead right now."

Westlake didn't appear especially grateful, nor did his aim waver.

"All right," Kaz said after a moment. "In point of fact, Hunt did tell me something useful before some guy snuffed him out."

"And what would that something useful be?" said Logan.

"The location of one Matthew Hayes."

Logan and Westlake exchanged glances.

"I'd call that useful," Westlake said.

"How'd you find Hunt, anyway?"

"I suspect the same way you did. And with so many people being led to him, I have me a funny feeling that it set off some alarms with the wrong people, and they're the ones who capped him. But they didn't do it in time to stop him from spilling his guts to me—right before a bullet spilled his brains."

"And you're working for the mother."

Kaz seemed ready to reply to that in one way but then cast a sidelong glance at Westlake and clearly thought better of it. "Among others, if you want to know the truth."

"Who else?"

"Mazone."

"Ah," said Logan. "Because he doesn't want a presidency that's a result of the terrorists winning."

"Exactly."

"Why go to the mother, then?"

"Just working all the angles. The mother approach gives me sentimental cred. Bounty hunter sees mother in distress and country in need and steps in. And if Mazone wins . . ."

"Then you have the appreciation of a grateful president."

Kaz acknowledged the truth of that with a slow nod.

"Fine," said Logan. "So where's the kid?"

"You have to be kidding."

Logan popped out a claw and held it to Kaz's head. "Do I look like I'm kidding?"

Kaz didn't seem concerned. He shifted his gaze ever so slightly to take in the weapon and then said coolly, "You know, you're liable to put an eye out with that thing."

"Where. Is. The kid?"

"Sit. On your claw. And rotate."

Logan was about ready to jam the claw through Kaz's head and be done with him, when Westlake finally spoke up. "He's not going to tell us, Logan."

"Oh, he will."

"Planning to torture me, Wolverine? That the plan?"

Suddenly, catching Logan completely off guard, Kaz turned and grabbed Logan's wrist. Logan's instinct was to pull away, but Kaz yanked with surprising strength and drove the claw directly into his own upper arm. Westlake gasped when he saw it. Kaz's grim smile never budged. Blood trickled down his chest.

"Now, maybe you want to twist it a little . . . like that," said Kaz, and he twisted Logan's wrist. It opened the wound further, causing the blood to flow more freely. He didn't cry out. He actually seemed amused.

Logan retracted his claw and yanked his wrist clear. Kaz made no effort to hold on to it. Instead, he reached toward his arm and squeezed hard, stanching the flow of blood.

"What else you got planned? Going to try and cut me to pieces? Maybe dangle me off a cliff? Lots of possibilities. And who knows? Maybe after a few days, you'll manage to break me. But I wouldn't bet on it. Of course, what you'll be betting is the boy's life, because—"

"Shut up."

Kaz did so. He grinned as he lifted his hand to check on his arm and saw that the bleeding had stopped.

"I think I see where this is going," said Westlake.

Logan did as well. "You want in, don't you?"

"Depends. Do you want the boy?"

"Obviously."

"Then we go to Mazone."

"Mazone?"

"My deal with him is that if I acquire major information, I report to him. Then he passes it on to the authorities."

"You're kidding."

Kaz shrugged.

"So you'll tell Mazone but not us."

"Right."

"Call him."

"No way in hell. Use phones to relay important information? God knows who's tapping what. No, I have to do it in person."

Logan weighed the downside of lopping off Kaz's head versus the uplifting feeling it would give him and decided—just barely—to leave Kaz intact.

"Fine," he said.

The road beneath them rumbled slightly. They turned and saw a flatbed truck coming around the curve. It showed no intention of slowing down.

Logan stepped out in front of it and put up his hands.

The driver, talking on a cell phone, wasn't paying attention. His eyes widened at the last second, and he hit the brakes. It wasn't nearly in time, and Logan would have been struck broadside had he not moved.

Instead, he leaped forward, bounding up the hood of the cab and coming face-to-face with the astounded driver. The truck lurched to a halt, and the driver stared at him, dumbfounded.

"Need a lift to the airport," Logan said. "National emergency."

The driver had gone deathly pale. When he found his voice, it was laced with anger. "You—you could've got yourself killed, you lunatic!"

"Prob'ly not."

"Get off my truck! Get the hell out of the—" Then he caught sight of Kaz, and his expression completely changed. "Is that—are you the TV bounty hunter?"

Kaz doffed an imaginary cap. "Be most obliged, sir, if you could give us a lift to O'Hare. Like the man said, it's a national emergency."

"Sure! Sure, hop in! Am I gonna be on your TV show?"

"Bet on it," said Kaz.

The three of them clambered into the back, and Logan glared at Kaz. "Not sure who I want to kill more right now, you or the driver."

"Do you always have an impulse to kill people you need?"

"Occasionally."

"Terrific," muttered Westlake as the sixteen-wheeler embarked on the challenging task of making a U-turn on a mountain road.

13

"THIS BREAKING NEWS STORY JUST IN. IN WHAT *observers are referring to as a shocking turn of events, authorities have arrested presidential candidate Winston Mazone in connection with the kidnapping of young Matthew Hayes, the crime that, as you know, is designed to derail the entire electoral process. We go to Stu Cabot, who's on the scene in the nation's capital. Stu?"*

"Thank you, Pamela. Washington is abuzz with speculation regarding the announced arrest of Senator Mazone. [Footage of Mazone being led out of campaign headquarters.] Although Mazone clearly wished to address the crowd that had gathered when word of his arrest got out, his attorneys prevented him from doing so. At the moment, although formal charges have not been filed, the FBI has declared the senator a person of interest, and he is currently being interrogated at FBI headquarters."

"Stu, do we have any details as to why the FBI has named Mazone as a suspect, other than the obvious perk, if you will,

that he would benefit from the president being voted out of office?"

"Pamela, the FBI has yet to release an official statement. However, we have obtained information from confidential sources that there is the equivalent of smoking-gun video footage showing the senator in a planning session with coconspirators, plotting the kidnapping."

"That's a shocking claim, Stu."

"Shocking to all concerned, Pamela. Even his political rivals state that although they knew Mazone was a determined and implacable opponent, they never would have believed him capable of such a scheme."

"Has Mazone's running mate, Steve Sanders, also been implicated?"

"Not at this time, Pamela. My sources say that not only does Sanders not appear on the video, but Mazone makes specific mention of keeping Sanders, and I quote, 'out of the loop. He's too much of a damned moralist to get involved in this,' end quote."

"And the FBI is in possession of this video? How did they come to acquire it, Stu, do we know that yet?"

"No, we don't, Pamela. What we do know is that the Mazone camp is asserting that the tape is a complete forgery. FBI analysts are going over the tape image by image to determine whether some sort of digital trickery is involved or if it is, in fact, genuine. I'm told that at this point, there is high confidence, repeat, high confidence, that it is an accurate visual representation of a planning meeting between Mazone and several coconspirators."

"Do we have identification on any of the others involved in the scheme?"

"No, Pamela. Mazone is the only one visible in the video."

"For those of you just tuning in, a shocking development in the Matthew Hayes kidnapping, one that would seem to indicate that Winston Mazone—considered to be the most logical beneficiary of a national blackmail scheme that would put him into the Oval Office—may well be the one who masterminded the scheme. It's my understanding that we are going now to the White House, where we will be getting a statement directly from the press secretary . . ."

Passengers forgot about their flights.

Normally, Chicago O'Hare airport was bustling with thousands upon thousands of people running, pushing, shoving, hustling to get from one end of one terminal to the other end of another terminal. That wasn't happening now. It was as if the determination to get wherever they were headed had been overridden by intense curiosity about the events that were now transpiring.

A few people were moving through the hallways of the vast airport, but many were doing exactly what Westlake, Logan, and Kaz were doing: standing bolt still and staring at one of the countless television monitors at various gates that were tuned to CNN. Usually these merely served as a diversion for passengers as they cooled their heels waiting for their planes to be ready for departure. Now, though, everyone was watching with mixtures of amazement, anger, and disbelief as the story about "that traitorous SOB" (as one waiting passenger so colorfully put it) was broadcast on a seemingly infinite loop. It had been all Mazone, all the time, for the last half-hour, which was how long the three of them had simply stood there and watched.

It wasn't as if they needed to catch a plane. Their helicopter was safely stored in a separate hangar, waiting for them to return. They had been cutting through the terminal to get to the special exit they'd been shown that would get them to their chopper. But when they had spotted the story being covered on CNN, it had brought them to a halt in their tracks.

For half an hour, the three of them said nothing. They just watched.

Westlake finally broke the silence as he turned to Kaz and said, "Now what?"

"We drop ten yards and punt," said Kaz.

"Where's the kid?" said Logan. "No reason keeping it to yourself anymore."

"No reason?" Kaz barely managed to keep back a laugh. "There's every reason, beginning with the fact that if I tell you where he is, you two will head off and get him without me."

"That's not true," said Logan.

Westlake immediately turned red. The transformation was noticed by a couple of stray passengers, but they simply stared in confusion and then either kept on walking or returned to watching CNN.

Logan, naturally, noticed and scowled fiercely. "Can't you ever turn that off?"

Westlake shook his head.

Kaz seemed amused. "If the whole Army thing doesn't work out for you, kid, you'd make a great partner. You'd be a handy guy to have around."

"Sorry. Not interested," said Westlake.

"Well, keep your mind open, is all I'm saying." He turned to look smugly at Logan. "So, you were gonna have me tell you where the kid is and then ditch me, huh?"

Logan's scowl deepened. "Got no reason to trust you."

"Feeling's mutual. So I guess that makes us even, don't it?"

"Not from where I sit."

"Where you sit," said Kaz, "is the passenger seat while I lead us to the boy. Then we go in and get him and fix this thing, and after that . . . after that's all done"—he grinned—"how about you and I strap on some good old-fashioned boxing gloves, step into a ring, and settle once and for all who's the better man? How's that sound to you? Unless you think the only thing that makes you better'n me is those shish-kabob sticks you got popping out of your hand."

"I got nothing to prove to you."

"That's what you say," said Kaz. "But me, I've got a feeling that you have a need to prove a whole lot, not just to me but to the whole damned world."

"You," said Logan after a moment, "are in more desperate need of getting your ass kicked than anyone else on the planet."

"I'll take that as a compliment."

"Take that any way you—"

"Excuse me," said Westlake, losing patience, "but could we please back-burner the testosterone fest until later? You know, after we've managed to save democracy?"

Logan and Kaz stared at each other.

"Sure," said Logan.

"Whatever," said Kaz.

14

"HOW IS IT POSSIBLE THAT THEY GOT ORGANIZED this quickly?"

The president was looking out the window of his private residence in the White House, out across the great lawn. Far away, almost as if it were in another country entirely, he could see the demonstrators massing outside the fence. Soldiers were assembled on the other side, standing silently but with their guns at the ready, making a mute but firm statement: Endeavor to climb over the fence at your extreme peril.

Even from this distance, the president could make out the fact that they were holding signs. He could not determine exactly what they said, but he didn't have to be a genius to figure it out.

"They want my head, don't they?" he said.

"The more polite ones are asking for it, yeah," said

his chief of staff, hovering near him like the angel of death paying a social call.

"And the less polite ones?"

"Various other parts of your anatomy."

"Terrific."

"I'm not concerned about them."

"Well, good for you," said the president. "Then again, you can afford not to, since you're not the one who's got various parts of his anatomy being called for. What are you concerned about, then?"

"This."

The chief of staff held up a DVD. The president looked at it blankly as the chief of staff walked across the room and slid it into a player. The television lit up. The president recognized what he was seeing immediately: Larry King's show. The gabfest host was leaning forward, elbows on his desk, fingers intertwined, and he was saying, "And is that really how you feel?"

The president didn't recognize the woman across from him. Her name appeared below her in small glowing yellow letters: "Ellen Hayes." The name didn't mean a thing to him. As she spoke, however, it all became painfully apparent.

"Yes, Larry, it's absolutely how I feel. This president, these policies, they are responsible not only for the deaths of thousands of young Americans, but now my own son's life is at risk. And what makes him different from all those soldiers is that at least they volunteered to go where they've been sent. Matthew was dragged kicking and screaming from our home. He was . . ."

She stopped and looked as if she were doing everything she could to keep herself together.

"Do you need a moment, Mrs. Hayes?" King said gently.

"Oh, God," said the president with a moan. "It's the mother."

"No . . . no, I'll be fine," she said. "It's just that—"

"Pause it."

The chief of staff did as he was ordered. Ellen Hayes froze on-screen, mouth open, her face a picture of barely restrained anguish.

The president reached behind himself, found a chair, and pulled it over. He flopped down onto it like a marionette with cut strings. "What the hell is she doing on television? I thought she was in her house waiting for word of her son."

"She was. But an antiwar organization made contact with her. They're using her, Mr. President. Using her to stoke their agenda. It's disgusting, really, seeing her manipulated in that fashion."

"I wish we could help her. If I could see her, talk to her . . ."

"Considering that, from what I understand, she's going to be joining the protesters outside, you may well get your wish."

"Great." He gestured for the chief of staff to unfreeze the image.

"When I think of Matthew," Ellen Hayes continued,

"caught up in this—this terrorist game, he's probably so scared. He has no idea what's going on. If you're listening"—she turned to the camera—"if the people who took my son are listening, please, I beg you, let him go. Don't make him a part of this. Please." She was losing control, the tears flooding down her face.

The president picked up the remote control and shut off the DVD, unwilling to witness any more. Nothing was said for a moment, and then he asked, "Was this before or after Mazone was arrested?"

"Before."

"Do you think he's involved?"

"I don't know."

"I'm not asking what you know," said the president, "I'm asking what you think. I trust feelings much more than I do facts. Facts can be manipulated, changed. Just look at science. They present things as facts one day, and next thing you know, there's a brand new fact. We can't even make up our damned minds whether Pluto's a planet or not. Feelings . . . feelings come from the heart and soul. A man's heart and soul doesn't change. It's pure. That's what I'm saying. So tell me your gut instinct. Is Mazone up to his neck in this or not?"

"My gut instinct, sir, is that he's not."

"Really?" The president's face sagged in disappointment. "Damn. But how do you explain that video, then?"

"Videos can be faked. Seeing isn't always believing."

"Still, that's a very convincing video. Well, we have to

let the investigation proceed. This could wind up leaving the voters with quite a dilemma, though."

"That's true enough," said the chief of staff. "As much as we preach the notion of innocent until proven guilty, the fact is that people tend to assume guilt unless someone else comes along and is proven to be the guilty party."

"Meaning that even if Senator Mazone is cleared of the charges . . ."

"With Election Day so near, the notion that he masterminded it will still be hanging over him in people's minds. It's just as I've always said, Mr. President, repeat the charge often enough, and people will forget the accuracy of it. They'll just remember the charge."

The president looked questioningly at the chief of staff. "You didn't have anything to do with the video, did you?"

"No, sir, of course not."

"Would you tell me if you did?"

"No, sir, of course not. But I didn't."

"That's a relief."

The chanting from the protesters floated across the lawn. The president returned to the window and saw that the crowd looked larger than before.

"Once upon a time," he said softly, "people could just walk into the White House and visit the president. Regular citizens. They'd have their horses or their goats grazing right out on the lawn. Right there. We didn't have this great divide between us. Can you imagine what it would be like if we went back to those days? Where just anyone could walk in and speak to me about whatever was bothering them?"

"You'd never get any work done, sir."

"Most days, I feel like I'm not getting anything done now. Nothing of consequence. Nothing that's really going to make a difference to the world. Maybe spending half my day just talking to everyday, ordinary citizens would be the best work I could possibly do."

"If that's what you want to do, Mr. President, then I'll see that it's done."

The president looked at him with interest. "Would you really?"

"Absolutely."

"You're lying to me right now, aren't you?"

The chief of staff hesitated and then said, "A little."

"That's what I thought." Slowly, his mind turned in a direction that he found most unpleasant. "This is going to come down to a show of arms, isn't it? I'm going to have to postpone the election, or allow it to be held and then petition the courts to have the results set aside. And it's going to drop a huge match into an even bigger tinderbox. Isn't that right?"

"That's entirely possible, Mr. President."

"You already have National Guard troops at the ready, don't you?"

"Yes, sir, Mr. President."

He looked out across the lawn and imagined it studded with goats and horses grazing. Then that was wiped away, and he envisioned it as a battleground, with citizens storming the fences and young men with guns being forced to open fire on their fellow Americans.

"This is going to end bloody," said the president. "I can feel it in my gut."

The chief of staff did not contradict him.

15

THE SMOOTH, BLUE WATERS OF THE PACIFIC SPED past beneath them as Westlake sent the Black Hawk hurtling across it at top speed.

The Black Hawk normally required two pilots, and Westlake had to admit to himself that he was impressed with how effortlessly Logan had fulfilled the requirements of the copilot. He had asked Logan where he had picked up chopper experience, but Logan had just looked at him and expressed no interest in responding, and Westlake had wisely decided not to press the issue.

They'd had to refuel twice along the way before embarking on the Pacific crossing. Even so, Westlake was keeping a wary eye on the fuel gauge. The Hawaiian Islands were not an option, well beyond the maximum cruising range of the Black Hawk. That meant that they were counting purely on finding the island where Matthew Hayes was allegedly being held—the one Kaz insisted was within the Black Hawk's range. For his own safety, Kaz had withheld the specific longitude and latitude until the chopper was well under way.

"I'm going to take it on faith that you won't try to push me out en route," Kaz had said.

"You do that," Logan had told him in a way designed to convince Kaz that he was laboring under a false sense of security. Westlake wanted to believe he was kidding. He wanted to believe it a lot.

Now, Westlake's check of the gauge confirmed for him exactly what his instinct had already warned him. "We're reaching the point of no return," he said over the comm set. The Black Hawk was so noisy that the three of them had to wear earphones and speak over microphone headsets. "If we drop below the half mark, we won't have enough fuel to return to the mainland."

Logan nodded and turned toward Kaz, who was crouched behind them. "Now or never, chief."

Kaz hesitated and then gave them the coordinates.

Westlake instantly entered them into the flight navigator. He wasn't thrilled when he saw the results. "We reach this destination," he said, "and we have twenty-two percent of fuel left."

"Which means," said Logan, "that we either have to be able to refuel on the island or figure they have other means of getting back to the mainland that we can nab. Assuming that the island is there to begin with."

"It's there," said Kaz.

"You don't know that for sure," said Westlake. "For

all you know, Hunt just spat out some random numbers, and this is a wild-goose chase that's going to land us in the middle of freaking nowhere."

"He was telling the truth. I could see it in his eyes."

"Maybe his eyes were lying."

"I've been doing this a long time, kiddo."

"And I'd like to keep doing this for a long time," said Westlake, "and if I wind up having to ditch in the Pacific, that greatly reduces my chances. Logan, what do you think?"

Logan studied Kaz for a long moment, seeming to weigh all the options. Finally, he said, "If it's me, I keep a steady course."

"We could die for no good reason."

"Ain't no good reasons to die, kid, no matter what the books may tell you. Martyrs, self-sacrifice, all that stuff, it's bull. When you die, you get no more chances. Me, I'm all about having more chances. But life ain't life if you ain't willing to risk tossing it away once in a while."

Westlake shook his head, convinced that he was never going to understand how Logan's mind worked. It didn't deter him from keeping the chopper on course for the coordinates Kaz had told them.

Time went by quickly, and the fuel supply was dwindling with more speed than Westlake liked. Logan didn't seem especially perturbed. He could afford it; he had a healing factor. Then again, that wasn't going to do him a whole lot of good if he wound up on the bottom of the ocean. As for Kaz, he had actually slid down in his chair with his head slumped back, eyes closed and mouth open. He was snoring softly. Nice to know he could be that relaxed, considering that his ass was as much on the line as any of theirs—

The warning systems on the Black Hawk lit up.

Alarms began screaming at them, and Kaz immediately came to full wakefulness. Logan was sitting forward, studying the controls, and clearly not liking what he was seeing.

"We got bogies," he said.

They were moving quickly. Westlake didn't have a visual confirmation on them yet, but the radar was picking them up loud and clear. Missiles, surface to air, moving fast. Three of them.

"You got countermeasures on this boat?" said Logan.

Westlake pointed at the release buttons.

Logan began to say, "Bring us around," but Westlake was already doing so. The Black Hawk banked hard and turned tail, the missiles right after it.

The blinking lights tracking the missiles' positions in comparison to their own indicated that they were drawing closer, still closer, and then Logan said, "Launching countermeasures."

He triggered the countermeasures, and the flares shot out underneath the ship's fuselage. Two of the missiles wavered, their radar thrown off by the flares as they tricked the heat-seeking instrumentation into believing that they themselves were the target. One exploded on impact with the flares, and the other struck the surface of the water and erupted, sending a geyser hurtling upward.

The third was not fooled one bit and came for the chopper.

"Hard kill! Only chance!" shouted Logan.

Westlake whipped the Black Hawk down and around and took the only option he had left. He fired a bank of missiles directly at the oncoming one, hoping to blow it out of the sky.

He was partially successful.

A mere thirty feet away, one of his own missiles intercepted the oncoming one. They erupted in midair, creating a massive fireball, sending shrapnel in every direction.

And one mass of tangled metal slammed into the Black Hawk's propellers.

For half a heartbeat, Westlake thought he had escaped danger, and he suddenly felt the sickening jolt. He knew what had happened even before he wanted to admit it to himself. There was no denying the truth, though, as the engine coughed and then died. The entire array of warning lights turned to crimson on his boards. The chopper shuddered violently, pitched, and started to fall.

"We've got a problem," said Logan coolly.

"Y'think?" shouted Kaz.

Westlake, never losing his composure, was sending out a Mayday, even though he was reasonably sure there was no one within range to hear it. The cabin was filling with gray and black smoke. Undoing his restraining belts, Westlake grabbed oxygen masks off the wall, jamming one onto his own face even as he hurled the other two to Logan and Kaz. Logan, yanking off his own restraints, caught it on the fly.

"There's a raft!" Westlake shouted. "A life raft in the—"

"I got it!"

But as Logan started to stagger toward the back of the chopper, Kaz looked frightened for the first time. He was pulling frantically at his restraints, and they weren't coming loose.

"A little help!" he called.

Logan hesitated. Then he snapped out his claws, about to slice through Kaz's restraints.

Suddenly, the chopper spiraled into a death roll.

The nose plummeted, hurling Westlake and Logan around and slamming them into the windshield. Logan's adamantium-laced body shattered the glass on impact, and he fell through and out.

Westlake had only enough time to scream Logan's name before the chopper struck the Pacific Ocean.

Water blasted in with the force of a hurricane. Westlake had no chance. The surge dragged him backward, past the struggling Kaz, who had managed to yank the buckle clear—or so Westlake thought. Pinned at the far end of the doomed vehicle, Westlake desperately tried to swim back in the other direction, but there was no time. The oxygen mask had been ripped from his face by the impact of the water, and he barely had time to take a deep breath of air before he was completely submerged.

He spotted a life raft, anchored to the wall in a web harness. He clambered toward it, although he had no idea what possible good it could do. Seconds later, he had managed to remove it from the harness and tried once again to thrash his way toward the front of the chopper. Deafened by the weight of the water, he could barely make out the faint sound of crunching metal. His lungs were beginning to ache from the pressure of the air building up within them, demanding release.

No chance, no chance in hell, no chance . . .

Suddenly, a blast of light flooded the cabin; the tail section of the Black Hawk had been torn away.

He had no idea what the hell was happening, and then someone grabbed him by the back of his uniform shirt and hauled him through the jagged opening. Astonished, he saw that it was Logan and realized what had happened. Logan had cut through the chopper with his claws.

The surface of the Pacific seemed miles away. Westlake clutched the life raft. Blindly, he pulled on the handle, having no idea if it would work underwater. Instantly, it began to inflate. Logan retracted his claws, and Westlake immediately knew why. The last thing they needed was Wolverine accidentally poking a hole in their ride.

Within seconds, the raft had fully inflated. Logan and Westlake kicked toward the surface, aided by its buoyancy. Below them, the Black Hawk continued to sink. Westlake pointed frantically at the wreck and mouthed the word *Kaz* to Logan. Logan shrugged. He didn't seem particularly concerned about the fate of the bounty hunter.

Seconds later, they broke the surface of the water. Gasping for air, Westlake pleaded, "Kaz is stuck down there!"

"Kid, we got our own problems."

"You don't leave a man behind!"

"He's not our man!"

"I'm not arguing this!"

Westlake took a deep breath and was about to drop below the surface when Logan grabbed him by the front of the shirt and shoved him up and into the bobbing life raft. "Stay here, you idiot," said the clearly annoyed Logan as he inhaled and then dove.

Long moments passed as Westlake waited with growing concern. He started second-guessing himself. What if he'd just sent Logan down to his death? Anything could be happening beneath the waves. What possible chance did he have of accomplishing his mission if he was on his own? He was just one soldier. It wasn't as if he were some cinematic killing machine. If he wanted to have a hope in hell of pulling this off, he needed Logan with him.

He looked at his watch. It had stopped. A few thousand pounds of water would do that. He had no idea how much time had gone by, but he was becoming convinced that it was far longer than anyone who didn't possess gills could possibly survive.

Suddenly, Logan broke the surface of the water. He took in deep gulps of air. His hair was flattened, which Westlake had to admit he was almost relieved to see. Considering all the circumstances under which it had held its shape, he'd been starting to wonder if even Logan's hair was laced with adamantium.

The fact that he wasn't hauling Kaz with him answered Westlake's questions before he could ask them.

The corporal had already hauled himself up into the life raft; now Logan did the same.

"It was too deep," Logan said. "I tried to get to it. I couldn't."

"Maybe he got out," said Westlake.

"Maybe he did."

"You really think so?"

"Sure."

Westlake promptly turned red.

Logan stared at him. "You're really starting to piss me off, kid, y'know that?"

"I do that with a lot of people."

Logan grunted.

"So," Westlake said, "somehow the words 'What now?' don't really seem to capture the situation."

"Now we start rowing."

"Which way?"

"That way."

The life raft was equipped with collapsible oars, and Logan and Westlake deployed them. As they began paddling, Westlake said, "How long you figure it's going to take?"

"It'll take as long as it takes."

"Yeah. That's helpful."

"Not trying to be helpful."

"Well, you're succeeding beyond your wildest expectations."

"You're giving me a lot of lip for someone whose life I just saved."

Westlake fell silent at that, knowing that Logan was right. "Sorry. Thanks for saving my life," he said after a time.

"Don't mention it. Just keep paddling."

Westlake glanced over the side of the raft at the final resting place of the helicopter. "You know, they're probably gonna bill us for the Black Hawk."

"No worries. I got Amex."

16

DAY ROLLED OVER INTO NIGHT AND THEN INTO the following day, bringing the election one day closer. Westlake drifted in and out of sleep during that time, yet it seemed whenever he was awake, Logan was still rowing. His stamina surpassed anything that Westlake would have thought possible.

An emergency rations kit had been attached to the life raft, with enough potable water to last them several days. When Westlake's stomach began to growl uncontrollably, Logan, without saying a word, dove into the water. He was gone for a minute or two, and when he surfaced, he had a still-quivering fish skewered on his claws. They ate it raw. Westlake had never been a fan of sushi, but in this instance, it was the best food he'd ever tasted.

"Is this what being with the X-Men is like?" Westlake finally asked as the sun climbed higher in the sky.

"No. Usually, we have a plane we fly around in. Should've used it in the first place. No way a couple of missiles would've taken out the Blackbird."

"Why didn't we use it, then?"

"Because your boss asked me to look into it, and sometimes I don't feel like running back to the rest of the team asking for help."

"So basically your pride stopped you."

Logan stopped rowing and stared at Westlake. "If you're planning to start psychoanalyzing me, please tell me so I can bury this oar up your ass right now and save time."

"I'm not trying to . . ." His voice trailed off, and finally he said, "I'm just trying to understand you."

"Forget it."

"Why forget it?"

"Because I'm not interested."

"But you're interesting."

Logan looked him up and down. "Sorry, kid, you're not my type."

"What? No! I just . . ." He shook his head. "You know what? You were right the first time. Forget it."

"Good," said Logan.

The two of them proceeded to row in silence. Westlake had questioned how Logan could possibly be keeping track of not only where they were headed but where they were. Logan had assured him that his sense of direction was such that there was no danger of getting lost.

Finally, Westlake got up the nerve to say, "If you're trying to persuade me to join up with your team, you're picking a damned strange way to do it."

"I'm not trying to persuade you to do anything, kid. Just want you considering all the options. Whatever decision you wind up making, that's up to you."

"That's not how you came across to me back at the base."

"I just don't want you getting the crap kicked out of you 'cause you're a mutant. That kind of thing turns my stomach. Gets me pissed off. I don't feel like getting pissed off. For one thing, it's too nice a day." Then his nostrils flared. "Uh-oh. Spoke too soon."

Westlake spotted it as soon as Logan had spoken, and his heart sank. It was still far off on the horizon, but it was visible, nasty, and coming their way. A vast span of dark clouds, stretching as far as the eye could see in either direction. Westlake thought he could see flashes of lightning within.

Then his spirits suddenly rose as he spotted something else. He had almost missed it against the darkness of the oncoming storm. "Is that . . . ?" and he was pointing.

"Good eye, kid," said Logan. "That matches up with the coordinates that Kaz gave us. Must be where they're holding the boy."

"It looks so far away."

"It is. Keep paddling. We want to get as close as we can before the storm hits us."

Westlake increased his efforts. Logan appeared to be continuing to do exactly what he'd been doing all along, but his strokes were so firm and steady that it was unlikely he could have improved upon them.

"I wasn't trying to be nosy, by the way," said Westlake.

"You really think this is the best time to discuss it?"

"I'm just saying . . . it must be incredible to be you."

"Not really."

"But all the things you can do!"

"Didn't ask to be a mutant, kid. I am what I am. No big deal."

"What if you didn't have to be? Would you be normal if you could?"

"Nobody's normal, kid. All there is are different levels of abnormality. We're all freaks, Westlake. Every damned one of us. It's just that some of us aren't afraid to admit it."

At least an hour passed. It felt as if they were drawing no closer to the island, but the storm was already bearing down on them. Westlake had an increasingly sinking feeling that they weren't going to make it. Or at least, he wasn't. Under no circumstance would he bet against Wolverine. Wolverine probably could have survived the great deluge—which, considering the storm that was rolling in, might well be coming at any moment.

The storm moved toward them like a vast dark ghost. The clouds swirled overhead; the winds became so fierce that Westlake was certain the life raft was going to capsize.

That was when the storm fully hit them.

It came in so fast and so hard that it was all they could do not to get heaved out of the life raft, much less keep steering it in the same direction. The waters chopped wildly beneath them. Westlake and Logan ceased rowing, instead holding on as tightly as they could. As it so happened, the waves were pitching them in the general direction of the island, albeit far more violently than either of them would have liked.

Lightning ripped across the sky. The rolling clouds had blotted out the sun. Westlake felt as if he were trapped in the midst of an apocalyptic nightmare.

Then, as the ocean roiled around them—and as Westlake had the briefest bit of relief that his stomach was empty, for he certainly would have hurled up its contents by this point—he saw several dorsal fins moving through the water toward them. They would vanish briefly beneath the chop but then quickly resurface. They were not angled and gray like something out of a movie but brownish and rounded, with white crests at the very top.

He pointed and shouted to Logan over the booming of the thunder and the crashing of the waves, "Tell me those are some kind of dolphins!"

Logan looked where he indicated as rain began to cascade down on them. Astoundingly—or perhaps not so astoundingly, based on what he'd seen of the man so far—Logan didn't seem the least bit perturbed. Rather, he simply took note of it, as if he'd been in an airplane and was having the Grand Canyon pointed out to him from twenty thousand feet up.

"Nope. Sharks. Oceanic white tips, from the look of 'em."

"Are they dangerous?" He was trying to cling to some shred of hope.

"They're man-eaters, if that's what you mean."

"Yeah, pretty much!"

The sharks drew closer, coming toward them on a direct line, thereby trashing any hope Westlake had that they just happened to be in the area and were going to pass by.

A massive wave drove under them at that moment. Westlake clutched desperately onto the sides of the life raft and tried to keep it from overturning through sheer willpower.

Logan laughed. It was the first time Westlake had heard him do so. It was a sound that frightened him even more than did the sharks.

For half a second, the wave cut out from under them, and the raft hung in midair. Then it crashed downward, hitting the surface so hard that it jolted Westlake's teeth. Another wave blasted upward, and still another, and Westlake wanted to scream at God that okay, he got it, God was in charge, and they were mere flotsam in His ocean, nothing more than insignificant mites. But he had a feeling that either God wasn't there, or if He was,

He wasn't especially going to care about what Westlake had to say.

And suddenly, he was airborne.

The wave had hit them so hard that he'd had no possible way of hanging on. He was flying, with no sense of which way was up or down, and then he hit the water. Westlake struggled to breathe as he was thrust beneath the surface.

He had no idea how far under he was pushed. He had a brief mental picture of his remains lying on the ocean floor with tiny sea creatures darting in and out of his skeleton like some sort of piratical "Dead men tell no tales" decoration in the bottom of an aquarium. Then, with a determined scissoring of his legs, he kicked his way back to the surface.

The instant he got there, something struck him in the head. In his near-panicked state, he was certain it was one of the sharks. Then he realized that he was wrong; it was the edge of the life raft. The raft was bobbing right next to him, upside down. It almost sent him under again, but he managed to fight his way back to the surface. Coughing up water, battling the surging of the waves, trying not to let the pounding of the rain drive him under yet again, Westlake struggled to overturn the raft. It seemed almost impossible, since he couldn't get any leverage.

Something else bumped up against him.

He turned and saw a dorsal fin not three feet away from him.

He didn't scream, didn't panic. Instead, he dropped under the water and went face-to-face with the shark. The bump he had felt was the creature checking him out. The next thing it would do would be to grab itself a chunk of his leg or torso.

It stared at him with dead black eyes, and Westlake drew back his fist and punched the shark squarely in its sensitive nose.

The shark drew back, surprised, and Westlake opened his mouth and shouted as loudly as he could before clamping his mouth shut again, lest he start swallowing water.

The ocean was an amazingly quiet place. Sharks were unaccustomed to loud noises. Sharks were also unaccustomed to direct blows to the face. All the reading that Westlake had done on the subject told him that his actions might well drive the shark away.

Tragically, the shark had done no reading on the subject whatsoever.

Not knowing the proper and expected responses, the shark instead, after being briefly taken aback, came straight at Westlake.

Westlake barely had time to yank out his gun. He had no idea if it would work underwater. He brought the gun up just as the shark's mouth enveloped his outstretched right arm. Within half a second, the shark would bring its teeth together and rip off Westlake's arm at the elbow.

He squeezed the trigger.

The gun blew a hole through the back of the shark.

The corporal barely managed to yank his arm clear as the shark spasmodically clamped its jaws shut. It half rolled away from him, its tail whipping back and forth frantically. Blood started to seep from it.

Blood.

Oh, crap, thought Westlake.

Westlake motored to the surface. Seconds later, he was gratefully sucking in air.

The raft was right-side up. Logan was perched in it, his hand outstretched toward Westlake. Westlake grabbed it, and Logan hauled him in. As he did so, he saw the other dorsal fins in the area converging from all directions. But they were ignoring the raft, instead going for the blood generated by the mortally wounded shark. Seconds later, the water was filled with thrashing as they ripped their associate to small pieces.

"Nice work," Logan said, sounding just that close to being impressed.

"Where the hell were you?"

"Swimming toward you. I was about to carve him up. But you were able to take care of yourself. Who knew?"

Westlake wasn't sure how to take that, and then he gave it no further thought as another surging wave propelled them forward.

For the first time, they appeared to be drawing closer to the island. Not only that, but it seemed as if the worst of the storm had passed. The rain was starting to lessen. Westlake couldn't believe it. After everything they'd gone through, something was actually falling their way.

That was when something solid slammed up at them from underneath. Westlake somersaulted through the air and had only the briefest glimpse of another shark, far larger than the others. It had erupted from below them, grabbing the raft in its teeth and ripping it to shreds. Logan was propelled in the opposite direction and hit the water.

Westlake went under yet again, ocean water driving up his nostrils. He splashed to the surface and looked around.

There was no sign of Logan or the shark.

Suddenly, the shark exploded from the water. Logan was astride its back, gripping onto its dorsal fin, one of his clawed hands drawn back and about to slam back down. Then they disappeared beneath the water again.

Westlake was about to try to swim toward Logan, but he realized he had no idea where to go. They had submerged and could be anywhere. Seconds later, that became moot, as the surging waves propelled him toward the island.

Have to find the boy . . . have to . . .

He hated to tell himself that he had to prioritize, that Logan likely could take care of himself, but that was, in fact, the truth. Matthew Hayes needed Westlake far more than Logan did.

He began swimming with determined, strong strokes. As the storm subsided, he drew closer to the island, and he suddenly realized that his feet were touching solid ground.

Oh, thank God! he thought, trying not to dwell on the notion that a gracious God wouldn't have thrown a damned storm at them.

He hauled himself forward, staggering toward shore. The island loomed in front of him. There were still dark clouds above it, but rain was no longer pounding down.

Westlake was soaked. He had secured his gun in his holster. It gave him a sense of security that he then couldn't help but think was very likely false. His thoughts whirled back to movies he had seen, where James Bond emerged from the water in a wetsuit and stripped it off to reveal a perfectly pressed tuxedo. Or a Schwarzenegger film where Arnold stepped from the water, bare-chested with trousers that dried in seconds, hauling about half a ton of artillery without the slightest show of effort. Not for the first time, he wondered why life couldn't be that way.

He turned around and waited for some sign of Logan. He was certain that it wouldn't be long. There was no way that some damned shark was going to take out Wolverine.

But time passed, and more time, and there was no sign of him. A vague sense of concern slowly morphed into full-blown dread.

Night was beginning to fall, and Westlake felt he could wait no longer.

He had come in at the bottom of a small cliff. Since he had done a considerable amount of free climbing in his life, this cliffside—while formidable—didn't seem insurmountable. His uniform had dried off somewhat, but a chill was beginning to insinuate itself into his bones. He needed to do something to warm himself up.

He went to the bottom of the cliff and peered upward, assessing the climb. His practiced eye found cracks and crevices that would have been glossed over by someone who was less discerning.

Westlake began to climb.

It was meticulous, laborious work, but it was better than walking the length of the beach in hopes of finding some other way around.

The entire climb, he kept the mental image of Matthew Hayes planted firmly in his mind. It helped to keep him focused on what this was really all about. It was easy to get distracted by everything, from a country in constitutional crisis to the oddities of the man who had thrust himself rudely into Westlake's life and seemed to have taken it over completely. At the bottom of all this was one boy, one scared boy, who just wanted to go home to his mother. And Westlake was going to do his damnedest to make certain that happened.

His fingertips were starting to bleed, which wasn't helping matters. As he held on with one hand, he wiped the other on his shirt, then switched hands and repeated it. He feared that the slickness of his hands would sabotage his grip on the cliffside. Once he was certain that he'd halted the flow of blood, he continued the slow and steady haul up.

Finally, his legs and arms trembling from exertion, his questing hands reached the top. He rested them there for a moment, preparing for the final push in which he'd heave his body up and over.

Something grabbed him by the wrist.

He let out a startled yelp, an octave or so higher than he would have liked. Then something hauled him upward as if he weighed nothing.

It was Logan.

He looked bedraggled and, amazingly, even a little tired. Westlake took an odd solace in the knowledge that even the formidable Wolverine could be mortal.

He didn't question how in hell Logan had gotten ahead of him or on top of the bluff that Westlake had just beaten his brains out scaling. It was enough that he was there, which gave Westlake a tremendous swell of relief.

Aided by the silent Logan, Westlake found footing atop the cliffside within seconds.

"We've gotta stop meeting like this," he said.

Logan didn't reply. That deathly silence spoke volumes.

"What? What is it?"

"We're too late," Logan said, so softly that Westlake could scarcely hear him.

"Too late? What do you mean, too late?" The gnawing dread returned full force in his gut, as if something had just punched him there.

"Island's crawling with feds. Kaz survived. He got here first. Found transmitting equipment, managed to make contact." He shrugged.

A flurry of thoughts tumbled through Westlake's head. It didn't seem like Kaz's style to call in backup. He would go in first, commando-style, find the boy, get him clear, maybe try to take down the bad guys single-handedly. He was just that much of a showboat. Except, if he didn't, that meant—well, it could mean half a dozen things.

"The boy. Matthew. Is he here? Is he on the island? Is—"

"I'm told they already airlifted his body out."

A pounding began directly behind Westlake's eyes. "His body?" he whispered.

Logan nodded once. He didn't blink; his eyes were cold and almost lifeless. "Yeah. The place was empty by the time Kaz got here, except for the kid's corpse. Gun-shot to the head."

The pounding drove Westlake toward fury. Desperately wanting someone he could blame, he said heatedly, "Where's Kaz? I don't believe it. I want to hear him say it. I want to be standing there when he says what happened, because you know what I think? I think he was working with them. I think he was working with them, and he tipped them that we were on our way so they could clear out. I think he's a murderer! I think I'm gonna rip his freaking head off!"

He was completely losing control. Logan placed a steadying hand on his shoulder, and Westlake turned his fury on Logan, even though he knew it was wrong and unfair.

"How can you stay so damned calm?" he bellowed.

"You think I'm calm?" Wolverine's voice never wavered. "You think that right now, I don't feel like pushing you off the cliff? Popping my claws and cutting down half a dozen or so feds just because they're there? You think I don't feel like pulling out Kaz's spine and showing it to him? It's all there, kid. All there. And right now, that's where it's staying, 'cause letting it out is gonna accomplish jack. Now, you got yourself a good idea there, making sure Kaz is on the up-and-up. And if he's not—if you turn into the human thermometer while he's swearing he had nothing to do with this— then not all the feds in the world are gonna keep me off him. Until, if, and when that happens, though, you keep it buttoned up, because otherwise, you're not gonna be of help to anyone."

Westlake was still surging with rage, but he was starting to channel it inward. "Doesn't look to me," he said, "as if I've been much help to anyone so far, in any event."

"Yeah, well, join the club," said Logan.

● ● ●

The scene was much as Logan had described it. There were feds everywhere, a bizarre mixture of men in suits with soldiers crawling over every square inch of the facility. Westlake hadn't been entirely certain what he had expected to find on the island. No. Strike that. He knew exactly what he'd expected. He'd been figuring on some vast volcano fortress like something out of a James Bond movie, with an elaborate monorail transport system perhaps. This was hardly that. Instead, it was little more than a collection of Quonset huts, as minimalist an arrangement as anyone could imagine. This made sense to Westlake. These were trained mercs, not B-movie supervillains. They were accustomed to living in all sorts of brutal conditions. They'd have no need of luxuries.

One of the officials operating the scene, a portly full-bird colonel, strode over to Logan and, indicating Westlake, said brusquely, "This him?" When Logan nodded, the colonel said, "This way, Corporal." Westlake immediately followed. It almost felt like a relief to be responding to orders. Logan trailed them.

Kaz was seated on the stump of a tree, drinking from a mug of what Westlake took to be coffee. When he saw the three of them approaching, his face didn't change expression. "Had a feeling," was all he said.

"I wouldn't believe this," said the colonel to Westlake, "if I didn't have verification from your CO. You can really determine if someone is lying?"

Westlake paused and then said, "If you don't mind my asking, Colonel, how much do you weigh?"

The colonel harrumphed, and then, realizing what Westlake was up to, said, "Two hundred and one."

Westlake immediately shone red.

The colonel took a step back, harrumphed once more, and said, "All right, point taken. You. Bounty hunter. Tell them what you told me."

Kaz did so, describing his own survival at sea—although in the broadest possible terms—his arrival on the island, and his discovery of the empty huts and the corpse of Matthew Hayes.

"I had nothing to do with the boy's kidnapping," Kaz insisted, and during his entire litany, Westlake's skin never changed hue in the slightest.

Finally, the colonel nodded, apparently satisfied. "All right."

"All right?" Westlake said faintly. "With all due respect, Colonel, how is any of this all right? The boy's dead. God only knows what kind of impact this is going to have on the election. I don't . . ."

Westlake started to tremble, at a loss for words, and furious with himself over his own weakness in spirit and body. He felt for a moment as if he were going to fall over, and this was obviously clear to Logan, who stepped in and took him gently by one arm.

"You been through a lot, soldier," he said, not unkindly. "How about you sit down?"

He knew that Logan was right, but instead, he pulled

his arm away and drew himself up, saluting stiffly. "Permission to carry on, sir?"

"Permission granted, soldier," said the colonel, snapping back his salute.

Westlake turned and walked away. He went a short distance and finally slumped against a sizable boulder. Logan casually strolled after him and stopped a few feet away.

"You going Greta Garbo on me, kid?"

Westlake looked at him uncomprehendingly.

"Sorry. Before yer time. What I'm askin' is, you want to be alone?"

"I want that boy to be alive. I want what we did to mean something. And I want to get the bastards who did this."

"Can't do anything about the first. But the fact that we tried at all means something. As for the third thing"—Logan spoke with grim certainty—"that much I can promise you. In spades."

" . . . and for a live report, we go to Stu Cabot in Washington. Stu?"

"Pamela, as a nation mourns the tragic demise of young Matthew Hayes, Winston Mazone finds himself hip deep in a sea of legal troubles. With charges being filed ranging from first-degree murder to election tampering—and some are even calling for treason to be considered—the disgraced senator has entered pleas of not guilty to all charges and continues to steadfastly maintain his innocence."

"What about the video which would seem to indicate his guilt, Stu?"

"Naturally, details of the Justice Department's findings are yet to be made official, but my sources have indicated that the video has passed all tests to which it has been subjected. As near as can be determined by available technology, Winston Mazone is unquestionably one of the coconspirators involved in planning the kidnapping of Matthew Hayes. There is no indication of any sort of digital tampering. In the meantime, war protesters are capitalizing on the loss of Matthew Hayes. He has become something of a poster child for the antiwar movement's protests over the administration's current policies."

[Footage of black wreaths being hung outside the White House fence along with posters displaying Matthew Hayes's smiling picture.]

"There's so much unbridled anger, Pamela, that people don't seem certain which way to direct it: toward the president, toward Senator Mazone, or toward the Congress that has failed to rein in any of the administration's initiatives. In short, there's plenty of blame to go around. In the meantime, Winston Mazone's party is reeling from the revelations regarding its standard bearer, and the future is uncertain at best. All eyes now turn toward the vice-presidential candidate, Steve Sanders, who has largely flown under the public radar until now. With the authorities flat-out stating that Sanders is not a person of interest in the case, it now remains to be seen whether Sanders can position himself as someone of interest to a battered and suspicious electorate."

17

VICE-PRESIDENTIAL CANDIDATE STEVE SANDERS HAD the weight of the world on his shoulders, or at least it felt like it.

No matter where he wound up stopping as he criss-crossed America, Sanders—a self-professed physical-fitness nut—had insisted that workout equipment be available in his hotel room. His staff, for the most part, had been able to accommodate his wishes.

Now he sat on the edge of his desk chair, stripped to his boxer shorts, slowly raising and lowering a set of eight-pound weights. His chest was covered with a fine film of sweat, his muscles visibly twisting under his skin. He sported a set of six-pack abs of which he was quite proud, and he had not been shy about having been photographed during photo ops at beaches and such.

Polls had shown that some still believed that Senator Sanders, all blond hair, toothy smile, and youthful exuberance, was a bit too callow for someone who would be a heartbeat from the presidency. But Sanders and his people had endeavored to transform that liability into a benefit. America was a youth-centric country, and Sanders had been positioned as a symbol of young health and potency, as opposed to various senior citizens (or those fast approaching that status) who had been lobbying for the offices of president and vice president. The move had paid off to some degree, because while some candidates had been making themselves look ridiculous posing by Jeeps or tanks or other symbols of virility, Sanders had been having himself photographed while running marathons or engaging in pickup basketball games with the press corps (and, as many reporters grudgingly admitted, kicking their asses up one side of the court and down the other).

Still, there were some who were saying that this crisis with Mazone was going to be Sanders's first true test of leadership. Other candidates at least had the opportunity to get into office before finding themselves saddled with a catastrophic scandal. Not Steve Sanders. No, he had to deal with Mazone's entire campaign spinning right off the rails, leaving Sanders—well, where, exactly? No one seemed to know.

"All Eyes on Sanders!" That was what the headlines had screamed. "Sanders Considers His Next Step." "Is the Race Over?" All these and more, and Sanders was happily soaking up the attention.

There had never been an election like this one. With

Mazone out of the picture, it would seem the president would win reelection in a walk. But the country was boiling mad over the death of this one damned kid whose name nobody knew little more than a week ago. They blamed the president for the boy's death. Not that that made a lick of sense once any serious consideration was given. The president was no more responsible for the boy's death than he was for some hurricane-spawned disaster. His policies hadn't killed the boy; the kidnappers had done that. But people didn't distinguish. They were looking for someplace to put their sense of outrage, and the president was the unlucky recipient of that ire.

At this point, it seemed likely that Mazone's name would not even be on the ballot, although lawyers on both sides of the aisle were still trying to get that sorted out. Meantime, people didn't want to cast their votes for the president, either, with the ghost of the boy hanging on his reelection campaign like a death shroud. That left Sanders as the man of the hour, presuming he was willing to step up and do what needed to be done. The only difficulty lay in determining exactly what that was.

There was a sharp knock at the door. Sanders allowed the dumbbells to thud to the floor as he called out, "Yes?"

"Your room service, Senator."

Sanders had been a junior senator before being tapped for the vice presidency. His lack of experience was just another thing for his opponents to carp over, right up until both Mazone and the president lost their luster as viable candidates. Now, experience seemed a distant second when it came to consideration of such things as criminal charges or being blamed for a young boy's death. In both those regards, Sanders's hands were clean.

Having tossed on a bathrobe, he walked over to his hotel-room door, glanced through the peephole to make sure nothing untoward was happening outside his door, and then unbolted the locks and stood back. The room-service waiter rolled the tray in, smiling and telling Sanders what a pleasure it was to meet him. They chatted back and forth about what a shame it was about that poor little boy, and Sanders reiterated that he was positive Mazone eventually would be cleared of these heinous charges.

"I think something's wrong with the wheels," said the waiter. "Whole thing suddenly felt heavy. I'm going to leave it here, if that's okay, send up someone else to pick it up, maybe take a look at it."

"That's fine," said Sanders as he signed the check. Then he looked up as the waiter took the check—and almost let out a startled yell.

He caught himself an instant before doing so. The waiter had deftly removed what was now clearly a wig and prosthetics on his face, as deft a disguise as Sanders had ever seen.

"Brohn." Sanders let out an annoyed sigh. "What the hell?"

"Best way to get in to see you," said Eli Brohn, jutting out his scarred chin defiantly.

"Well, you still have a flair for the dramatic." He gestured toward the food. "Way more than I really need, if you're interested."

"Don't mind if I do," said Brohn, as he helped himself to some shrimp cocktail.

"It appears," said Sanders, "according to security briefings I've gotten, that there's some awareness of Dragon Corps' involvement in this matter. You should have disposed of the guy at the airport. You left a loose end."

Brohn shrugged. "I'm not a murderer. Not my style to ice a guy in cold blood."

"A merc with morals. Who would've thought?"

Brohn didn't seem amused by the comment. "Just because I do what I do, it doesn't make me immoral. Just means I've got my priorities in order."

"Don't worry about it," said Sanders. "They don't have anything on you definitively. Just one guy's word, and he never even saw you come through with the boy, right?"

"Right."

"What about Quince? Is Quince in place?"

"Yup. I know, this all hinges on him. He's fine."

"Good. As for the rest of it, it'll all work out. You see, these things always do," said Sanders. And he smiled.

18

GENERAL TIBERIUS DOYLE WATCHED LOGAN SITTING slumped in a chair in his office at Fort Randolph. Logan was holding a small stogie lightly between two fingers, watching the smoke waft lazily toward the ceiling. He hadn't said anything since walking in over the protests of Doyle's aide and taking a seat uninvited. Doyle had waved off his aide, assuring him that everything was under control, and then sat there and simply observed Logan not say a damned thing.

Finally, Doyle broke the silence. "Those things'll kill you, you know," he said, indicating the rolled tobacco in Logan's mouth.

"They'll have to wait in line."

Doyle paused and then said, in what he fancied was a tone both consoling and yet not patronizing, "You tried your best."

"I don't like coming up short."

"You can accomplish many things, Logan, but you can't move through time and space. It's not like the boy died before your eyes and you're blaming yourself that you didn't move quickly enough to prevent it. You got there—"

"Too late."

"Yes. Too late."

"Ain't made up my mind yet whether that's better or worse than standing there and seeing it happen." Logan leaned forward. "Gonna need another chopper."

"What?"

"Another chopper. And I could use Westlake for a while longer. His whole thing with being a walking lie detector is a great time saver."

"For what?"

"For finding the guys who did this. For tracking down Dragon Corps and making them pay."

Slowly, Doyle shook his head. "Logan—"

"Don't punk out on me now, General."

"It's not a matter of punking out. Believe it or not, Logan, even generals have to answer to higher-ups. I could justify the expenditure of personnel and equipment when the derailing of an election seemed imminent. But you lost a Black Hawk helicopter."

"It's not like we parked it at the mall and couldn't find it again. The damned thing was shot out of the sky."

"I know that. And I'll have to explain that. And I will. But that's not the point. The point is, Logan, I can justify anything when it comes to matters of national security. But a revenge mission is another matter."

"Could be more than that. There ain't nothing to stop Dragon Corps from grabbing some other kid. Starting this whole thing over again."

"True. But I can't justify the expenditure of equipment and manpower on a possibility."

Logan sat back in his chair and took a long, slow drag on his cigar. "Someone's been on your case, haven't they." It was framed a question, but there was no hint of questioning in his voice.

Doyle looked as if he were about to offer protests but then clearly opted not to bother. "Let's just say that the secretary of the Army had something to say to me about it."

"Courtesy of our friends in the Bureau of National Emergency, if I had to guess."

"As I said, Logan, everyone has someone else he has to answer to. Except you, perhaps. One of the advantages of being an independent operator."

"Guess so. It's weird. I let myself get dragged into this whole thing, and now I keep feeling like I should've done more. How's our corporal doing?"

"He seemed much like you after his debriefing. Frustrated. Angry. Wishing he could have done more." Doyle looked at him sidelong. "You were hoping he would want out of the Army after chasing around the country with you."

"Don't know what gave you that idea."

"Westlake said so."

"Oh. Well . . . okay, then. Yeah, that's true."

"The boy's a determined career Army man through and through, Logan. You weren't going to shake that out of him."

"Let's hope your other determined career Army men don't succeed where I failed."

"Yes, that was an unfortunate incident, and the men who were involved have been dealt with."

"There'll always be more."

"And you think the answer is to hide in that school of yours, behind protective walls?"

"What would you call what you do here? You call your training facility a fort; ours is a school. Are you hiding?"

"Of course not."

"Same thing."

"You know it's not."

"No, I don't, but thanks for assumin' I do."

Doyle felt as if he wanted to argue the point more but realized that it was more trouble than it was worth. Logan was a determined cuss, and there was very little that Doyle could say that would change his mind on just about anything.

"Thanks for your help," said Logan. He rose from his chair.

"Where are you off to now?"

"Washington."

"Why? What's there?" Then he realized. "The boy's funeral."

Logan nodded.

Because of the national attention that Matthew's kidnapping had gotten, Ellen Hayes had received the offer from no less than the Congress of the United States of America to have Matthew's funeral be a day of national mourning, with the actual viewing and ceremony to be held in the nation's capital. The government would naturally cover all costs. There were many who accused the Congress of playing politics with the tragedy of Matthew's demise. That the entire purpose of the endeavor was to milk Matthew's passing to further whatever their individual agendas might be, just as the antiwar groups hooking up with Ellen Hayes were targeted with the same accusation.

But by this point, Ellen Hayes no longer cared. Whereas before she had made herself available to whatever news outlets were interested in talking to her, now she had gone into seclusion. In any shots of her caught in passing, she looked vacant, empty, drained of enthusiasm and life. A small army of people whose main job appeared to be guarding her from the press seemed to have sprung from nowhere. She was trapped in the middle of a publicity maelstrom, but she was like the eye of any storm—it swirled around her without touching her. All the turmoil she was experiencing came from within rather than without.

She had agreed to allow her son's funeral to become a major national undertaking, and the general belief was that she had done so because she really didn't give a damn about anything anymore.

"You want me to clear the way for you to attend," said Doyle.

Logan nodded. "My understanding is that the president's going to be there. So a guy with claws in his hands wouldn't exactly be allowed to stroll in."

"I'll go through channels. Should be able to manage it. You wish to pay your respects?"

"Yeah. Figure it's the least I can do. And so far, the least I can do is all I've done."

"I suspect Corporal Westlake will wish to attend as well."

"Wouldn't surprise me."

"I'll arrange for military transport to Washington and a car to meet you there."

" 'Preciate that."

He started to rise, and then Doyle said, "And Logan . . ."

"Yeah?"

"Extend the sympathies of the U.S. Army to Mrs. Hayes on her loss, would you?"

"Sure. Why not? Sympathies are all we have to give these days."

Tony Westlake, sitting by himself in the PX, staring off into space, barely noticed when Logan stepped in behind him. Slowly, he became aware of Logan's presence. He still didn't bother to turn and look at him.

"What do you want?" he said hollowly.

"Heading to the funeral. Thought you might want to come. See it through."

"What is there to see through? The boy's dead."

"Have it your way." Logan didn't walk away.

"We failed," Westlake muttered.

"Yeah. Can't win 'em all."

"Is that what it all boils down to for you? A casual cliché?"

"What else?"

"It was a tragedy!"

"It was for the mother. Not for us."

Westlake turned and looked at him, revolted. "How can you say that?"

"Because we move on. Sooner or later—sooner, most likely—our lives, yours and mine, will go back to normal. Ellen Hayes's life never will. In a lot of ways, that kid was her life. We're just a couple of guys who tried to make a difference and didn't manage it. It was a job. We did the best we could. Tomorrow there's a different job."

"And the guys who did this?" There was cold fury in his eyes. "What about them?"

"I find them. I bring them down."

"I'll help."

"General won't hear of it. He's loaned you out enough. 'Less, of course, you'd care to resign. Get yourself sprung out of the Army. Doyle might be okay with that. Come join the X-Men, like I suggested to you before all this started."

"You mean, like you were hoping I'd want to do when I got done following you all over creation."

"Pretty much."

Westlake leaned back in the chair. His gaze was distant, as if he were looking off toward another time, another place. "What do you think I should do?" he said finally.

"Aw, no. You don't put that on me."

"Why the hell not? You seemed full enough of opinions when you first showed up. You were bound and determined that I should join up with you guys."

"I just didn't want you to get your head handed to you by your fellow soldiers. With the X-Men, ain't no chance of that happening."

"So, no one will attack me if I'm an X-Man."

"Oh, hell no, tons of guys will attack you."

"Well, thanks for your honesty."

"Honesty's easier than trying to keep lies straight." He paused and then said, "Kid, you did good work out there. You got nothing to hang your head over. Ain't our fault it went bad."

"Is that what you tell yourself?"

"What I tell myself ain't nobody's business but mine. Anyway . . . nice working with you."

With that, he started to leave. Before he could do so, Westlake called after him, "Is that invitation to the funeral still open?"

"Sure. General's setting it up."

"Okay, well . . . yeah. Yeah, okay. I'm in. Like you said, I should see it through to the end. Even if the end isn't what I was hoping for."

"The end never is, kid. It almost never is."

19

THE PRESIDENT HADN'T WANTED TO COME.

He had been quite certain, and indeed was correct, that protesters would be gathering outside the funeral home. Fortunately enough, they were being rounded up and isolated blocks away, in a "protest zone" where they wouldn't be able to interfere with the actual funeral proceedings and—more important—be less likely to show up during prime-time news coverage.

Still, facing the mother under the scrutiny of the cameras—a mother who doubtless blamed the president to some degree for the tragic fate suffered by her son—was not his idea of a good time. He had a lot of faith in his ability to charm people with his considerable personal magnetism, given the opportunity. But this was going to be a stretch, even for him.

The squad of Secret Service agents who always accompanied him had secured the area of the Santangelo

Funeral Home, the venue that had been carefully selected for the services. It had been the scene for several
high-profile funerals in the last several years and was
favored by the Secret Service as a place where they
could provide maximum protection, thanks to a variety
of considerations that the president didn't pretend to
understand.

The president made his entrance, wishing that he
could be just about anyplace else. He felt a steady
thudding in his temples. Absolutely nothing was going
right these days. With Election Day fast approaching,
the polling numbers were far from encouraging. And
the fact that people were still blaming him for what had
happened made him not want to attend the funeral.
But his chief of staff had insisted that failing to do so
would get him painted as insensitive and uncaring. It
was a clear damned-if-you-do, damned-if-you-don't
scenario, and the feeling was that the president had
nothing to lose by trying to be proactive.

The mood in the funeral home was subdued, as expected. The president was greeted with solemn nods.
The speaker of the House was there, as were a variety of
other political rivals. As if operating under an unspoken
accord, no challenges were issued, no blame was tossed
around. This was neither the time nor the place.

All eyes naturally turned in the president's direction
as he walked slowly toward the casket at the far end of
the room. He didn't like open-casket ceremonies, never
had. The entire concept of decorating corpses to give

them the appearance of someone in a deep slumber creeped him out. But he certainly wasn't about to convey that skittishness to anyone. He would deal with it, that was all. Just deal with it.

As was to be expected, the boy's mother was standing protectively near the casket. She was talking to two other women, both of whom had their backs to the president. Her eyes were red-rimmed and looked empty. When she saw him coming, she stopped talking. The other two women, sensing a shift in tone in the room, had turned and were regarding him with as much feigned politeness as they could muster. As for Ellen Hayes . . .

Nothing. Just blankness in her face.

If everyone hadn't had to pass through metal detectors on the way in—standard for this kind of memorial service, where high-ranking officials were expected to attend—the president would have been certain that she was about to pull out a gun and open fire on him. She had the sort of empty-eyed look that one would expect to see on the face of a killer, as if her mind were a million miles away, and her body was functioning on autopilot.

He took a deep breath to steady himself and then strode toward her. He reached out as gently as he could and took one of her hands in both of his. Her hand was cold, lifeless.

"I am so sorry for your loss," he said as softly, as meaningfully, as he could.

She mouthed the words *Thank you* but was having trouble getting her voice to accompany. She cleared her throat, and this time the actual words emerged from her mouth, softly and a little strangled.

"The sympathies of an entire country go out to you," he said. "I never had the opportunity to know your son. I wish I had."

"He was rooting for Mazone."

"Yes, well . . ."

All manner of alarms went off in the president's head. He had kept carefully silent and noncommittal over the legal problems that Mazone had landed in. If nothing else, the Justice Department didn't want the condemning words of the commander in chief tainting a potential jury pool. Plus, given the circumstances, it simply wasn't appropriate for the president to be commenting on Mazone's alleged involvement with the case.

Instead, playing it as safe as he could, the president said, "The senator's loss . . . is all our loss."

Ellen Hayes sounded like a ghost. "He deserved so much more than he was given."

Clichés came to his mind. *The Lord moves in mysterious ways. We're not meant to understand the grand plan. His killers will be found, dead or alive.*

Instead, all he said was, "I know." It was the simplest and, ultimately, most sincere thing he could have said. Her hand was still between his, and he squeezed it. "I'm a father. If anything happened to one of my children . . ." His voice trailed off.

She returned the tightening of his hand, the first sign of real life that she had displayed. "I'm glad you understand. And I hope that you never experience anything like this."

Then she released his hand and turned away, resting her hand on the edge of the casket.

He felt relief surging through him. He had braced himself for a flood of vituperation, and instead there had been nothing. Nothing at all. Perhaps she had decided to embrace the same decorum being displayed by the other politicians, believing that her son's funeral was no place to raise a ruckus, much less with the commander in chief.

He began to think that he was going to get out of this situation without any sort of trouble.

That was when the metal detector went berserk.

Logan stepped back from the detector, only the smallest hint of annoyance visible on his face. Westlake had already stepped through, and he watched as Logan stared blandly at the full-dress Marines who were manning the detector at the entrance to the funeral home.

"Sir, remove your belt, please."

"That ain't gonna do it, sonny," said Logan.

Westlake moved toward the Marine and said, "General Doyle was supposed to have cleared us through."

The Marine fired a look at him that spoke volumes: *Don't try anything, Army boy, or I will take you down.* "We have procedures to deal with, *Corporal*," he said, taking care to put particular emphasis on Westlake's rank, clearly intended to put Westlake in his place, since the Marine was a lieutenant. "I'm sure you can respect that." He turned back to Logan. "Sir, please remove your belt."

Logan shrugged, did so, placed it on a table next to the metal detector, and took one step forward. Once again, the detector began to howl.

"Imagine my shock," said Logan.

"He has metal inside his body," Westlake said. "That's what's setting it off."

"You mean, like a pin in his hip?"

"Among other places," said Logan.

The lieutenant stepped forward with a metal-detection wand. Logan calmly put his arms out to either side. People lined up behind him were clearly annoyed at the delay, but there was nothing they could do to speed matters along. Another Marine with a printout in front of him was nodding and saying to the lieutenant with the wand, "They're both on the list. They have proper ID."

"We still have to clear them," said the lieutenant. He started running the wand along Logan's body.

It never stopped going off. His eyes widened as every square inch of Logan's frame caused the wand to beep in protest. Those behind Logan took a step back, looking concerned and confused. Through all of it, Logan never appeared other than distantly amused.

"How the hell are you walking?" the lieutenant finally said.

"I'm not," Logan said reasonably. "I'm standing here."

"Haven't you done enough?"

Logan looked up, and a familiar scowling face appeared before him. "Agent Craig," said Logan. "Pleasure as always."

"I should have you arrested."

Indicating the equipment with a nod of his head, Logan said, "For what? Beeping?"

"You know damned well what for, you—"

"Agent Craig—Lieutenant—I'll handle it from here."

The familiar voice instantly snapped the lieutenant to attention. Craig, for his part, held out for a moment longer. "Sir, this man represents a security—"

"I know who he is and what he represents," said the president. "On my responsibility, let him in."

"Sir, yes, sir," said the lieutenant again. The other Marines, and even Westlake, had likewise snapped to attention.

"At ease," said the president. He put out a hand and said, "Logan. Still causing problems, I see."

"Wasn't planning on it, sir. Just kind of happened."

"As it typically tends to do with you." He glanced at Westlake, who was looking goggle-eyed at Logan. "Friend of yours?"

"Tony Westlake," said Logan. "Future head of the Joint Chiefs of Staff. He helped me out looking for the Hayes boy."

"Quite an achievement there, Corporal," said the president, putting out a hand. Westlake shook it numbly.

"Logan isn't always amenable to people helping him. You must be something special."

"He is," said Logan.

"May I ask . . ." Westlake hesitated.

"Go ahead, son," said the president.

"I was just wondering where you knew Logan from."

"There was a . . . situation that Logan attended to. He and several of his teammates. Sorry I can't go into more detail. The whole national-security thing. You understand."

"Oh, yes, sir. Of course."

"I'll tell you later," Logan said in a low voice. "If you'll excuse me, Mr. President," and he nodded in the direction of Ellen Hayes.

"Yes, of course," said the president, stepping back.

Logan and Corporal Westlake moved past him. The president watched as Ellen Hayes, who had taken a seat, looked up at the two of them with a face too exhausted even to display emotion.

The president stiffened slightly as his attention shifted back to the main entrance, and he saw who was next to come in through the metal detectors. Steve Sanders was nodding in the direction of photographers who were snapping his picture as fast as they could. The president hated to admit it, but Sanders had been fielding this situation perfectly. The only person whose reputation had not been dragged down as a result of this fiasco, he was also the only person who looked to benefit from it.

Sanders saw the president and, annoyingly, headed straight toward him. He did so slowly, his hands out where they could be seen easily. Obviously, he wasn't stupid; in a situation such as this, the Secret Service was watching everyone suspiciously. That was their job, after all, and nobody faulted them for it.

"Mr. President," said Sanders formally, putting out a hand.

"Senator." The president shook it. Sanders had a very firm handshake.

"A tragedy, sir. Tragedy for all concerned."

"Couldn't agree more."

"And I am certain," Sanders said, "that Senator Mazone will be exonerated."

Tread carefully . . . tread very carefully . . .

"I know that the investigation will get to the bottom of it," said the president noncommittally. It was as neutral a statement as he could have made, but Sanders's head bobbed like a floating cork. "I have confidence that all will be revealed in due time."

"As have I," said Sanders. "It just sickens me that these monsters were convinced they could derail the electoral process through their actions."

"Americans will not give in to terrorists." The president intoned it like a mantra.

He glanced over at Logan and Westlake, who were deep in conversation with Ellen Hayes. She appeared to be looking right through them. He wondered if she was hearing them or, for that matter, hearing anyone.

"Tell me, Mr. President," Sanders said, "who do you think the voters will blame for this tragedy?"

"The terrorists. Who else?"

"I think we both know who else, Mr. President."

"Senator," the president said sternly, "I certainly hope you don't have any intention of trying to score political points as a result of this terrible turn of events."

"No more than you do, Mr. President."

The president looked at him levelly and got the feeling that there was more to Sanders than the senator was letting on. Previously, Sanders had seemed like little more than an empty suit who wouldn't pose any sort of threat to Mazone's spotlight. Now, though, there was something about him . . .

That was when the screaming started, and the shouting, and suddenly, the president felt his feet actually leaving the ground. The Secret Service had clustered in tightly around him, and there were shouts of "Secure Eagle! Secure Eagle!" He tried to see what was happening, but it was impossible to make out anything between the broad shoulders of the Secret Service detachment. Seconds later, he'd been ushered out of the funeral home without the faintest idea of what was going on.

"You said you were going to get him back," Ellen Hayes said tonelessly. Westlake felt as if they were invisible to her, that she was looking right through them. It was clear, though, that she was addressing her comments to Logan. "What happened to that?"

Logan said nothing in response. Westlake saw the hesitation and decided to step into the breech.

"Sometimes, ma'am, even the best isn't good enough."

"He had so much to live for. And they took it from him." Slow anger began to build in her voice as she showed signs of life. "I want the bastards who did this. I want them found. I want them punished. Can you do that?"

Westlake was about to give a response that would leave them some leeway, but Logan said curtly, "Yes."

"Logan," whispered Westlake. He tried to take Logan by the elbow, to pull him off to the side so he could speak with him privately.

Logan shook off his hand effortlessly. "I'll find them. I'll find them and take them down. They won't do this to anybody else."

Westlake half expected her to dismiss his promise out of hand. After all, he had spoken with similar confidence when it came to rescuing Matthew, and they all knew how that had worked out. To Westlake's surprise, however, she nodded. Her face was still an immobile mask, but there was cold determination in her eyes.

"Good. That would mean a lot to me." She glanced toward Matthew's corpse. "And I like to think it would mean a lot to Mattie as well."

Logan was staring at the boy's body in the coffin. His

eyes narrowed. Westlake noticed that something had changed in Logan's deportment. He had tensed, like a stalking lion, and it was as if the air around him were filled with a sort of feral energy.

"Logan?" he said.

He had no idea if Logan even heard him. Slowly, the mutant was approaching the coffin. Matthew's face was in peaceful repose, so peaceful that he looked more asleep than dead.

A TV cameraman was moving in close on Logan, until Logan glanced at him in a way that made him back off. At that point, Westlake noticed that there were, in fact, several camera crews present.

"Mrs. Hayes," said Westlake in a low voice, "if you want, I can try and have all these cameramen tossed . . ."

"They're here because I want them here," she said. "The world should know the human cost of terrorism."

It was Westlake's opinion that the world already had a fairly clear idea of that, but he kept that notion to himself.

Meantime, Logan had drawn closer to the coffin. His nostrils flared. He leaned in toward the corpse and sniffed it. Other people noticed what he was doing, and their reactions ranged from confused to appalled.

"Logan!" Westlake said again, and he moved toward him. "What's going on?"

"This ain't him."

He was just loud enough for Ellen Hayes to have heard him.

"What? What are you saying?"

"This ain't your son."

"What?"

"This ain't him. The scent is completely different from what I picked up in his room."

Ellen Hayes looked stunned, unable even to begin to phrase a response to that.

Westlake said, "Logan . . ."

Logan wasn't listening to him. Instead, to the horror of all onlookers, he grabbed the corpse of Matthew Hayes by the front of its neatly pressed shirt and yanked it upright. Its head lolled back. People began to scream. Secret Service men and police officers started toward him.

"Who are you?" Logan wasn't shouting, not even coming close to losing his temper. But there was quiet fury in his voice, which seemed insane, considering that the object of his fury was dead.

Cops drew within a foot of him, and that was as far as they got. Logan didn't even bother to glance their way; instead, his claws snapped out with a frightening *snikt* sound. They froze, looking at one another, unsure how to proceed, particularly since Logan wasn't threatening anyone except for someone who was beyond harm.

"We do this the easy way," said Logan to the corpse, "or the hard way."

He's lost his mind, thought Westlake. *He's lost his freaking mind.* But at the same time, the cold confidence with which Logan had approached every obstacle that had arisen in their path came back to him. Westlake, who had been about to try to talk sense into Logan, kept his mouth shut—which was probably fortunate, since it was doubtful he'd manage to sway Logan one way or another.

"Fine," said Logan. He retracted two of the three claws on his right hand and jabbed down into the shoulder of Matthew Hayes's corpse.

There were screams from Ellen Hayes and various family members and attendees, and several of the cops lunged toward Logan to try to take him down, claws or no. But those screams paled next to the scream that emerged from Matthew Hayes as he grabbed at his shoulder, and shrieked, "Son of a bitch!"

Everyone froze. Everyone, that is, except Logan, who grabbed Matthew Hayes from the coffin and yanked him clear. He drew him nose-to-nose and snarled, "You're good at playing dead, I'll give ya that. How'd you like to go for the real thing?"

Matthew gave him a look that was pure hatred, and then his skin suddenly rippled. His features remained the same, but he grew larger, more massive. The little suit ripped down the middle, the sleeves tearing loose of the shoulders. His lower half remained exactly the same, presumably to keep his pants intact. But from the waist up, within seconds, he'd swollen to three times his original size. Muscles stood out like cables against his back and along his arms. He picked up the startled

Logan, twisted fast, and heaved him into the nearest crowd of police officers. The cops went down, Logan on top of them.

Ellen Hayes's face had taken on the shade of curdled milk. She looked ready to pass out.

Cops and agents were moving in toward Matthew Hayes, or the thing calling itself Matthew Hayes; others had already gotten the president the hell out.

The camera crews had no idea where to point their cameras first and were swerving this way and that, trying to get everything.

No one was pulling out a gun to try to shoot the thing, and Westlake instantly understood why. There were too many innocent people, not to mention high-profile politicos and VIPs, milling together. Stray bullets could result in some very prestigious obituaries.

The creature with a distorted version of Matthew Hayes's face charged forward, tossing aside anyone who tried to get in its way. It lurched from one side to the other, seeking a way out. Everyone was screaming, shouting, either trying to stop it from leaving or trying to get out of its way.

It then went straight up.

For a heartbeat, Westlake thought that it had flown, but that wasn't the case. Rather, it had leaped skyward. There was a skylight overhead through which the sun's rays had been filtering, carefully tinted so that it would have a quieting, mellowing effect on anyone below. It had exactly the opposite impact now as "Matthew

Hayes" crashed through it, sending glass tumbling and everyone scattering for cover.

Westlake looked around, tried to find Logan, and couldn't.

"My God," someone said, staring at Westlake. "What the hell happened to you?"

Westlake initially had no idea what he was referring to, and then he glanced at his own hands. They were red. His skin had changed color.

Someone had lied. In all the screaming, someone had lied about something.

But what?

20

LOGAN SPRINTED DOWN THE STREET, ON THE SCENT. He rounded a corner, and there was the guy, just ahead of him. He was shrugging off the remains of the tattered shirt and glancing over his shoulder to see if he was being chased. Logan made no effort to be stealthy; this was a full-out pursuit, and there was no time for subtlety.

The quarry's (for that was how Logan was thinking of him) legs began to lengthen, tearing through the trousers that had easily accommodated Matthew Hayes. This guy was definitely some sort of shape shifter, Mystique and Mister Fantastic rolled into one.

Cars veered out of the way as the quarry took seven-league strides right down the middle of the street. Logan kept in pursuit, running up the fronts of cars, bounding off car rooftops, doing whatever he could to close the gap between him and his target.

They rounded a corner and ran headlong into protesters.

The White House sat in the distance, and there was a
mob scene of people waving signs declaring everything
they felt was wrong with the current administration
and its policies. Just beyond the fence were soldiers
lined up. None of them had a weapon out and aimed,
but they looked prepared to do what needed to be done
should a confrontation arise.

All reacted much the same, however, when they saw
the long-limbed shape shifter coming their way. They
shouted, screamed in confusion, pointed—did all the
things that a typical mob does.

The quarry promptly reduced his size and thrust
himself straight into the heart of the crowd.

Oh, perfect.

Logan never slowed. Instead, he hurled himself right
into the midst of the bewildered crowd, although he
took the precaution of retracting his claws, lest he accidentally skewer somebody.

"Out of the way! Out of the way, you idiots!"

Logan was shouting, but it was like one pebble trying to make itself heard over the thundering of an ava-
lanche. The vast majority of the people there believed
that they were under attack. Because of that, they were
moving every which way, providing a formidable assault
on Logan's senses.

Logan stopped moving. He closed his eyes, slowed
his breathing. Within seconds, everything around him

had faded to a distant buzzing. There was only him and the scent of his quarry, one single thread floating through a massive tapestry of aromas.

There was no way that anyone or anything living could have sorted out one scent among so many.

Logan did it anyway.

His head snapped around, and he angled sharply to his right. People were surging around him, but they may as well have been gnats for all that they impeded him. Logan shoved them aside and never slowed; most of them never even saw him, because one instant he was there, and then he had moved through and beyond.

He cut through like a shark and then saw his quarry, just ahead, still bare-chested, his trousers now little more than tattered shorts. The shape shifter glanced back, saw him, turned, and decided to take a stand. His torso and legs swelled, Hulk-like, and he shouted, "Fine! Bring it!"

Logan's claws snapped out.

He did not, however, charge. His instincts were to leap forward and, claws swinging, rip this idiot to pieces. But he knew that would be a bad move; he needed him alive so that he could question him about what was going on.

"Where's your tattoo?" he said as he began to circle his prey. The shape shifter countered, his feet moving as Logan's did but in the exact opposite pattern. "You're with Dragon Corps, right? What's your name?"

"Sure. Right," said the shape shifter, and then he charged.

Logan leaped over him and swiped down with his claws, slicing across the shape shifter's back. He let out a roar of pain and swung blindly with a huge fist. He got lucky, striking Logan in the chest as he sailed past. There was a loud *clank* as the fist made impact with the adamantium-laced skeleton. Logan spiraled through the air and landed in a crouch, ready to charge again. The shape shifter turned to face him once more.

His arms suddenly lengthened, and his fists became gargantuan mallets. He brought them repeatedly down, slamming all around Logan, causing him to jump from one side to the other. As Logan dodged, he lashed out with his claws, slicing into his opponent's arms. Logan was annoyed to see that the cuts kept healing over, even faster than Logan's own healing factor would have permitted. Either the shape shifter was impervious to harm (although he obviously could feel pain), or else he was shifting his skin around to cover the places where Logan was scoring on him.

The protesters had managed to get largely out of the way, and many of them had run off. But some had remained, forming a rapidly expanding semicircle as they watched the proceedings. Had the battle involved Captain America or Iron Man slugging it out with some evildoer, they wouldn't have hesitated to shout out encouragement. As it was, they weren't entirely sure who was the good guy and who was the bad guy, and thus whom they should be rooting for.

They also served to block the soldiers who were on the other side of the fence. Seeing the turn that events had taken, the soldiers had unslung their weapons and had them at the ready. But they couldn't aim at either Logan or the shape shifter, because the protesters were blocking them, completely ignoring the commands of senior officers to get the hell out of the way. Even if they had done so, the soldiers wouldn't have known whom to shoot at, or even if they should shoot anyone, since neither Logan nor the shape shifter was making the slightest attempt to attack the White House. They were far too focused on each other.

Asphalt imploded under the crushing blows of the shape shifter's hands. Logan snatched a couple of pieces in either hand and flung them as hard as he could, smashing them into the shape shifter's face. He staggered, bellowing in fury, and Logan took the opportunity to leap. At the last moment, the shape shifter lashed out, but Logan twisted in midair and eluded him. He landed on the shape shifter's chest, gripping the side of his head to stay on.

"Where's the kid?" he snarled.

"Go to hell!"

"You must've had a getaway plan. You were going to head out after the funeral, after the 'body' had been buried. Where to?"

The shape shifter, instead of answering, dissolved in Logan's grasp. One moment he was there, the next it was like trying to hold on to melting Silly Putty.

And suddenly, he had reared up from all sides and enveloped Logan.

Everything around Logan was black. The shape shifter, his body amorphous, had completely surrounded Logan. He was trying to end things quickly by smothering the embattled mutant.

He was attempting to keep Logan's arms pinned at his sides, but Logan wouldn't have any of it. No matter how much pressure he put on Logan from the sides, it couldn't deter him from bending his wrists. Logan retracted his claws, angled his wrists, and snapped the claws out again. They emerged on a horizontal line, stabbing in both directions. He heard a low, smothered moan and knew that he'd done damage. It was no effort at all for him to rotate his hands so that he was effectively digging a wider and wider hole into his adversary, thwarting the shape shifter's attempts to repair the damage.

Suddenly, just like that, the pressure was released, and Logan was alone. He swayed a moment, pulling himself together, and sucked in air greedily as he looked around to see where the shape shifter had gone.

He couldn't say he was thrilled when he spotted him.

The shape shifter was seeping down into a sewer grating.

"Oh, no, you don't!" shouted Logan as he leaped the distance and brought his claws swinging down just as the last of the shape shifter morphed through the grating. Logan was about to cut apart the metal when he realized there was no way he would fit through. He looked around quickly and spotted a manhole cover a short distance away. He darted over and rammed his claws down into it, gritted his teeth, and yanked as hard as he could. Slowly, maddeningly slowly, the sewer cover came free from the hole. He swung it to the right and withdrew his claws. It thudded to the ground, rolling in place for a moment before settling down.

"Why is it always sewers?" he muttered before he dropped feet-first into the tunnels.

He landed shin deep in liquid, the contents of which he didn't want to think about. The smell from the place assaulted him, threatening to overwhelm his senses in a way that even the crowd aboveground hadn't managed. He stopped trying to follow the scent and instead reached out with his other senses, all as keen. He screened out the distant sound of water running, pouring out from assorted junctures and combining into the main flow. He listened hard, trying to detect the sound of a body sloshing through the sewers.

Nothing . . .

Nothing . . .

And then, very faint . . .

A splash. A series of splashes.

Gotcha, thought Logan.

He sprinted through the tunnel, trying not to let the stench overwhelm him. At first, he had proceeded cautiously, but the sounds were becoming more distant, harder to pick up. So he tossed that aside and broke into a dead run, splashing through the sewage as quickly as he could. He knew it was risky; if the shape shifter heard him coming, he might lie in wait, try to ambush him.

Let him. Beats the hell out of this.

He turned a corner and came to a halt.

The tunnels went off in two branches. The sound of his target's splashing footsteps was in the distance, and the echoes made it damned near impossible to figure out which branch the shape shifter had gone down.

Making his best guess, Logan darted off down the lefthand tunnel and into the darkness.

Quince was cursing to himself almost nonstop.

As he slogged through the tunnels, trying not to pass out from the stench, he couldn't help thinking that he should have seen this coming, especially with that damned Wolverine sticking his nose into this.

The moment Quince had learned of Wolverine's involvement, unease had crept through him. He'd never had the occasion to cross swords with the legendary runt, but Wolverine's reputation definitely preceded him. His coconspirators had been far more sanguine about the prospect, but Quince had been the sole voice of reason, saying, "This could go wrong. This could all go so wrong with Wolverine involved, you have no idea."

But they hadn't listened, and now Quince was suffering the brunt of their miscalculation.

He was sore in all the places where the runt had stabbed him. Standing and squaring off against him had been a mistake, but what else was he supposed to have done? Wolverine wasn't going to back off.

The whole operation had gone straight to hell. "So easy," Brawn had promised. "A cakewalk. In and out. No problem."

So now where were they? Everyone knew that the supposed corpse of Matthew Hayes was actually a shape shifter who could feign death well enough to fool just about anyone. The cause of "death" had seemed so obvious, courtesy of his morphing skills, that no autopsy had been performed, just as expected. He'd lain there in a deep, self-induced trance while they'd prepped his body for the funeral. Embalming had posed no threat to his morphing form. And once buried, well, getting out of a coffin wasn't *that* much of a trick for a shape shifter.

So simple. All so simple.

Until bloody freaking Wolverine.

And by now, everyone would know that Matthew Hayes was likely alive and that someone with a direct link to his whereabouts was running around the nation's capital. In the meantime, they'd had to dump Hunt, who'd become a liability. To top it all off, Quince had been reduced to mucking around in the sewers, of all places.

Still, if Wolverine was tracking him by scent, as he most likely was, this seemed the best way to go about losing him.

And so Quince slogged onward, silently plotting all the things he was going to do to wreak revenge on his associates when and if he managed to get back to their lair.

He kept listening for sounds of pursuit and every so often even thought he heard something. But it was hard to be absolutely certain. He briefly considered stopping and taking a stand but quickly dismissed the idea. That tactic hadn't worked out very well for him before, and he wasn't interested in a repeat performance.

The sad irony was, everyone was supposed to come out a winner in this. Everyone. Dragon Corps was going to be the unsung heroes in this entire operation.

Quince loved America. Loved it more than anyone he knew, possibly more than anyone alive. It hurt him, physically hurt him, when he thought about what was happening to this country. The wavering of faith, the deterioration of values, the failing of the people's resolution to take a stand against terrorism, and—most problematic—the current administration's flailing around in terms of its own handling of terrorist threats. All he had wanted to do was help. That was all any of the members of Dragon Corps wanted to do. Get the right man into the job so he could do what needed to be done. When the true history of everything that had happened eventually came clear, fifty, maybe a hundred years from now, they would be hailed as heroes and patriots.

For the time being, though, it was a major pain in the ass to be hunted as if they were criminals and villains. All of those mindless protesters, scattering out of the way and shrieking in girlish terror—even the men sounded like teenage girls—it almost made him embarrassed to be an American. They had substituted signs for true national fortitude, substituted slogans for spirit. They were the true villains here, not him. Not Quince.

He had no idea where he was. If he kept at it, he might well wind up heading in a complete circle and finding himself face-to-face with Wolverine again. That was not a confrontation that he was eagerly seeking.

Quince banged up against a ladder and looked up. There was a manhole cover some feet above. There was no light filtering through. That meant one of two things. Either a car was parked over the manhole, or else night had fallen. He had lost track of time.

He felt worn out, exhausted, in no shape to fight should he emerge in the middle of a group of National Guardsmen or something. But he decided it would be best to take the chance.

He clambered up the ladder and pushed against the manhole cover. It wasn't light, but Quince's strength was still formidable enough to shove it out of the way with little difficulty. He peered out tentatively. The last thing he wanted to do was spring out of the manhole and get himself hit by an oncoming truck.

The street was deserted. The sun was indeed down, and long shadows were stretching across rundown buildings. He had managed to surface in one of Washington's lousier sections of town. So much the better.

A small group of swaggering youths was grouped around a lamppost. Several had cigarettes dangling from their mouths. They were wearing gang colors. *Wonderful.* They pointed and laughed when they saw the mostly unclad Quince haul himself out of the sewer. He had resumed his normal, human shape, no longer adopting the form of Matthew Hayes.

They started to strut toward him, several of them making loud "Whewww!" noises in response to the distinctive odor that was radiating off him. He supposed he couldn't blame them for that; he'd been wandering around in sewers for God knew how long. One look at his tattered clothing, and it was obvious he didn't have any money on him, so robbery clearly wasn't their motivation. Instead, they were going to hassle him out of concern for protecting their territory, or maybe they were just bored and looking for some amusement.

Either way, Quince wasn't interested in playing along.

He took two steps toward them and tripled his size.

That was more than enough for them to fall back, tripping over one another, and one of them shouted,

"It's the Hulk!" *Good.* Let them go running to the nearest police station howling that the Hulk was in town. The more confusion that could be generated, the better he liked it.

He checked the street signs to see where he was. He knew the layout of Washington quite well; all he needed to do was orient himself, and he could find the way to his destination with little trouble.

Once he had his location down, he started off at a slow jog, keeping close to the shadows. As he passed an alleyway, he spotted a homeless guy slumped against a wall. When Quince slowed pace, the guy pathetically put out a hand in a mute request for change.

You want change? I'll give you change.

Moments later, the homeless guy was lying deep in the darkness of the furthest reaches of the alleyway, stripped of his clothes. Quince finished pulling on the oversized coat, and his nose wrinkled from the smell. Trust him to find something capable of obscuring the stink of the sewers. It wasn't easy, but this guy's wardrobe had managed it.

Still, it was better than running around in clothing so scanty that sooner or later, some passing patrol car would surely notice him, pull over, and ask him what was going on. A fight would ensue, backup would be called, and he'd be right back in a big steaming bowl of mess. He simply didn't need the grief.

He continued on foot. He easily could have flagged a

cab and then made off with it, but he was determined to get through the rest of the damned city with his head as far down as possible.

Eventually, he made it to the bank of the Potomac River. He followed it until he arrived at the private dock.

Then he waited.

And waited.

Finally, far off in the distance, he saw it slowly approaching. Actually, he heard it before he saw it: the distinct high-pitched whine of its twin engines.

The seaplane descended from the night sky, lower and lower, until its pontoons gently touched down on the water. Even though he knew there should be no pursuit, Quince still scanned the skies overhead to see if there was any sign of fighters in the air. Nothing. Save for a few dark clouds, the skies were empty. He was relieved. He knew that Haze's power should have kept the incoming plane off D.C. radar, but the way things were going, he wasn't willing to take anything for granted.

The airplane slowly glided to a halt mere feet away from Quince. The propellers had slowed but had not stopped; they were idling. The side hatch door opened, and Quince, elongating his legs, sprang toward the plane. He landed inside and pulled the door shut behind him.

Haze was sitting in the pilot's seat. He had a grin on his face and that annoyingly smug look of satisfaction that Quince frequently found hard to take.

"I hear you had a rough day. Love the ensemble, by the way."

"I should rip your head off," said Quince, who was in no mood for what Haze considered to be witty repartee. "I should just rip your damned head off and use it for a basketball, is what I should do."

"Aw, c'mon, Quince."

"*You* c'mon! Do you have any clue what I went through?" Even as Quince ranted, he made his way to the vacant passenger's seat and strapped himself in.

"Of course I do! It was on the damned news! The footage is everywhere. Brawn's furious."

"Brawn can bite me. He wasn't the one who had Wolverine breathing down his ass."

"Wolverine," Haze said, shaking his head. "Why the hell did he get pulled into this in the first place, anyway?"

"I don't know why, but whatever the reason, he's in the middle of it, and I'm damned lucky he didn't chop me into small cubes. The guy's an animal."

"Where is he?"

"Still wandering around in the sewers, with any luck."

"The sewers. That explains the smell. Here I thought it was just the clothes."

"No. It was me, running through the sewers with that lunatic tracking me. This is all your fault, Haze."

"My fault?"

"You said this would go easy."

"How could I have known Wolverine would get involved? If he hadn't stuck his nose into it—literally—this would be a cakewalk."

"Well, you *should* have known."

"How?"

Quince had no response for that. Instead, he folded his arms, scowled fiercely, and said, "Just get us airborne. And keep making damned sure that no radar picks us up. We sure as hell don't need Air Force jets showing up."

"Have I ever let us down on that score?"

He had to admit to himself that Haze, in fact, had not. His code name was well founded. He had the mutant ability to create a field around himself or his surroundings that defied the ability of any electronic device to detect him, like a foggy haze that hid them from view. Washington, D.C. was far too secure an area when it came to tracking incoming and outgoing small aircraft. Any crazed terrorist who thought he could fly a single-engine plane loaded with explosives into the middle of the Capital Beltway and blow up Congress or the White House would be in for a very rude awakening the moment a couple of F-16s pulled alongside him, gave him one warning to veer off, and then blew him out of the sky without a second's hesitation.

But Haze, among other things, created holes in radar. It didn't matter how advanced the tracking systems surrounding Washington were, they were going to be oblivious to Haze's presence.

The propellers revved up as Haze guided the plane forward. It picked up speed and within moments was barreling down the Potomac. Pedestrians pointed in amazement. Even if the cops were alerted, and they in turn alerted the Air Force, it wouldn't matter. None of their instruments would be able to track them. They'd be depending entirely on making visual contact—and even that wouldn't do them a damn bit of good, because Haze's power extended beyond merely eluding radar. He could create genuine invisibility fields. He wasn't bothering at the moment, because it wasn't an easy thing for him to do; it took a hell of a lot of concentration, and he couldn't sustain it indefinitely. He'd employ the ability on an as-needed basis. So, if a squad of Tomahawks was suddenly bearing down on them, then the seaplane would vanish like a snowflake in a desert. Until such time, however, he was content merely to scramble radar and call it a day.

The plane continued to climb, and minutes later, Washington was left far behind them. Quince didn't realize that he'd been holding his breath since takeoff, but he finally let out a relieved sigh. "Maaaaan . . ."

"What? You weren't *really* worried about Wolverine, were you? I mean, yeah, sure, he's got the reputation. But he's a midget with claws. He's no match for you."

"You didn't see him," said Quince. With the tension ebbing from his body, he was allowing the full impact of the confrontation to come back to him. "I swear, the look in his eyes—no mercy, man. When he comes at you, there's no mercy in him at all. It's like . . . like he's dead inside. When you're in his sights, then it's you and him, and the rest of the world can just go to hell. He's one spooky bastard."

"Shake it off, man. You ditched him in the sewers. We're heading back to the lair. You'll kick back, have some hot coffee, take a shower—probably not in that order—and then we'll figure out what our next move is."

"Yeah. Yeah, sounds like a plan."

The plane arced off into the night sky.

21

THE SCENE AT THE FUNERAL HOME CONTINUED TO be a zoo long into the late hours of the day, and Agent Craig had finally had it with Corporal Westlake.

When the umpteenth "Agent Craig, you've got to listen to me!" rang in his ear, Craig turned to Westlake, pointed at him, and said to his men, "Arrest this man."

"What?" Westlake practically exploded. *"On what charge?!"*

"This is the United States," said Craig. "We'll think of something."

·They dragged Westlake off at that point, and Craig continued to have his forensics team turn the place upside down.

Ellen Hayes was practically catatonic. Craig had tried to question her, but the woman was barely capable of stringing a coherent sentence together. The most anyone could get out of her was a soft, repetitious "No, no, no."

It wasn't as if anyone else they interviewed was of much more help. Everything had happened so quickly that most of those present had been scrambling blindly to get the hell out of the way. The general parameters of the eyewitness accounts matched up: the boy had come back to life, transformed into a monster, and jumped away. And the TV news reporters were naturally having a field day with it. Craig would have shut things down if he could, but it was too late. All of the TV cameras had been generating live feeds, so as soon as it happened, it was already in the news stations' databases, to say nothing of the Internet.

Ah, for the days when the government could come down like the right hand of God and just censor whatever it wanted.

There was a tap on his shoulder, and Craig saw that Agent Keith was standing next to him. "Yeah, what?"

"It's the soldier."

For a moment, Craig had no idea what he was referring to. "What is? What's what soldier?"

"Corporal Westlake. He's demanding to see you."

Craig rolled his eyes and started to say, "Tell him to—"

"He wants to confess."

That brought Craig up short. "Confess? To what?"

"His involvement in the kidnapping. The whole plan. But he says he'll only confess to you."

It was a trick. It had to be a trick. There was no way it

wasn't a trick. Yet with all that certainty in Craig's mind, he couldn't allow this to pass.

Fifteen minutes later, he was at headquarters. He strode into a small room, where Westlake was seated with his hands resting on a table. His spine was perfectly straight. He certainly sat like an Army man. Craig sat down and pulled a notepad over. He clicked open a pen and was poised to write.

"Why are you bothering with that?" Westlake said. "Isn't everything I say in here being recorded on hidden microphones?"

"Yes," said Craig. "But you can never be too cautious. I'm a big believer in not putting all my trust in mechanization."

"Sound philosophy."

"So . . . you were going to confess?"

"Hmm?" Westlake looked puzzled for a moment, and then his face cleared. "Oh. Right. That. No, that was complete bull. I just needed to get you here."

Craig laid down his pen and scowled fiercely at Westlake. "You know, I wasn't really going to charge you with anything. I just wanted to get you the hell out of my hair. But I'm tempted to slap you with obstruction of justice just on general principles."

"Look," said Westlake intently, "you know what I can do. You know I'm a walking lie detector. When everything was going nuts—"

"I don't have time for this," said Craig, and he rose from his chair.

Westlake remained seated, but he raised his voice. "My skin turned red! When that creature was escaping and everyone was shouting, my skin turned red!"

"So?"

"So somebody said something within my hearing that was a lie."

"Like what?"

"Like 'Who is that?'"

Craig still had the urge to dismiss what he was being told out of hand, but his determination to get to the bottom of all this prevented him from doing so. Instead, he remained standing, his hands resting lightly on the table. "Saying 'Who is that?' isn't a lie."

"It is if you know perfectly well who it is. It means you're saying it in order to try to cover up knowledge you already have."

"Maybe," said Craig. "On the other hand, you could have somebody shouting 'I don't want to die!' except they have suicidal tendencies."

"True. But what if that's not what happened? What if someone who was there had direct, firsthand knowledge of whoever or whatever it was that came leaping out of the coffin?"

Craig paused and then said, "Well, what did you have in mind? Bring back everybody who was in the room, march them in front of you one at a time, and have them claim whether they're guilty or innocent while we wait to see if you turn into a cooked lobster?"

"That shouldn't be necessary," said Westlake, ignoring the sarcasm. "I've had a lot of time to think about it. There were several TV cameras there. They were shooting in all directions, so I'm thinking they had pretty much every angle covered. Do you think you can get all the raw footage that all of them were recording?"

"Of course we can," said Craig, and now his mind was starting to move quickly. "And we go through them, have everything transcribed and time-stamped. It'll be tricky to sort out what people were saying individually, since everyone was shouting at once, but we can wash it through our instruments a few times and get a pretty clear idea. Then, with any luck, we'll have a visual of exactly when your skin changed color, and we can match it up to what was being said right when that occurred. And, more important, who said it."

"And then we bring in that one person."

"Exactly." He drummed his fingers for a moment on the tabletop and said, "I'm going to have you moved to a vacant office. Just temporary, you understand. But it'll be more comfortable than the holding cell we've had you stuck in."

"Thank you."

"Don't thank me. I'm about to turn your life into a living hell of research. You'll thank me when it's over."

22

QUINCE WASN'T EVEN THINKING ABOUT THE FACT
that the sunrise was ushering in Election Day. Odd,
really, considering that the entire plan had hinged on it.

Plan. Was that really even the right word? *Plan* would
indicate that there was some grand scheme that was
going to lead toward personal benefit. Certainly, that
was the way Dragon Corps typically operated. They
weren't a group dedicated to public works or benefiting
the commonwealth. They were mercs, for crying out
loud. They went where the money was. But this whole
endeavor had been undertaken purely out of altruism.
It figures that they had encountered the amount of grief
they had. No good deed ever goes unpunished.

He realized that he'd drifted in and out of sleep as
the sun crept up over the horizon. He glanced toward
Haze to make sure that he was still awake and focused.
He sure as hell didn't need the pilot falling asleep at

the stick. But no, Haze simply glanced at him as he stretched and said, "Welcome back to the land of the living. I was having a whole conversation with you at one point before I realized you'd fallen asleep."

"Sorry about that."

"Don't apologize. It's the best chat we've had in years."

Quince made a sneering "ha ha" expression. He stretched once more and said, "How much longer?"

"We're about five minutes out. There, you can see it."

Quince looked at the rolling waters of the Atlantic beneath them and saw their destination in the distance: the craggy island that they had dubbed the Dragon's Lair.

It once had been the private domain of a prominent drug lord. That was until the Corps decided it would make a superb base of operations for them. So they had moved in and simply eliminated everyone who was residing there, correctly assuming that no one would care what happened to a drug lord. To other drug lords, he was one fewer competitor to deal with, and the federal agencies that had been tracking his activities assumed that some rivals had disposed of him. There had been a small bit of unpleasantness when one of the drug lord's rivals had shown up on the island, seeking to seize the property for himself. The Dragon Corps disposed of him fairly efficiently and left just enough of his henchmen alive to spread the word that the island was off limits. No one had dared to bother them since.

The property itself was expansive. A mansion, of

course, with far more than enough living accommodations. The drug lord had been considerate enough to leave behind a fully stocked weapons arsenal, which the Corps had augmented. The mansion was surrounded by a forest populated by small game that the Corps would occasionally hunt for either food or sport. And beyond the edges of the forest was a range of mountains that encircled the island, providing no easy means of access save for hidden passages that the drug lord had been good enough to construct before his tragically premature demise.

Quince had come to think of it as home.

He glanced out the window of the plane and smiled. "Hey, check it out. Dolphins."

"You and dolphins," Haze said with a sigh, and shook his head.

Quince didn't care about Haze's casual dismissal. Call him a sap, call him an animal lover, whatever. He loved watching schools of dolphins as they leaped and played through the waters of the surging Atlantic. He sometimes—

His reverie ceased as he continued to stare down, uncertain that he was actually seeing what he was seeing.

From the angle they were flying at, he was now able to see the shadow of the airplane below them on the water. But it didn't look right. It appeared asymmetrical somehow. As if one of the pontoons were larger than the other, or the strut was broken, creating a bulge, or . . .

Or something was hanging on.

Quince immediately fumbled at the straps of his restraints. Haze looked at him in confusion and said, "What the hell's the matter, man?"

"Shut up! Just shut up!"

He pulled free of the restraint and stumbled to the back of the plane. There was a holster with a gun dangling from a hook nearby. Quince yanked the gun clear of the holster and checked the clip to make sure it was loaded. Then he went to the hatch and started pulling at the locking mechanism.

"Quince! What's going on? What are you, bailing out? I don't—"

"I told you to shut up!"

Pushing against the wind resistance, he managed to shove open the door and crane his neck to look down. His eyes widened at what he saw.

Wolverine was clinging to the right pontoon.

His legs were wrapped around the pontoon itself, and his arms were around the strut. He'd been dozing, but the instant the door opened, he came fully awake and made eye contact with Quince.

"Sonofabitch!" shouted Quince.

Knowing the jig was up, Wolverine gambled everything on one quick move, scrambling to his feet and leaping up toward the open door. But Quince had the gun out and leveled, and he opened fire.

The slugs slammed into Wolverine's chest. A couple glanced off his skull. Wolverine twisted in midair, and even under the barrage to which Quince was subjecting him, he managed to get the tips of his right claws into the door frame. He looked up, and Quince shot him in the face.

Wolverine slumped back, and yet the claws kept him embedded in the plane. Quince kicked at the claws, knocking them loose from the door frame, and Wolverine fell. He struck the nearest pontoon and rebounded off it, looking helpless and lifeless as he tumbled down and struck the water far below.

"What's happening? For God's sake, Quince—"

"It's Wolverine!" shouted Quince as he slammed the door shut. He was breathing heavily, the air rasping in his lungs. "It's the goddamned Wolverine! He was hanging on to the pontoons!"

"That's impossible!"

"Don't tell me it's impossible! I just shot him in the face to get him off the plane!"

"How did he trail you through the sewers? And the streets? You're a pro, Quince. You're one of the best! There's no way that he could have kept up with you or tailed you on the surface without you spotting him. No way!"

"Yeah, well, thanks for the vote of confidence, which, by the way, means nothing. Because he did trail me through the sewers, and he did follow me on the surface, and I have no clue how he managed it other than that he's Wolverine." Quince was buckling himself back in. "Get us down to the ground. Alert the rest of the Corps. Let 'em know we're under attack."

"Under attack? What are you talking about? You said you just shot him in the face."

"I know I did."

"So you shot him! In the face! How does that make us remotely under attack?"

"Because he's Wolverine, and from what I hear, shooting him in the face just pisses him off."

"You're crazy, Quince!"

"Damned straight. I was crazy to agree to this harebrained scheme that had no back end, no payout, nothing!"

"Getting Sanders into office should have been pay-out enough . . ."

"Well, it's not!" Quince's face was almost red with fury. "Screw this whole king-building idea. You ask me, we should just take a flame thrower to the whole damned capital and be done with it."

Haze was shaking his head. "He's gotta be dead, man. I'm telling you, I don't care what his reputation is. Reputations are overblown. That's the whole point of them. People exaggerate."

"Considering what I've just seen with my own eyes, everything I'd heard about him before yesterday barely scratched the surface. Come on"—he thudded the side of the plane—"get this crate down."

Haze angled the seaplane downward, bringing it in

fast and tight. Minutes later, they were skidding along the surface of the Atlantic and soon had glided to a halt within range of the island.

A pier extended from the narrow shoreline. Haze cut the engine, leaped out of the plane, and clambered up the ladder. Then he tossed a rope out to Quince, who caught it and anchored the plane to the pier.

They sprinted down as if the devil were on their heels—which, as far as they were concerned, was far closer to the truth than either of them cared to admit.

They had ceased all unnecessary conversation. They'd been working together long enough to know when it was time to focus on a mission. And in this instance, the mission was to get back to the mansion as quickly as possible.

"He's going to track us there," said Quince.

They approached an outcropping of rock, and Quince looked for a particular outthrust piece. He found it and pulled down on it hard. Unseen gears ground together, and a small section of the wall opened.

"You shot him in the face. Presuming he's even alive, which he's not, he's not going to be in shape to track a damned thing!"

"You know what, Haze? You're really not going to get it until you find yourself face to face with the guy. Let's hope, for your sake, that never comes up."

They stepped through, and seconds later, functioning on a timer, the rocky wall swung shut. The camouflage was seamless; it would have been impossible for just about anyone to tell that there was any sort of hidden entrance there.

Quince, however, was greatly concerned about the entire concept of "just about anyone," because he was nearly certain that if there was anyone who could beat those odds, it was Wolverine.

Logan spent the entire plunge from the airplane roundly cursing himself for being caught so easily.

He knew he should have been faster off the mark than that, but he'd been pushing himself almost non-stop since this endless escapade had begun. He'd slept not more than a few minutes at a time, and even someone with a healing factor needed some shuteye once in a while.

And this had been the result: getting shot in the face and sent plummeting to the bottom of the Atlantic Ocean.

He struck the water and sank.

Blood seeped from his wounds, inking the seawater. He hoped that the holes that had been blown in him would heal before any sharks caught the scent. He was still a bit disoriented and nauseated, but he knew it would soon pass.

Logan hung in the deep for a moment, trying to get his bearings. He released a few air bubbles from his mouth, watched which way they went. He was glad he did, because they floated in the opposite direction from what he'd guessed was up. Just went to show that even the mighty Wolverine could be thrown for a loop, even if it was for less than a minute.

He propelled himself toward the surface. Seconds later, he emerged, gulping in air. He looked around, orienting himself, and saw the plane in the distance. It was heading toward the island and was just now coming in for a landing.

Logan began to swim.

After about ten minutes, fatigue began to pull at him, but he shook it off. There was no way he was going to let himself get tired. He was Wolverine. He didn't get tired. He didn't get killed. All he got was the job done, whatever it took, and that was what he was going to do here.

He glanced to his right and couldn't believe the luck. A school of dolphins was swimming alongside.

Quickly, he reached out and snagged the nearest one, a large male, by the dorsal fin. The dolphin bucked slightly in surprise and tried to pull away as quickly as it could. Logan didn't let go. Then the dolphin tried to go deep, but Logan wouldn't have any of that, either. Instead, he snagged the underside of the dolphin's nose and pulled it upright. Pointing the animal in the direction he wanted to go, he waited for it to conclude that the only way to shake this unwanted passenger loose was sheer speed. The next thing he knew, Logan was hurtling toward the island at a far greater velocity than he could have achieved on his own.

A swim that would have required the better part of

an hour took mere minutes. As soon as he had drawn within an easy swim of the island, he released his reluctant mount. The dolphin turned away with an annoyed flip of its tail that Logan could only imagine represented an obscene gesture in dolphin language.

He saw the seaplane bobbing near a pier and swam toward it. Once ashore and assured by the sight of the seaplane that he was in the right place, he faced the challenge of following the members of Dragon Corps to the inner sections of the island.

He could have tried to climb up the rocky escarpment facing him. After all, if Westlake had managed a similar feat back in the Pacific, then certainly this would present no real difficulty for Wolverine. But unlike the cliffside that Westlake had faced, this was a damned mountain range. Besides, he didn't think for a moment that the others would leave their plane tied up someplace that was inaccessible to the recesses of the island. There had to be some other way through.

He started to sniff around, and it didn't take him long at all to pick up the shape shifter's trail. Considering that he reeked of a combination of sewer and alcohol, it wasn't hard to do. Logan had been a silent witness to the shape shifter's rousting of a homeless guy. He had desperately wanted to intercede but had to weigh the needs of one poor bum against the opportunity of tailing the shape shifter back to his nest. It was the more surefire method, rather than capturing him and hoping that he could pound the information out of the guy.

Not that Logan hadn't been willing to give that angle a try should the necessity have arisen.

The trail led him to what appeared to be a wall of solid rock. But then he studied the traces of movements their feet had made in the sand, where they'd stood, what they'd touched. It took him only seconds to find the triggering piece of rock that caused the wall to slide open. Darkness beckoned within.

He didn't detect anyone inside waiting in ambush. Even if someone were there, he'd make sure it went badly for him or her; darkness was a second home to him. He entered cautiously, not the least startled when the wall swung shut behind him.

A length of tunnels opened out before him. He touched the sides, inspected them, and figured out that they had not developed naturally. Perhaps there had been a network of caves to begin with, but someone had built on them, expanded them, and transformed them into genuine passageways. He had no idea if it was Dragon Corps or someone else who had done so. Ultimately, he didn't care all that much. He just needed to get through them and learn what was on the other side.

What if the kid's not here? What then? What if he was never here? What if there never was a kid? If he always was a shape shifter and a member of Dragon Corps . . .

No. None of that made one lick of sense. There had been too much publicity about him, too many people investigating his particular situation. It was preposterous to think that the kid was somehow a part of all this rather than a victim . . .

And yet . . .

And yet it had never sat right for Logan.

Even as he made his way through the cave, he kept coming back to the same question that had plagued him since day one: *Why Matthew? Why this particular kid?* The notion that it was random didn't track for him. Random was a car filled with explosives being driven into a crowded restaurant. This kid was targeted. Typically in such endeavors, it was someone who knew the kid. Despite the view of the world held by some that it was filled with lunatics in vans driving around preying on random children, the fact was that most crimes against kids, including kidnapping, were committed by people who already knew the children or even had some sort of personal relationship with them.

The problem was that there didn't seem to be any evidence to support that theory in this case. The mother was a single mom, clearly devastated by the fate that had befallen her son. Logan didn't believe that she could have arranged the whole thing. Her emotions had been far too raw to be faked, even if it had been possible for her to elude detection by Westlake's truth-telling abilities. The father was dead, out of the picture. Logan had gone over all of the files back in General Doyle's office and hadn't found anything out of the ordinary with the rest of the family. No one seemed to have any motivation to make off with the kid, particularly in such a flamboyant and rabble-rousing manner.

Which left Logan still frustrated and still in the dark—both figuratively and literally.

However, in the literal sense, there was light at the end of the tunnel. He came out the other end and shielded his eyes, needing a moment for them to recover against the glare of the sun overhead.

A forest loomed, barring his way.

It was of little consequence to Logan, though. This was actually the sort of environment he preferred. He could easily blend in, be invisible. He would be calling the shots. Their spoor was still clear to him, so he could track them easily and, once he overtook them, attack them if need be or, even better, continue to follow them to wherever they were hiding the kid.

All of that went through Logan's mind as he entered the forest. And as soon as the green closed around him, he lost the scent.

Logan froze in his tracks, unable to understand what had just happened. How could he have lost the scent? It had been right there a second ago.

That was when something struck him in the side of the head with incredible velocity. By the time he realized that it was a bullet, he already had dropped to the ground. Blood was pouring from a wound in his forehead, and, even more alarmingly, the wound wasn't closing.

"What the hell?" he murmured.

There was a rustling of brush nearby, and he barely

managed to look up in time to see Kaz approaching him. He had a gun out, smoke still wafting from the barrel. There was an amused smile on his face.

"Welcome to the Dragon's Lair, Logan," said the bounty hunter. "Hope you enjoy the stay. I've got the perfect place picked out for where we'll bury your corpse."

He brought the gun level with Logan's eyes and fired.

"Stu, what's the feeling there in Washington?"

"In all my years, Pamela, I've never seen this sort of tension. Even though we're hours away from declaring a winner, Washington is acting like a town under siege. Police are on highest levels of alert. There are National Guardsmen at every election site. Politicians walk around with haunted looks in their eyes, as if having trouble believing that something like this could happen in the United States. There is a general consensus that the entire electoral process has been compromised. No matter what the outcome, I think we can anticipate court challenges for months to come."

"Do we have any sense of what that outcome will be?"

"Nothing definitive, of course, but exit polls throughout the country are showing a significant lead for dark-horse candidate Steve Sanders. With Mazone forced to withdraw his name from the race because of the ongoing investigation and a tremendous amount of voter resentment being focused on the president because of the plight of Matthew Hayes, many voters seem inclined to go for the candidate who seems untainted by the entire scandal."

"What about third-party candidates?"

"Definitely a better showing than in years past but still not mathematically significant insofar as can be determined. No, at this point, it appears to be Sanders's election to win or lose."

"Unless, as you said, Stu, the issue winds up being decided by the courts."

"No one wants to see that happen, Pamela, but it certainly seems to be a possibility."

"Have spokesmen for the president offered any glimpse of what we can expect should the election go to Sanders?"

"At this point, the official line is that the American people should have the opportunity to make their wishes known. Beyond that, Pamela, your guess is as good as mine."

23

IT WAS JUST THE PRESIDENT AND THE CHIEF OF staff.

They were not in the Oval Office; they were in the chief of staff's office. Smaller. Less intimidating.

The fact that the president was feeling intimidated by the Oval Office at this particular point in time was sort of an inner warning system to him. He always felt that way when he was contemplating something that he knew, deep down, was wrong or at least was something that he was conflicted over. The Oval Office was for decisive action to be taken in defense of the country and the Constitution. When he was considering something that the Founding Fathers might have frowned on, he preferred to be elsewhere.

This was one of those times.

From the chief of staff's office, he was able to see all the way to the edge of the front lawn. The protesters had lessened in number for a short time during the supposed demise of Matthew Hayes. But after the insanely bizarre "resurrection" and the realization that an imposter had taken the boy's place—putting his entire fate in limbo once more—there had been a resurgence of voters expressing their anger and frustration at being yanked around by unknown lunatics—and apparently superpowered lunatics at that. Given the now evidently supernormal manner of the threat, the Avengers were being brought into the mix, and the president had every reason to think that matters were going to sort themselves out.

In the meantime, however . . .

In the meantime . . .

He had a serious problem on his hands, and he damned well knew it.

The president spoke so softly that the chief of staff didn't hear him at first and said, "Pardon me, Mr. President?"

"I said, what would I be required to do? Would I have to file some sort of formal lawsuit? Request an injunction? Something like that?"

"No, Mr. President, this would go completely outside the judiciary. The fact of the matter is, as we've discussed before, we're at war."

"At war." The president chuckled at that. "Yet there hasn't been any sort of formal declaration, and damned if I know which country we're at war with."

"It's a new kind of war. A new kind of mentality

that we have to cope with. There will be definite grow-ing pains within our system as we try to make those adaptations."

"All right, well, if we're not going through the judi-ciary, then what?"

"You'll use your powers as granted you under the War Powers Act to set aside the election results. It's that simple."

"It's easy for you to say that it's simple. No one's going to remember your name. I'll be the one who goes down in history books as trying to usurp the govern-ment."

"You're not usurping anything, Mr. President. You have the power to take whatever steps you feel are nec-essary to repel attacks against this country."

"Attacks? There are no troops. No one's landing at-tacking platoons on our shores."

"Nevertheless, the attempted skewing of this elec-tion by terrorists constitutes, in our opinion, an attack. If you're going to repel it, as you are authorized to do, then the first step in doing so has to be to say that the results of the election don't count."

"You mean take away the right to decide from the American people."

"The terrorists did that, Mr. President." He came around his desk, his fist clenched, not threateningly but urgently. "They got into our citizens' heads. The only question that anyone should have had to deal with was who was the best choice for the office of the president.

Instead, everyone has to examine his soul and wonder if he wants the death of a young boy on his conscience. That simply isn't right. They shouldn't have to cope with such things."

"So I know the mind of the American people better than they do?"

"Of course. When has that not been the case?" The chief of staff tried to sound soothing. "People think they know what they want, but most of the time, they really don't. They depend on leaders—true leaders, not people who determine their plans by whatever the latest polling sample says—to have a vision of what should be done. That's why you were elected. That's why they count on you."

"Count on me? How can you say that?" he said skeptically. "Even before this entire tragic business surfaced, so many people hated my guts . . ."

"Heh." The chief of staff shook his head.

"What? What is it?"

"Have you ever read the newspapers that were published the day before John F. Kennedy was shot?"

The president frowned. "No. I don't think so. I mean, maybe I read them at the time, yeah, but . . ."

"Find some. To be specific, find the ones in which there are editorials about JFK's policies that are critical. And trust me, there's plenty of them. You can't believe the number of newspapers that were tearing him a new one about this, that, and the other thing. But the day after he died, those very same newspapers did a one-eighty. The editorials talked about what a great president he was. How his youthful vigor energized a nation. They talked about all the promise that wasn't kept."

"So you're saying I should go to Dallas and ride in a motorcade, is that it?"

"I'm saying," said the chief of staff, "that you can't worry about the here and now. Opinions shift, and history has a way of seeing the truth of things."

"The truth of things?" The president leaned back in a chair, drumming his hands uneasily on the armrests. "The truth of things is that you're proposing I do what no president before me has ever done: refuse to abide by the wishes of the electorate. How is this going to make me any better than some two-bit Third World dictator?"

"Because they're only interested in retaining power no matter what. That's not your motivation here. Your motivation is to protect the process, not undermine it. Your motivation," he said solemnly, "is to not let the terrorists win. And if you just roll over, shrug your shoulders, and say, 'Oh well,' when clearly these results are distorted, then that's exactly what you'll be doing."

"So you say. But I have a funny feeling that the American people aren't going to see it that way. I think they're not going to distinguish me from any of those two-bit dictators grabbing power and clutching on with both hands."

"Screw the American people!" said the chief of staff in exasperation.

The president stared at him. "Oh, yeah," he said dryly. "That'll make a great sound bite on the evening news."

"I wouldn't say it for the benefit of the evening news. Nor would I say this: the fact is, Mr. President, that you don't owe the American people anything. They're like weeds: they spring up in abundance, and they bend with the wind. Your first loyalty has to be to protect the Constitution. Everything else is secondary to that, and I'm telling you, this entire affair is endangering the Constitution. Because if we just go belly-up on this, then there's nothing—absolutely nothing—to stop future terrorists from doing the exact same thing. Election after election can be tampered with through these sorts of pressure tactics. We need to draw a hard line here and now. We need to send a message that says that we're not going to accept the results foisted upon us by terrorists. Instead, we will fight to make certain that the American public has the right to speak its mind at the voting booth without the pressure of guilt trips and terrorist maneuvering. Yes, yes," he said, putting up a hand to head off the president's uncertainty, "there are those who will condemn you. No question. But years from now, you'll be seen as a saint. The man who made the tough decisions that no one else could or would make."

The president let all that sink in. Finally, he said, "I'm going to have to speak to the Joint Chiefs. There's no way—no way—this is going to work if the military doesn't line up behind me."

"I've already spoken to them, Mr. President."

"Really." The president wasn't surprised. "And what did they say?"

"They serve at the pleasure of the president, and you are the commander in chief. There were some initial concerns, but they see the wisdom of our position."

"Oh, so it's *our* position? I find that interesting, considering I hadn't fully decided whether I was coming around to it or not."

"I took the liberty of . . . based on previous discussions . . ." For the first time, the chief of staff seemed a bit flustered. "If I overstepped myself, Mr. President, I sincerely apologize."

The president waved it off. "It's all right. I think you know I was going to come around to your point of view sooner or later."

"I wouldn't say that, Mr. President."

"You don't have to. I just did."

He simply stood there for a long moment that seemed to go on forever. He felt the weight of history crushing down on him, and he kept stumbling over the same fact over and over again: *This is wrong. It feels wrong.*

He knew all the reasons that it was wrong, and yet . . .

And yet . . .

"Call in the speech writers," he said. "I want to work with them."

"Work with them, sir?" He sounded confused.

"I'm going to go on television to tell the American people that I'm setting aside their perceived will and substituting my own. They're going to crucify me. They're going to freaking crucify me. You know it as well as I. And the least I can do, if I'm giving what may well be the last speech of my presidency, is use as many of my own words as I can."

"Very well, sir. And sir . . ."

"Yeah?"

"The thing to emphasize is that this is only a temporary fix. Once this business with Matthew Hayes has been resolved, once feelings have had the opportunity to subside, then a new election will be held. The people's voice will be heard."

"I very much suspect they won't be waiting until the new election for their voice to be heard. They're going to let me know what they're thinking, and it's going to be loud, and it's going to be . . ." His voice trailed off, and when he spoke again, he felt much older. "From the very beginning, I was worried this thing was going to end bloody. And if you lie to me about that, then I swear to God, I will demand your resignation right now."

The chief of staff met his gaze and then looked downward. "I'll tell the writers to expect you."

"You do that."

The chief of staff left his office, and the president

stood there, continuing to look out the window. It seemed to him that the mass of protesters was taking on a life all its own. The individual personalities of the people were blending into one vast mob mentality.

He envisioned soldiers having to open fire on fellow citizens.

This thing is going to end bloody . . .

24

LOGAN HAD NEVER MOVED AS QUICKLY IN HIS LIFE.

It seemed impossible that at point-blank range, Kaz could possibly miss.

As it turned out, it was indeed impossible.

Although he avoided the bullet going squarely between his eyes, he wasn't fast enough to avoid it entirely. The bullet ricocheted off his forehead, and Logan fell backward, stunned, his brains rattling around inside his skull.

His face was now completely covered with blood that poured from the two wounds he'd sustained. They were showing no signs of slowing down.

His head was buzzing. Becoming totally disoriented, Logan—who'd been trying to stand—succeeded only in falling forward again. As it turned out, that was the only thing that saved him, as Kaz's next shot went over his head, missing him by inches.

He's damping my powers somehow . . . he's a mutant . . . he's one of them. Stupid, stupid, stupid, how could I not have realized . . .

Kaz swung the gun around, and Logan snapped out his claws.

He screamed.

The claws punctured his skin, and it hurt like hell, just as it always did. But this time, it was agonizing. And more, there was no healing of the wounds. Instead, blood flowed freely from the tops of his hands.

He fought through the pain and swung his claws. Kaz stepped back, yanking his gun clear, but Logan followed up with an upward swipe. He got lucky. The adamantium claws sliced through the gun, shattering it.

Then he charged. Blinded as he was by the blood, by the pain, it was still contrary to Logan's nature to fall back. Instead, he attacked.

Kaz reached out and caught Logan's wrists before the claws could strike home. They struggled for a moment, strength against faltering strength, and a smile spread across Kaz's face.

"Beating yourself up about it, ain'tcha, punk," said Kaz. "Figuring you should have seen it coming."

"You should've, too," snarled Logan, and he thrust his head forward. His forehead slammed into Kaz's nose, and Kaz let out a startled howl. There was a satisfying crack of cartilage as Logan's head rearranged Kaz's nose.

Then he brought his knee up with the intention of nailing Kaz in the crotch. He came close to doing it, but

Kaz twisted his leg at the last minute and intercepted the thrust. Frustrated, angry, he shoved Logan away to get himself some distance.

Logan rolled to his feet and faced Kaz. He dragged his arm across his face to clear the blood out of his eyes. "Got your abilities from aliens, huh?" he said with a contemptuous laugh. "What? Afraid you wouldn't be so kid-friendly if Mr. and Mrs. America knew that you were one of those scary mutant freaks?"

"Something like that," said Kaz.

"Why? Why were you playing all sides?"

"Because that's what I do. You never know how these things are going to turn out. Never hurts to have friends in all camps."

Then he reached behind his back and produced what looked like a high-tech riot gun. Logan had no desire to be on the receiving end of it.

Despite his every instinct to the contrary, Logan turned and ran. He moved just quickly enough that the gun blew off the side of a tree.

He ran for all he was worth. His mind was racing faster than his feet.

He dampens powers. Except he's not like Leach: He must be able to turn it on and off, because this is the first time I'm around him that I feel this way. So . . .

Dammit! He was the one who killed Hunt! And when he lied around Westlake, he just shut off Westlake's powers so that they wouldn't react. Or he only let them react when it served his purposes. And we had no way of knowing!

Logan furiously beat himself up over becoming overly dependent on Westlake and his amazing ability to distinguish truth from falsehood. Logan had been sure that Kaz wasn't on the up-and-up, but he hadn't trusted himself. Now he was paying the price—and quite possibly, Matthew Hayes was paying it as well.

He kept his claws out even though blood was seeping down them. The trees seemed to fly past him as he ran. Then he became aware that the pain was beginning to ease. He stopped briefly, leaning against a tree and looking at his hands. The blood had stopped pouring out. He touched his head where the wounds had been, and they were just finishing healing over.

"Excellent," he muttered.

Suddenly, his senses warned him, which was a welcome change from before. He ducked just as a blast ripped through the air above his head. He wasn't certain what the range of Kaz's power was, but he wasn't about to let him get close enough to find out.

He also didn't need to make it easier for him.

He swung his claws, slicing through tree trunks. The trees tumbled over, one on top of another, blocking Kaz's path. Then he kept moving.

Suddenly, he skidded to a halt.

There was a sheer drop directly in front of him. Far below, a river was racing along at the bottom of a steep ravine. He cast a glance over the intervening distance to the other side of the ravine and made some fast mental calculations. It took him only moments to ascertain that there was no way he would be able to jump it.

That wasn't going to stop him from trying.

He took a few steps back to get a running start, sprinted as fast as he could, and leaped off the edge of the ravine.

He was hoping that even if he came up short, he'd be able to sink his claws into the far side. If he could do that, he'd need just a few seconds to pull himself up.

Logan sailed over the ravine in an impressive arc, his claws stretched to the fullest. The far wall loomed close, tantalizingly close—

And then a shotgun blast echoed through the stillness of the forest.

It took Logan across the back. He cried out as the impact sent his jump off angle. Instead of driving his claws into the far side, as he needed to do, the tips of them scraped against it, knocking a few chunks of dirt loose. Seconds later, Logan was in free fall.

He withdrew his claws; he certainly didn't want to fall on them accidentally. It wasn't that he wouldn't heal, but it would be embarrassing if he impaled himself with his own claws.

Ohhh, this is gonna hurt, he thought as he plunged. He uttered a very short prayer that the water was sufficiently deep to cushion his fall; then he realized that he wasn't heading for the water. His trajectory was taking him toward the rocky shore.

Displaying astounding muscle control, Logan twisted himself in midair, shifting his descent so that he was in fact coming down into the water. Of course, if the water was only a foot deep, then the difference in the impact would be minimal at best.

He hit the river and sank like an adamantium-laced rock. It wasn't all that deep; his feet touched the bottom, and then he sprang upward. The water was moving quickly, and Logan, although a strong swimmer, couldn't fight the current. Still, there were benefits to that. Treading water, he looked up at the point from which he'd jumped. Kaz was standing there with his gun, trying to take aim. But Logan was moving too quickly and was too far away for Kaz to be able to do anything to impede his escape.

"So long, Kaz," muttered Logan, and suddenly he heard a distant thundering that was coming very close, very quickly. He tried to see what was ahead of him and realized it too late to do anything about it.

Seconds later, Logan was swept over the top of a waterfall. He plunged a hundred feet to the bottom and disappeared into the churning water.

Kaz cursed to himself as he watched Logan tumble down into the waterfall. Not for a moment did he believe that it would be enough to kill the irritating runt. Anybody else, yes, but not Wolverine.

He snapped open his comm device. It was short-wave, designed to function on the island. He punched in a code and held the device to his ear.

"Yeah?" came the curt greeting from Haze.

"He got away."

"He got *away?* Dammit, Kaz, I thought you said you could handle him!"

"I did handle him! I shot him over and over again, and he wound up going over the falls."

"Over the falls?" Haze sounded as if he couldn't understand why Kaz was wasting his time with this. "If he went over the falls, then he's dead. Why're we even talking about this!?"

"Because all the times I shot him, it didn't kill him, that's why!"

"So what do we do?"

"We find him, that's what. He's still somewhere on the island, but he's hurt, banged up. We should—"

"Be able to take him?" Haze didn't bother to keep the sarcasm from his voice. "Because you've done such a terrific job of that so far."

"I don't need your crap, Haze. I'm going to tell Quince and Brohn what's going on. You activate all the perimeter booby traps."

"What, you don't think I already put them on?"

"I don't know what to think, Haze, especially considering that you're the one who got us into this fix in the first place."

"Now, don't start that again . . ."

"I'm going to start it and keep starting it until this insanity is over! Understood?"

"What about Matthew? Should I go out looking for Logan as well, or . . ."

"The more, the merrier," said Kaz. "But first, get the kid down to the safe room. If Logan makes it to the compound, I don't want him to be able to just waltz in and grab the kid."

"Right. Right, the safe room. Got it."

"And Haze . . ."

"Yeah?"

"Keep smiling," Kaz said mirthlessly before severing the connection.

Haze was feeling the onset of a pounding headache. It was strange to think that a mutant mercenary would suffer from tension headaches, and they typically didn't bother him. But with everything that was going on, Haze sensed the familiar flashing patterns behind his eyes and prayed for the strength to push his way through the discomfort.

The compound was routinely referred to as "the lair" just because that sounded snappier than "the compound." To look at it, one would never have known it for what it was: the headquarters of a formidable group of mercenaries. The floors were covered with plush carpeting; the furniture was in a postmodern style. True, many of the walls and shelves were fake, capable of rotating to reveal various weapons-storage facilities and such, but that didn't distract from the homey ambience.

He ran through the lair to the rec room and found Matthew Hayes exactly where he thought he would.

Matthew was seated in front of a television with his legs crossed, playing a video game. At that moment, he was steering what appeared to be a racing car through a series of increasingly challenging obstacles.

"Mattie," said Haze.

Matthew looked up and grinned. "Hey, Dad. What's up?"

Robert Hayes, a.k.a. Haze, far more alive than dead as had been believed, crossed the room to his son and rested a hand on the boy's shoulder. "We've got to get you someplace secure," he told him.

"Secure? Why? Isn't this secure?"

"It's secure but not secure enough. Come on."

He took the video-game controller from Matthew's hand and started to usher him out of the room. But Matthew pulled away, looking concerned and confused. "Is someone coming, Dad?"

Haze hesitated, considering the possibility of lying. But then he decided that it wasn't going to work. Matthew was simply too smart a kid for him to be able to pull something like that. "Yeah. Someone's coming."

"Who? How many?"

"One."

"*One?*" Obviously, Matthew could scarcely believe it. "One guy against all of you? How is this any kind of a problem?"

"Because it is, and you'll have to trust me on that."

"Dad . . ."

He hesitated, and Haze was starting to get edgy. "Matthew, come on, don't make me drag you—"

"Drag me?" Matthew had to laugh at that. "For crying out loud, Dad, you already dragged me out of my house!"

"We've been over all that, Matthew. It was the only way to—"

"To what? To scare the living crap out of Mom?"

Haze took him firmly by either arm, crouching so they were eye to eye. "I didn't have a choice, Matthew. She couldn't know that I was still alive. I need to be able to do what I do."

"I know, I know," said Matthew in frustration. "To function as a secret agent. You told me."

"She never understood. She was going to break up the family, Matthew. She was going to divorce me and make sure that I never saw you again. I didn't want that for us. This was the only way."

"The only way? Kidnapping me was the only way?"

Haze couldn't help but feel that they were running out of time. He felt as if Wolverine were already there, hiding in the shadows somewhere, preparing to spring out at him and rip him to pieces in order to take Matthew and get him out of there.

He hated doing what he was about to do—hated it. It was an aspect of his power that he had no trouble utilizing on others when he saw the need, but he was trying not to do it with his own son. But Matthew had left him no choice.

Running a loving hand along the side of Matthew's face, Haze said soothingly, "You know that I only did what was best for all of us. You know that, don't you, Matthew?"

A sort of white noise settled in on Matthew's brain. It blanketed his concerns, shielding them away, and he smiled listlessly at his father. "Of course, I know that, Dad."

"If that's the case, then you'll come with me right now."

"Sure, Dad."

Without another word of protest, Matthew took his father's hand. Haze hurried him through the lair, down a flight of winding stairs toward the safe room. The chamber loomed before them, and Haze escorted his son in and sat him carefully in the center of the room. "Here, see? Video games here, too." He gestured toward the large TV. "And eat anything you want. There's plenty." That was also true; the safe room was stocked with an ample larder that could see them through anything up to and including a nuclear holocaust (not that they were expecting someone to drop a nuke on their island, but one could never be too careful).

He stepped out, knowing that soon the vague white noise would lift from Matthew's brain, and the boy would never know it had been there. He had done the same thing the night they'd removed him from the house. Once they'd gotten him on the plane, Matthew had reacted with shock, horror, even terror when he saw his supposedly dead father very much alive. Then he struggled mightily, howling that he wanted to go back to his mother, and Haze—at Quince's urging—used his abilities to calm the boy. He swore to himself that he wasn't going to keep doing so, but he had nevertheless. He felt guilty about it, but he really didn't have any choice. Sometimes, out of love for one's children, fathers have to do very difficult things. Very difficult.

Every time he exerted his influence over Matthew, he made him more and more passive. He disliked that development; he didn't want to do permanent brain damage to his son. What kind of father would that make him? Still, he had to do what was necessary to keep him under control. He just prayed that such mental exertions eventually would not be necessary, and Matthew would grow to accept and even appreciate the new life that Robert Hayes was creating for him.

Haze stepped out of the safe room, set the time lock for twelve hours, and triggered the closing code. He instructed the computer to use a random series of numbers rather than picking an assortment himself. That way, Matthew would be in the safe room for half a day no matter what. There was no way that Wolverine was going to be able to wrangle the code out of him.

Just thinking about Wolverine made him whip his head around, suddenly paranoid. His back tensed as he imagined that homicidal lunatic leaping in out of nowhere and burying his claws in Haze's back. *Hurry up, dammit,* he urged the door, which seemed to be taking its own sweet time swinging shut.

Eventually, the door closed, releasing a hiss of air as it sealed itself, and a relieved Haze echoed with a prolonged "Phewwwwwww."

So it was attended to. Matthew was secured. Now it was just a matter of tracking Wolverine down and disposing of him once and for all. Either that or allowing the assorted booby traps around the island to attend to him on their own.

Haze was prepared to do whatever it took to stop Wolverine. No father would do any less to protect his son.

25

WESTLAKE FELT AS IF HIS HEAD WAS SWIMMING AND that he'd been staring at videos for days instead of hours.

Agent Craig, on the other hand, didn't seem the least bit fatigued. His focus remained remarkably consistent as he scanned through all the images.

It had not been all that difficult for the Bureau of National Emergency to acquire the raw footage that various cameramen had recorded at the wake. And several of them had managed to capture the moment when the body of Matthew Hayes sprang to life, started morphing into bizarre shapes, and launched into a slug fest with Wolverine. Oh, sure, the news stations had tried to claim that the government had no business confiscating the footage, but Craig's people simply stormed into the places, flashing badges and warrants and making it clear that this could be done the easy way or the hard way. So it made sense to cooperate and save everyone time and aggravation. Unsurprisingly, cooperation had been forthcoming in short order.

Westlake was starting to wonder if it had been worth it.

There had been so much screaming, so much back-and-forth, that it seemed impossible to determine who had been saying what and what single false phrase might have triggered Westlake's reaction. Craig was methodically checking each video frame by frame, but it seemed to be taking forever.

"Look," Westlake finally said, stepping back from the bank of monitors that festooned the wall. Craig, who was seated at the video-playback controls and was manipulating them with the dexterity of a concert pianist, looked up at him with an expression of curiosity. "Maybe we're going about this all wrong. Maybe we should just round up everyone who was there and question them."

"Round up everyone." There was faint incredulousness in his voice.

Westlake ignored the faint sarcasm. "Yeah. We round them up and bring them into a room one by one and question them. The moment they try to lie, I'll catch them at it, and then we've got them."

"If we round up everyone," said Craig, "then we're going to have to round up *everyone*. Do you see the problem inherent in that?"

"Well, it's a lot of work going out and finding every-one . . ."

"No, that's not the problem. The problem is that 'everyone' would have to include . . ."

Westlake stared at him blankly, but then suddenly the light dawned. "The president. We'd have to bring in the president."

"Exactly. That's problematic on the best of days, which this most certainly is not. Which reminds me, have you voted?"

"What? Uh . . . no. No, I haven't. But I'm nowhere near my base. There's no way . . ."

Craig tapped an intercom and said, "Miller? This is Craig. Prep an absentee ballot for Corporal Westlake, would you, please?"

"Yes, sir."

"An absentee ballot?"

"Sure. Bring it out to any polling place, and drop it off. They'll attend to processing it. Just consider it an extra service from the BNE."

"You mean I'm free to go?"

"We didn't really have anything to hold you on any-way," Craig admitted. "This is going to take a while longer. No point in you sitting around and not accom-plishing anything. Go vote, and then come back here. I can take your word for it, as a member of the armed forces, that you will return here?"

"Yes, of course. Certainly."

"Okay, fine."

Another agent, who Westlake assumed to be Miller, walked in with an absentee ballot. He proffered it to Craig, who in turn handed it to Westlake. "Miller," said Craig, "see Corporal Westlake out, and leave word that he's to be permitted to return to me here."

"Yes, sir," said Miller.

Minutes later, holding a card with an address for the nearest polling place, Westlake was walking through the streets of Washington. He didn't know how much of it was his imagination, but he felt as if he could feel tension in the air. The sun was setting; he'd had no idea that it was so late in the day.

He wondered what was happening with Logan. He had to think that Logan was hot on the trail of that whatever-it-was that had erupted from Matthew's coffin and torn through the funeral home.

What if he's dead? What if his body's floating somewhere and Matthew Hayes is . . .

He shut down that line of reasoning. It wasn't going to accomplish anything, and besides, he had trouble envisioning Wolverine's dead body. He had seen Logan survive incredible hardships and come springing back as if they were nothing. Logan was a survivor. Logan was a winner. Logan was—as he was quick to inform anyone who listened—the best there was at what he did. There was no reason, short of incessant negativity, to believe that things were going to turn out differently for Logan this time.

Logan didn't fail. Failure was for lesser mortals.

He arrived at the polling place and was astounded to see a line stretching out the door. In all his years of going to the polls—first brought along by his parents, who considered it a lesson in civic responsibility, and then on his own once he turned eighteen—he had never seen one so crowded. Typically, the lackadaisical approach that so many Americans took toward elections resulted in low voter turnout. That wasn't the case today, though. Instead, the country had been galvanized into action as a result of the events surrounding Matthew Hayes. He dwelt on the irony of the notion that terrorists had yet again brought the country together. He didn't understand why that was. The name of the damned country was United States. Why were they only united when they were under assault, and the rest of the time there seemed to be an unmistakable sense of "I've got mine, and everyone else can go hang."

He considered that maybe he was being too hard on his fellow Americans. Or worse . . . maybe he wasn't.

The sound of a chanting crowd in the distance caught his attention. He looked in the direction from which it was coming and realized that its origin was the White House. He knew that protesters had been in position there since all of this had happened and that the crowd was likely only getting larger.

His parents always had spoken fondly of the many demonstrations they'd either witnessed or attended in the 1960s. Westlake naturally had been born far too late for that. Now, even though his every instinct told him that it would be a spectacularly bad idea to do so, he tossed one last look in the direction of the polling place and then turned his back to it, heading instead for the White House.

Later, he would consider the irony of that. That if the polls hadn't been so crowded, he likely would have gone in to vote and then headed straight back to Craig. Had events transpired in that manner, he wouldn't have wound up in front of the White House just as everything was going to hell and wouldn't have held a bleeding woman in his arms.

There were some who believed in parallel universes, where everything that happened in one particular way in this universe turned out entirely differently in another because a choice took the decision maker down one path instead of the other. Westlake had never believed in such philosophies; to do so made life seem—to him— utterly barren of purpose. What point was there in free will if nothing that anyone did mattered?

Still, when everything fell apart, he found himself wishing that not only were such parallel universes real but that he could transport himself to the one where he had simply gone in and voted and kept his nose out of the debacle that was to follow.

But they weren't, and he couldn't.

The closer he got to the crowd, the more convinced he was that something really bad was going to happen. But

Westlake wasn't looking at the crowd. He was looking at the soldiers on the other side of the fence.

He knew soldiers. He knew that in circumstances such as this, they were far too trained and far too proud to display any sign of nervousness, at least overtly. But there were telltale signs that the corporal could discern. The little sideways glances at one another. The way that although they were holding their weapons at parade rest across their bodies, their hands were moving around on their rifles ever so slightly, as if caressing them. The position of their elbows, a bit outthrust, indicating that they believed they were going to have to bring their weapons to bear and fire in a split second.

As he drew closer, Westlake began to get angry looks and reactions from protesters. No surprise there: he was still wearing the distinctive gray "digis" Army uniform, and his weapon was in plain sight. People snarled and spat and told him to go away, and he found himself repeatedly saying, "I wasn't sent here! I just came to see what was happening!" Most of them continued to throw distrustful looks his way, but a few appeared to nod approvingly, and one even tried to thrust a protest sign into his hands, which he politely declined.

Then, amazingly, despite the huge agglomeration of voices all around him, one voice nevertheless leaped out at him. On the other hand, perhaps it wasn't that big of a surprise, because its owner was standing on a makeshift platform. She was facing the crowd, implor-

ing them, riling them up, and when she spoke, their
volume lessened slightly so that they could hear her.

"Mrs. Hayes?" he whispered.

Sure enough. Ellen Hayes, who, to the best of his
knowledge, had been so devastated by what she'd witnessed that she'd retreated to some private and hidden
location where she could try to battle back to finding her equilibrium, obviously had recovered. Which
wasn't to say she was looking well. Quite the contrary:
she looked awful. Her skin was sallow, her hair askew,
and her eyes burned with inner fury, not to mention
the glassy exhaustion of someone who hadn't slept in
days.

He couldn't even understand much of what she was
saying. Her words weren't hanging together coherently.
She kept saying "my son" and upbraiding the president
and talking about children being the real victims of
a government spiraling out of control, and the crowd
kept cheering at random moments that seemed to be
more luck of the draw than anything really responsive
to what she was saying.

It was clear to Westlake that they didn't give a damn
about her as a person or as the beleaguered mother of a
missing child. She was a convenient symbol and nothing more, and they were going to milk that for all it was
worth.

A dull rage burned in his chest at the way she was
being manipulated, and Westlake started making his way
through the crowd with renewed vigor.

Apparently realizing where he was headed, members of the surging mob seemed bound and determined to prevent him from accomplishing his goal. "She's a friend of mine!" he shouted, but they didn't seem to give a damn. Probably they didn't believe him, or if they did, they simply didn't care.

A burly man blocked his path. He had some sort of official identification dangling in a lanyard around his throat. Clearly, he was working for some central agency that facilitated this gathering. These things didn't happen spontaneously. There was organization— buses chartered, arrangements made. This guy wasn't just a crowd member; he was someone entrusted with responsibility to make sure everything went off as planned.

"Get back, soldier boy," he said with an unmistakable undertone of threat.

"She's a friend of mine."

"Here's me not caring."

A woman who was almost as burly stood next to him. Westlake noticed that they were wearing matching wedding rings. "Tell me, fella, you ever cheat on your wife?"

"What?"

The man looked ready to slug him, and so did his wife, but Westlake kept his cool and said, "I'm a mutant. You've heard of mutants, right? My whole thing is, anybody tells a lie around me, my skin turns red. I'm a human lie detector. So, you ever cheat on your wife?"

"You're fulla crap!"

But his wife was looking at Westlake with consideration, and suddenly she said, "I love my mother."

Instantly, Westlake's skin went beet red.

The woman gasped, and the man's eyes widened. Others had been listening in with half an ear, but when they saw this display of Westlake's ability, they were clearly taken aback.

Westlake knew he was taking a terrible chance. Certainly, this crowd had no love of Army personnel. Now he was adding into the mix the chance of antimutant sentiment? It was criminally bad strategy, but it was the only thing that occurred to him, the only card he had left to play. It was either that or pull out his gun and threaten to shoot, and that wasn't an option.

The color change subsided, and he fixed his gaze on the man and said, "I'm telling you again. She's a friend of mine. I want to help her. She's not well, and you just need to look at her to see it. But if you don't want to let me through, then let's play truth or dare, you're so tough. Have you ever cheated on your wife?"

"No," said the man defiantly, and Westlake's skin remained exactly as it was. That was a bad piece of luck; he was hoping that the ensuing argument between husband and wife would be enough to cause a distraction.

"Let him through," said the wife with newfound urgency.

"Dolores, what the hell?"

"Let him through," she said again. "I mean, obviously, he's sincere. Anyone can see that. He wants to help, and that poor woman clearly is on her last legs."

She cast a desperate glance at Westlake, and he instantly understood. The husband had been faithful, all right, but the wife hadn't. And she was in a panic that Westlake would ask her the same question that he had just hurled at her husband.

The man stared at her, and Westlake could almost see the wheels turning inside his head. Slowly, he was coming to the same conclusion that Westlake had. The only question was, would he try to seek out the truth at the risk of public humiliation?

Without breaking his stare, the man said to Westlake, "Fine. Go talk to her. But," he continued, turning to face him, "if she acts like she doesn't know you, or tells you to get out of her face, and you upset her, I'm hauling your ass out of here whether you like it or not. And you damned well better be ready to use that gun, 'cause that's the only way you'll stop me."

"You needn't worry about that," said Westlake, but he had the feeling that his words weren't remotely consoling. He also suspected that, despite their surroundings, the man's thoughts had turned to matters of a far more personal nature. Westlake allowed himself one moment of guilt over having come in out of nowhere and potentially thrown a monkey wrench into the marriage of these two strangers, and then he was past the burly man and his wife and approaching the makeshift podium. Other people had witnessed what had just happened, and they were clearing out of his way. Apparently, lots of folks had their secrets.

He waited until she took a breath in her ranting and then called, "Mrs. Hayes!" She stopped talking and looked around, unable to determine from where the voice had originated. "Ellen!" he said even louder, and this time, her gaze fell upon him. He waited for some sort of reaction from her: hatred, disinterest, contempt, something. Instead, it was just blankness, as if she knew she should have some kind of response to his presence but couldn't recall what it ought to be.

"It's Tony Westlake," he said, not at all sure if she remembered him or not. "Can I talk to you for a few minutes?" He gestured for her to come down from the platform.

"Let her speak!" someone shouted, and then others took up the cry, as if Westlake were endeavoring to censor her words. Westlake ignored them, focused instead on Ellen.

She continued to stare at him with that same eerie emptiness, and then she said in a hollow tone, "You said you were going to save my son. And you didn't. Then you stood there and said how sorry you were that he was dead. Except he's not. At least, we don't know that he is. Why should I listen to anything you say now?"

"Because I care about you," he said as fervently as he could. He gestured toward the crowd crushing in from all sides. It was difficult making himself heard over the mounting chants, but he thought she could still hear him. "I care about you as a person! These people . . . they care about you as a symbol! They just want to use you. Exploit you."

"Let them," she said. "I don't care what happens to me anymore."

"But you have to care! You have to, because you want to be there for your son when he comes back."

She laughed humorlessly at the words.

And then someone who was looking at some sort of PDA—another group organizer, clearly, as the lanyard tipped off—clambered up onto the podium. Westlake tensed, certain that the man was going to start laying into him, trash-talking him. But the man didn't even glance at him. Instead, he spoke into the microphone. "The president just announced that he's going to address the nation at nine-thirty!"

That made no sense to Westlake. None. What in the world could the president have to say to the American people at nine-thirty at night? Would it be possible for the networks to call the election that quickly? He supposed so; nowadays, the speed with which they were able to compile information was absolutely astounding. Still, why? Hell, the polls would only close at nine P.M. in the Eastern time zone. There would still be many hours of voting throughout the rest of the country.

What could he possibly say about an election that had been neither concluded nor finalized? Unless, of course, private polling had convinced the president's

people that they had a pretty good grasp of how it was
going to turn out.

Think it through . . . think it through . . .

The shouting from all around him subsided to a dull
roar as he tuned it out, and he thought, *If he thinks he
lost, would he come on so quickly to concede? That makes no
sense. If he thought he won, then why make a speech at all? Was
it intended to be some sort of a pep talk or a thank you to the
American citizens for not being browbeaten into refusing to vote?
Possible . . . but still . . .*

But still . . .

People were too busy babbling, wondering what was
going on, and he heard a number of people grinning
and saying "Concession!" as if that made any sense at
all. No one seemed to be doing what he was doing,
which was just standing there and thinking about it.

But these thoughts were leading him in a particular
direction, a direction that he disliked intensely.

He wouldn't do that. He would never do that.

That was when Westlake saw choppers moving in,
large transport choppers that were used for moving in
troops. They were increasing the number of soldiers
who were guarding the White House.

Oh, my God.

He walked right up to Ellen. Someone tried to get
in his way, and Westlake shot him a look of such pure
ferocity that it prompted the guy to take an intimidated
step back. He drew in close to her and said in a low
voice, "Ellen, we have to get out of here. Now."

"I'm not leaving."

"You don't understand. I think I know what's going to happen at nine-thirty. I think I know what the president is going to talk about. And I think anyone who's here stands a really good chance of being hurt."

"I don't care."

"Ellen, that's the wrong attitude to have. You want to be all right. You want to survive for the sake of your son."

"My son is dead."

He was taken aback by the hopelessness in her words. "No. No, you can't believe that. You have to believe in—"

"I don't believe in anything anymore. I don't believe in a government that failed to protect him. I don't believe in the people who promised they'd get him back and couldn't do it. And I don't believe in any God who would have allowed this to happen."

"Please don't say that."

"What difference does it make whether or not I say it? I believe it; that's all that matters."

He could have just tried picking her up, slinging her over his shoulders, and forcing his way out of there. He did have a gun, after all. But the thought of aiming his weapon at civilians, at fellow Americans . . . and it would go off. There was no doubting that. Someone would make a stupid, rash move, and Westlake would fire, and the crowd would go berserk. Ellen would be hurt in the melee, which would run totally contrary to what he wanted to accomplish, and he would very likely wind up dead.

"All right. Fine. But I'm staying near you at all times. Understood?"

She shrugged. His proximity to her was simply something else that she didn't care about.

Westlake stayed by her side as the time ticked down toward the president's national address. He felt as if he were watching a freight train derail in slow motion. The only thing he wasn't sure of was whether he was a bystander witnessing it or one of its doomed passengers.

26

I CAN'T SWIM!

You crazy? The fall'll probably kill ya!

For some reason, that exchange from *Butch Cassidy and the Sundance Kid* flashed through Logan's mind as he plummeted the length of the waterfall.

The truth was, of course, Logan *could* swim. And the fall would very likely not kill him, because Wolverine was practically unkillable.

That, however, didn't mean that Logan was incapable of suffering so much pain that he wished he *would* die. There was only so much that the body could tolerate before it went into shock or shut down or even begged for death.

His body slammed onto the jagged rocks below. He repeatedly smashed into them and lay helpless as tons of water hammered down on him, knocking him off the rocks. Logan, his body lifeless to anyone who might have been looking on, simply tumbled off.

The pounding water was at once deafening and then a hushed gurgle as Logan's body was driven under. He sank below the water's surface, and the current of the stream took hold of him and pulled. He was powerless to try to prevent it. He could sense his brain sending commands to his arms and legs, instructing them to move, to swim. But the synapses refused to fire. He simply bobbed beneath the water in silent agony.

He caught a break, if it could be termed that. As the current carried him, an uprising of rock projected from the riverbed, directly in his path. When Logan's paralyzed body struck it, the angle sent him floating toward the surface. It wasn't for long, but Logan took the opportunity to draw in a deep breath of air before he resubmerged, allowing him a momentary reprieve.

As he drifted down the river, he could feel the repairs transpiring. His fingers twitched as the weakness drained from his core. Within seconds, his arms were fully mobile. He tried not to make any motions that were too dramatic, however, because for all he knew, somebody was tracking him with a sniper scope. Not that bullets would kill him—at least, probably not. But even Logan had reached his pain threshold, so he was hoping to be given at least some breathing space for a few minutes.

Another outcropping protruded from the water in front of him. This time, as he bumped up against it, he pushed off it with a thrust of his submerged hand, sending him angling toward the shore. He knew that he would have to show signs of life sooner or later, so he waited until the water became shallow beneath him, planted his feet against the silt, and pushed up toward the riverbank. His shoulder blades tensed in fear that a bullet might wind up lodged between them.

Nothing happened.

It didn't prompt him to lessen his guard, but he did allow himself one quick sigh of relief as he finished hauling himself out of the river.

He looked around and then closed his eyes. Having initially gotten a sense of the lay of the land during his first overview of the island, he simply needed to take a moment to reorient himself. It took a hell of a lot more than getting chucked over a waterfall and sent tumbling down a river to throw off Logan's internal compass.

He opened his eyes after a few moments and smiled with a look of determined satisfaction. He knew where he was. He knew where he was going. Now it was just a matter of getting there.

He took some time to sniff the air, all of his senses on high alert. He couldn't perceive anything that presented a threat. There was some wildlife in the area, mostly small animals, rabbits and such. No humans—or mutants, for that matter—were nearby.

Mutants. Kaz was a mutant. Kaz was part of Dragon Corps.

He shook his head, irritated beyond measure that

he hadn't seen that coming. Well, now that he knew Kaz for what he was, he wasn't about to let himself get caught off guard a second time. If it came down to Kaz and him again, the outcome would be very different.

Deciding that the best strategy would be to hug the shoreline, Logan started moving while keeping a wary eye out for anyone who might be in the area.

Even as he did so, his mind was assessing the situation. Whom was he going to have to face? Kaz was definitely there, with his ability to short-circuit Logan's mutant powers, including his senses. But not even that could make the claws in Logan's hands go away. Get him close enough to Kaz, and he'd make short work of him.

Quince, the shape shifter, was also there. Still, no matter how well he could disguise his appearance, his scent wouldn't change. As long as Logan could lock onto that, he'd find him.

Then there was the guy flying the airplane. He remained a question mark. Logan didn't know who the guy was or what he could do. He simply had to hope he could react quickly enough to counter whatever the guy could throw at him.

Plus, there was the matter of Eli Brohn, or Brawn. His dossier had indicated a being of formidable speed and strength. That didn't worry Logan too much. He'd had so-called *gods* come at him with fists flying and lived to tell the tale.

Still, there were unknowns, particularly the whereabouts of the boy, Matthew. This wasn't a simple search-and-destroy mission. Were that the case, Logan would try to find some sort of munitions depot and see whether he couldn't just blow the whole damned island off the face of the globe. Obviously, that wasn't an option here. He had to make certain that he left *someone* in working order so that they could guide him to Matthew Hayes.

Still, Logan wasn't intimidated. He'd faced greater odds than this, and—

Suddenly, the hairs on the back of his neck stood on end. He tensed, looking around, trying to spot the source of his reflexive reaction.

He saw the flash of the muzzles half an instant before the bullets started flying.

He had known there was some sort of danger in the immediate vicinity. He had been in these types of situations too many times not to have developed a kind of sixth sense about such things. And so it happened that he was looking in the general direction of a grove of trees when bullets suddenly started to rip out of some concealed point overhead.

He hit the dirt as the bullets tore up the ground around him. He felt two thud into his arm, and he let out a roar of fury as he started rolling, trying to put some distance between himself and the bullets.

Booby trap. He wasn't sniffing any humans around there. The damned thing was automated. Worse, it was "smart" automated. Most weapons systems wait until you get within range to trigger. Not this. It had waited until he was already well within the perimeter and then opened fire. That way, it would be that much tougher for him to get out of range again.

His skin healed up, pushing the foreign matter of the bullets out of his arm as it did so. Logan continued to hug the ground, but when another bullet grazed his leg, he knew he couldn't simply continue to lie there. He bounded to his feet and, in a low crouch, charged toward the river.

He leaped into it, trying to make a getaway. The instant he hit the water's surface, electricity ripped through him. He tried to reverse course in midair, but his suddenly rigid, clenched muscles betrayed him as he fell beneath the water's surface.

An endless series of jolts rammed into his body, twisting and turning him. A charming backup to the machine-gun nest—the river had been electrified, as if someone had dropped a giant radio into it. He felt his blood boil as his body was being fried from the inside out.

His muscles failed to obey his commands at first, but as the current drove him to the opposite bank, he managed to resume control. Racked with pain, he hauled himself up. Bullets thudded into the river from the distant trees. He recoiled, trembling, his body still reflexively spasming from the jolts he'd just received. The bullets tracked his movements and then abruptly stopped.

His back pressed against an upraised stretch of rock. He heard a slight scuffling from overhead, a few pebbles falling to his right. It was all the advance warning he needed. He rolled out of the way just as an enormous figure slammed down from overhead, landing right where he'd been.

Logan started to turn to face him, but his muscles still weren't responding the way they should. So he got only partway around before something sliced across his face. He barely managed to get his head back in time; had he not done so, he belatedly realized, his entire face might have been sliced off.

It was Brawn. He had weapons in both hands: Japanese punching daggers. Vicious weapons with crossways handles around which the user wrapped his fists. Triangular blades stretched out from the handle; they acted more like deadly extensions of the user's reach than like traditional daggers. Plus, because of the way they were wielded, they were much harder to knock out of the user's grip.

"You should never have come here," Brawn said.

"I get told that a lot," said Logan.

"Too bad you haven't gotten the message yet."

Brawn came in fast and strong, pinwheeling his arms, creating an almost impenetrable wall of blades. Logan dodged this way and that, looking for an opening. He thought he saw one and lunged with his claws, hoping to slice Brawn's blades apart. Instead, they struck against one of the blades, snagging it but not breaking it. He didn't know what they were made of, but they were certainly tougher than standard metal.

Brawn stepped forward, his left blade scraping the length of Logan's claws, as he tried to bring the right hand blade slamming home. Logan blocked it, and they struggled for a few moments, strength against strength, neither uttering a word but instead grunting and growling under their breath.

Suddenly, Logan was airborne, Brawn having lifted him off his feet and chucked him back into the river. Logan braced himself for another round of shocks.

Nothing happened.

Not knocking his luck, Logan scrambled out of the river on the far side. The gap didn't slow Brawn at all. He took a few steps and vaulted across. He landed ten feet away from Logan and looked ready for more.

"Take me to the boy," said Logan.

"Oh, is that all?"

Brawn came at him even faster this time. Logan backed up, assessing the attack, watching for patterns, seeing how Brawn repeated himself during the assault. The fighting computer in his mind analyzed everything within seconds.

Then he left an opening—ever so slight but enough that he was sure Brawn would see it.

Brawn did. He lunged, taking advantage, and Logan sidestepped, swinging his claws around and raking them across Brawn's chest.

Brawn let out a startled cry. He clutched at his

chest, blood bubbling through the wound, and Logan took the opportunity to drive his foot straight up into Brawn's chin. The impact made a loud crunching noise as Brawn fell backward heavily, hitting the ground with a thud.

As he lay there, moaning, Logan brought his foot down hard on one of Brawn's wrists. "Let go of the blade," growled Logan, "or I cut it off at the elbow."

Brawn promptly did as he was told. Logan kicked it away, along with the other one, then grabbed Brawn by the throat and drew his face close to his.

"You're going to save me some time. You're going to bring me to the boy."

"Oh, am I?"

"Yeah. You—"

Logan was suddenly struck from behind.

He had no idea how that could have happened. No one should have been able to come up behind him that close and get the jump on him. It should have been a flat-out impossibility.

He was caught just enough off guard that Brawn was able to yank himself clear. A split second later, Brawn had vanished right in front of Logan's eyes.

He took a step forward, bewildered, and suddenly was punched in the side of the head with a blow that felt as if he'd been hit by a Mack truck. Logan staggered but did not fall. He swept his claws in the direction of where the punch had just come from. He connected with nothing, but now he was struck from the other side, just as heavily, a one-two punch, and this time it sent him to his knees.

With a growl, rather than try to get to his feet, he lunged, arms outstretched, hoping to take whoever or whatever had hit him right around the waist. Again, there was nothing there, or perhaps he had just missed his attacker clean.

He let the forward motion of his thrust carry him as he somersaulted to his feet and quickly backed up against a large and sturdy tree. He braced himself, convinced that no one could come at him from behind, or at least they'd have a much tougher time of it.

Logan had no idea what was happening, other than that someone in the Dragon Corps had some sort of invisibility power and was capable of extending it to someone else. He didn't think Brawn had it; otherwise, he could have just come after Logan directly.

Still . . .

There was a lot more to screening someone's presence than what can be perceived by the eye.

Logan closed his eyes. They weren't going to be of any use to him and would probably misguide him. He let his sense of smell and his sense of hearing do the work instead. He didn't make the slightest motion of his own. He stood there, claws at the ready, poised to strike. He could have been a statue for all that anyone seeing him for the first time would have known.

He waited for something: a crack of a branch, a bending of a blade of grass, the faintest scent.

There . . . right there . . .

Logan suddenly reached up over his head and sliced through the upper portion of the tree with his claws. He hoped that such an odd move would freeze his attackers in their tracks as they looked on in confusion.

He yanked forward on the tree as hard as he could. It instantly gave way and crashed down.

There was a satisfying, startled outcry from about ten feet in front of him, and a second later, two forms appeared. One of them was Brawn, standing off to the side. The other, pinned under the tree, was another guy Logan didn't recognize but suspected might be the pilot of the plane that had picked up Quince.

Brawn didn't hesitate. He picked up the tree as he charged and slammed forward with it like a battering ram, catching Logan squarely in the chest. It lifted Logan up and off the ground. Having by now regained his full strength, Logan backflipped, landed on his feet, and tore off down the length of the tree, claws slicing away lower branches as he ran straight at Brawn.

Realizing the impending danger, Brawn hauled back the tree and threw it as hard and as far as he could. Logan held on as it soared through the air toward the cliffs edge. Logan leaped clear of it and watched as it plummeted and clattered its way to the bottom of the drop.

He let out a sigh of relief as he turned once again to face his attackers.

Seconds later, a string of explosives detonated directly in front of him. He took a step back reflexively; he realized that it was the wrong move, but the realization was belated. The cliffside crumbled away beneath his feet, and another drop, even more cataclysmic than the first one, yawned beneath him. Far below, there was no sign of a watery body to absorb the impact, just solid ground.

As he fell, Logan twisted his body, thrashing with his claws. He sliced into the angled mountainside as it hurtled past, blasting chunks of dirt, rock, and shrubs everywhere. He managed to haul his feet forward so that he was now sliding down the side of the rock face, gritting his teeth, straining every muscle.

Gradually, he managed to slow his descent and was soon clinging batlike to the side of the rock face.

Then he heard a distant *fwooof* sound, a sound that he recognized all too quickly: something had been launched.

He didn't have to take two guesses about who was the target.

He twisted around just in time to see what appeared to be a short-range ballistic missile spiraling right toward him.

Terrific, he thought.

He stayed where he was, seeing no advantage in trying to outrun it. It moved far more quickly than he possibly could.

Then he saw a second roaring in right behind it, and a third. *Oh, better and better.*

He hugged the rock side, pacing the missile's approach, counting it off, waiting. Two seconds before the missile struck, he released his hold. He fell down and away from it and then kicked off from the rocks, sending himself hurtling in another direction. The first missile struck, as did the second, each impact sending debris raining down on him.

Then he caught what qualified for him as a break. The combined shock waves of the first two missiles slammed into Logan, shoving him out of the way of the third missile, which thudded into the stone side, sending an explosion of rocks and dirt all around him.

Now too far from the rock side to use it as succor, Logan settled for somersaulting through the air and letting the momentum carry him toward a grove of trees. He hit the uppermost branches, which snapped under the impact of his descent. They continued to break under the weight of his body for a few seconds, but then he was slowed enough that he came to a halt, suspended about fifty feet above the ground.

He took a deep breath. Then he took a mental inventory of himself and found that he was evidently in one piece. That was good. He was going to take his triumphs wherever he could find them.

He dropped to the ground and, the instant he did so, realized he'd made an error.

The ground went out from under him.

He tried to leap clear of it, but it fought back against his efforts to escape. It was some sort of quicksand, except it wasn't; it had been manufactured. Not only that, but he was certain that seconds earlier, the ground had been firm. They must have run some kind of current through it that changed the molecular structure. Yet another booby trap designed just for him.

But how was that possible? Weren't the members of Dragon Corps subjected to the same sorts of hazards? It wasn't as if the traps could differentiate.

Except, well, maybe they could.

What if the Dragon Corps members were carrying some sort of devices on them that deactivated any booby traps in the area, that identified them as friends rather than foes? That would certainly explain why, for instance, the machine-gun nest shut down the moment one of the Dragon Corps was launching an attack.

It was a fascinating idea, one that Logan would be very interested in exploring, provided he didn't die within the next few minutes.

He offered no resistance against the quagmire that was pulling him down. He knew that thrashing about would result in his being sucked in faster. Instead, he kept his body perfectly relaxed until, finally, the sand stopped dragging him down. Unfortunately, it wasn't until the surface of the pool was just under his chin that he finally bobbed to a halt, so he didn't have a good deal of leeway.

He paused a moment to make sure that he wasn't sinking anymore. Then, very slowly, very tentatively, he allowed his body to drift into a horizontal position.

He kicked gently toward what he hoped was the nearest shoreline. The sand lapped around him, as if trying to decide whether or not he was actually there. Logan continued to kick in a scissors fashion until he saw what he was fairly certain was a solid edge. He reached out for it, grabbed it, and pulled himself forward and out of it.

He lay on the ground for a minute or two, pulling himself together. Even as he did so, he reviewed how things had been going thus far and decided he wasn't at all satisfied with his progress.

He figured that the way they might well be tracking him was to wait for him to fall into booby traps and then show up after the fact to try to seal the deal. That being the case, there was no advantage in it for him to continue accommodating them.

Now, all he had to do was stay put and wait for one of them to come to him.

The one downside of the idea was that it was going to eat up even more time, and he wasn't entirely certain how much time he had left insofar as Election Day went. But he decided to put the consideration out of his mind. His first and foremost concern had to be getting the boy out alive, and he couldn't operate on a timetable.

Besides, if night fell while he was on the island, then the tactical advantage was going to shift to him. These guys were formidable, no doubt about that. And he was reasonably sure they had night-vision goggles, which they likely believed would tilt the scales back and make them even.

But they were wrong. Because no infrared goggles, no flashlight, nothing in the world was going to enable them to even up the odds once Logan was on the prowl in darkness. And if they didn't realize that, well, so much the better.

And as for booby traps, they weren't the only ones who could whip those up.

"This may be the most difficult speech that I have ever made, not just in my presidency but also in my life. The most difficult for me to make and the most difficult for you to hear. But I am asking you to listen to it all the way through before jumping to any sorts of conclusions. Better still, take a day to consider my words before being motivated to take any ill-considered actions. Because I firmly believe that once you have given them due consideration, you will see that I speak the truth.

"The fact of the matter, my friends, is that, despite all our endeavors to the contrary, the terrorists have won.

"The moment that young Matthew Hayes was kidnapped from his bedroom, the moment that his fate became intertwined with the outcome of the presidential election, terrorists seized hold of the American electoral system. They seized hold with both hands and put a stranglehold on the will of the American people.

"Not a one of us—not a one—has been able to put the fate of Matthew Hayes out of our minds in the voting booth. We are supposed to be alone once we pull that curtain closed, but that wasn't the case here. Not only was Matthew Hayes in there with us, but so was the specter of terrorism. It was whispering in

our ears, implying that a vote for me was a vote for the death of a helpless young man.

"Granted, there were those of you who were not planning to vote for me in the first place. There's never been a president in the history of the country who was elected unanimously. But there were many of you who would have voted for me and instead decided to stay home lest you had to wrestle with the dictates of your conscience. Or you were on the fence and had this latest terrorist threat tip you in the other direction. Plus, I'm sure that there were some who intended all along to vote for my opponent but chose not to cast your vote for him at all lest you feel that you were being compelled to do so by terrorist dictates.

"The Constitution of the United States guarantees full, free elections for the American people. It is my job to protect both the Constitution and the American people. How can I possibly be doing either job if I allow the election, as it has currently played out, to stand?

"Yes, my friends, the terrorists have won . . . this round. But I have no intention of letting their triumph be enshrined in the history books as a lesson for all future terrorists who will doubtless resort to similar tactics to try to steer elections toward those who sympathize with their causes.

"My only regret is that I did not take this step sooner. Frankly, I was hoping that the American people would be able to set aside the actions of the terrorists. But I have been shown irrefutable polling data that indicate that Americans have indeed permitted the actions of a few to dictate the choices of many. I do not blame you for this. You're only human. It is not your

fault that many of you have succumbed to the brutal tactics of terrorists and allowed them to have an impact on the way you vote. It is, instead, my own fault for failing to take action sooner. Preventive action that could have avoided all this. I did not do so, and I am willing to face the judgment of history for my lapse. But now, faced with the situation that we have, I am not going to stand by and continue to allow terrorists to run rampant over everything that we hold dear.

"As I said, I must protect you from this unholy ordeal, and I must protect the Constitution and the mandated means of orderly succession—means that have been irrefutably tampered with.

"To that end, I have just issued National Security Decision Directive 687, an executive order being issued in conjunction with the Department of Homeland Security. I have been advised that this is the right and proper means to pursue since the terrorists' attempt to usurp the proper outcome of an election can and should be considered an act of war, an action that stems from our ongoing war against terror. NSDD 687 states that any election outcomes that can be demonstrably linked to an act of terrorism or an act of war—as this one certainly can be—is not to be considered legal and binding and can be set aside at the discretion of the chief executive.

"Trust me when I say that this is not an action I take lightly. I know how some people are going to paint this decision. I know how some factions are going to attempt to politicize this and claim that I am acting out of an interest in holding on to power beyond my term's natural end. But I am trusting the wisdom of the majority of the American people to realize that I am act-

ing, not in my own best interests, but in the best interests of the citizenry of this great country.

"Matters will remain as they are until the predicament of Matthew Hayes has been resolved—resolved, we are still hoping, in a manner that will be a happy one for all concerned. Until that time, those holding office will continue to do so, indefinitely. The transfer of power will still take place two months after an election is held. But it will not be an election the outcome of which is dictated by terrorists. Instead, it will be an election where Americans, all Americans, are free to vote their minds, their wills, and their consciences. As are you all, I am hoping that that time will be soon. Until an election can be rescheduled, I am asking you to trust your duly elected leaders to see us through this national time of crisis. God bless you all, and God bless America."

27

BRAWN DIDN'T LIKE ANY OF THE WAY THIS WAS going. The sun was setting, and Wolverine was still out there. The longer that homicidal runt was running around the island, the greater the chances that he was going to screw things up.

Well, weren't things already screwed up?

"This is all your fault, Haze," he said.

Haze, who was moving through the forest next to him, stopped and looked at him in frustration. "Look, I had no way of knowing that Wolverine was going to get involved."

"Shut up. I've heard this all before," said Brawn, who was in no mood.

"Look, just knock it off, okay? I figured you'd appreciate that I'd be here covering your back. If it weren't for me—"

"If it weren't for you, what? Wolverine would have

taken me down?" He sneered. "Don't make me laugh, Haze. What would you do if you were on your own? Hide until he goes away?"

"Okay, fine! Then we'll split up and—"

Brawn grabbed him by the shoulder as he started to turn away and snapped him around. "Are you insane? Have you ever seen one of those movies?" When Haze stared at him blankly, he continued, "Where there's some lunatic stalking people in the woods. They split up, and the next thing you know, they're being picked off one by one. We'll stick together, thanks."

"Fine. And Eli . . ."

Brawn scowled, not normally liking the use of his first name in these situations—or, really, in any situations. "What?"

"Thanks. For . . . *you* know."

"Yeah, whatever," said Brawn impatiently. He already felt annoyed enough over allowing Dragon Corps to be pulled into this entire presidential race business. He certainly didn't need to be dealing with Haze's gratitude.

They made their way through the forest. With the light fading, Brawn pulled out a thermal detection visor from his backpack and strapped it across his eyes. It started giving readouts that were extremely helpful. They enabled Brawn to perceive the path through which Wolverine had recently crossed. It didn't matter how skilled or subtle Wolverine might be, he was still flesh and blood, and he was going to leave traces of himself behind. Slight imprints of his feet in the soil or places where small bits of brush had been broken back. All these and more were easily detectable.

What if he's making them easily detectable? What if he's doing nothing to cover his tracks because he's trying to draw you in? What if—

Brawn shook off his doubts. This was what happened when you found yourself going up against someone like Wolverine: his very reputation made you second-guess everything.

He had a high-powered rifle cradled under his right arm. He was hoping he wouldn't need it; certainly, if it came to hand-to-hand combat, he was still convinced he could take the runt. But it didn't hurt to have some insurance just in case. Haze was similarly armed and also had several hand grenades attached to his belt.

"Got anything on the motion detector?" he said to Haze.

Haze was carrying a compact sensor device strapped to his wrist. He was studying it intently. "Small creatures here and there, nothing large enough to be Wolverine. Nothing within a quarter-mile."

A quarter-mile should have been more than enough to detect Wolverine before he could get close enough to launch an assault. After all, his only weapons were those pig stickers on the backs of his hands, and he had to get a hell of a lot closer than a quarter of a mile to use them.

"Y'sure?" said Brawn. "He's pretty small. Might easily be mistaken for a woodchuck or something."

Haze looked at him in bewilderment, and it took a few moments for him to realize that Brawn was kidding. He did it so rarely. "Yeah, I'm sure," said Haze with a half-smile.

"Okay, then," said Brawn. He continued to study the images through his night-vision goggles. Now there was no track of Wolverine anywhere. But he was reasonably sure that the path of Wolverine's escape would have taken him in this direction. How was it possible, though, that he wasn't seeing any sign of him?

Suddenly, there was a high-pitched *twang* and a sharp rustling of branches. Brawn automatically snapped into a crouch and brought his rifle up to bear. He scanned the immediate area, looking for some sign of . . . something. But he couldn't spot anything.

"Haze, whaddaya got?"

There was no response.

Brawn turned and saw that Haze was gone. "Haze!" he whispered, figuring that his teammate had reflexively activated his invisibility shields and thus simply disappeared. But he called his name a second and then a third time, and when there was still no response, he abruptly realized what had happened.

Wolverine.

Above. That had to be it. No wonder there'd been no track of him on the ground; the runt had taken to the trees and was making his way via the branches like Tarzan.

He shouted into his comm link, "Haze is down! Haze is down!" He didn't need to provide location; all of their units had built-in GPS systems, so anyone else in the group would be able to track them. Then he aimed upward and opened fire. He was firing blind; his thermal unit wasn't giving him any sort of reading. But he figured that maybe he'd get lucky. Granted, there was always the possibility that he might wind up hitting Haze instead of Wolverine, but that was a chance that he was more than willing to take. If Haze ended up getting himself killed via friendly fire, that was just poetic justice as far as Brawn was concerned.

He emptied the clip and ejected it, slamming in another within seconds. There was still no movement from above. He opened fire again, spraying wildly in no discernible configuration. It was the best chance he had at nailing Wolverine: don't give him any set pattern to anticipate and react to.

He went through that clip as well. He hesitated, smoke wafting from the barrel, waiting for something— a moan, a falling body, anything.

Nothing. Just that same unsettling silence.

He ejected the clip, but just as he was about to ram the next one home, something fell at his feet. He looked down.

Brawn had just enough time to see that it was one of Haze's hand grenades. His eyes widened. Dropping the clip in his haste, Brawn leaped into the air, trying to distance himself from the grenade as much as he could.

He didn't manage to get all that far.

The concussive explosion from the grenade propelled him twenty feet through the air. He slammed into a tree. Brawn's body was not invulnerable, but it was durable beyond that of human norm. That was fortunate for him, because otherwise, the impact would have broken his spine. As it was, it broke the tree. It came crashing down, sending Brawn tumbling to the ground.

He barely had enough time to lunge to his feet, and then Wolverine was right there in front of him. Brawn was still holding the gun; fat lot of good it was going to do him, considering that he had lost his grip on the ammo clip. Instead, he swung the rifle like a club. Wolverine easily sidestepped it and knocked it aside, sending the gun hurtling from his hands.

Brawn lashed out with a foot, slamming Wolverine in the chest. It staggered him slightly, and Brawn came in fast, hoping to take him down with a flurry of fists. He landed a punch or two, blows that would have taken the head off a normal opponent. They snapped Wolverine's head around, but that was about all they managed to accomplish, as Wolverine caught Brawn's right fist and twisted it around behind his back. Brawn let out a grunt and drove backward with his legs. The reversal of thrust lifted Wolverine off his feet, and Brawn slammed the shorter mutant against a tree.

"Now you're just pissin' me off," Wolverine growled in his ear.

He clambered up and over Brawn, landing in front of him even as Brawn was twisting around to try to grab him from behind. Wolverine drove forward with his claws. Brawn countered the move, stepping to one side and deflecting the thrust, then slamming an elbow into Wolverine's skull. Pain laced through Brawn's forearm; it felt as if he had driven his elbow into a brick wall. Wolverine, for his part, didn't seem any the worse for wear.

Brawn tried one last-ditch effort, attacking with focused fury as he deflected Wolverine's claw thrusts with formidable countermeasures, backed up by his superhuman strength. But he could feel his energy starting to flag, and Wolverine didn't appear to be slowing down. Then one of Wolverine's thrusts got through Brawn's defenses, and there were three rips on his upper biceps. Brawn lunged, far less efficiently this time, and now he was stumbling, courtesy of more wounds on his right thigh. He turned to charge at Wolverine once more and suddenly found the points of Wolverine's claws pressed up against his chest. He froze. Wolverine was standing there with a focused look, as if there were no one else in the entirety of the world except himself and Brawn.

"This would be a good time to surrender," said Wolverine.

The funny thing to Brawn was that there was absolutely no hesitation in what he did next.

He shoved himself forward as fast and as hard as he

could. He treasured the look of surprise on Wolverine's face as Brawn drove the claws directly into his own chest. Instantly, Wolverine retracted the claws, but he was too late.

"Screw your surrender," Brawn managed to gasp out, and then he fell to the ground and stopped moving as blood pooled beneath him.

Haze's first instinct had been to struggle furiously in the treetops, but he had quickly thought better of it. The latticework of vines and branches on which Wolverine had perched him was such that if he managed to pull free of it, he'd have a far, bone-bruising drop to the ground for his reward.

He'd never even seen the snare that had come in out of nowhere and hauled him skyward. It actually had been multiple snares: one had drawn tightly around his throat, cutting off his ability to cry out, and the others had snagged him around the upper chest. He'd been damned lucky about the latter snares, because if it had just been the one that looped around his throat, he would have had his neck snapped instantly.

He heard sounds of skirmishes from below. His instinct was to try to render himself invisible, but that wouldn't have done him a bit of good. Wolverine knew where to find him; he was lashed to the overhead branches. Then he heard the sound of a concussion grenade and reasoned that it was one of his own; a glance down at his weapons belt confirmed that.

This is insane. None of it was supposed to happen this way. Why the hell did Wolverine have to get involved?

Then everything went deathly silent.

Wolverine had grabbed his comm device away from him, broken it with a quick flex of his fingers. He had no way of summoning help, although he wasn't entirely sure that help would have done him any good. If he summoned the others, he might well be leading them into a trap.

Suddenly, there was a rustling of the branches near him, and Wolverine was facing him. His face was inscrutable. Haze gasped; how the hell had Wolverine gotten that close to him without making the slightest noise other than some minor rustling of branches?

"Where is it?" he said.

"Wh-where's what?"

"You guys must have some sort of device that disables the booby traps, because they don't activate anytime you're around. I couldn't find it on your pal's body. Where's yours?"

"His . . . body?" His voice was hollow.

"Where's yours? Unless you want to wind up just like him."

"There's nothing. There's no device."

"Don't lie to me."

"I'm not lying," said Haze insistently. "You're right about that—the booby traps don't trigger when it comes to us, but there's no device. The traps are equipped with sensors that read our DNA."

"DNA?"

"Yeah. Keyed to each of us. So we can't . . ." His voice trailed off. "You killed Brawn?"

"He killed himself. Doesn't take losing very well. How about you?"

One of his claws was directly under Haze's chin.

"I'm okay with it," said Haze.

"Good. You stay here. Don't move too much."

"Wait! Take me with you! You—you can use me as protection." He spoke quickly, the words tumbling over each other. "My DNA will provide—"

"It won't provide anything that your dead pal can't give me. Plus, he won't be able to run away, besides."

"I won't run away, either. Trust me, you're going to need me."

"I really don't."

"Matthew won't want to go with you. You really want to drag the kid kicking and screaming across the island?"

"I'll knock him out if I have to." Wolverine hesitated and then, against his better judgment, said, "Why won't he want to come with me?"

"Because he won't want to leave me."

"And who the hell are . . . ?" His eyes narrowed, and something seemed to click into place in his brain. Resemblances that he was noting for the first time. "Wait a minute. You're not . . ."

"His father."

"Looking healthy for a dead man."

"It was the only way," Haze said. "The government was closing in on us. They didn't like the idea of a bunch of mutant mercenaries doing whatever the hell we wanted. Certainly, that should be something you could relate to."

"Yeah. But the stuff you pulled—his mother . . ."

"His mother wouldn't have understood."

"Understood that her husband was a merc?"

"That's the least of it. My wife—she didn't use to be that way. You gotta understand. I never would've married her. But as time passed, she got more and more frantic about mutants. If she had known—"

"Known that you were a mutant?"

"Not me. I mean, yes, me. But I'm not the problem. Matthew was the problem."

Wolverine stared at him. "Your *son's* a mutant?"

Slowly, Haze nodded. "Yes."

"What can he do? What's his power? How can she not have noticed it?"

"I don't know what it is. It hasn't manifested yet."

Wolverine made no attempt to hide the skepticism in his voice. "Then how do you know he's a mutant?"

"I just . . . I just do. From the moment he was born, I could tell. I could tell he was different from other kids. Maybe I'm extra-sensitive to it because I'm a mutant as well. I don't know."

"That's right. You don't."

"All I know," Haze persisted urgently, "is that when his powers do manifest, he needs to be with me. With his father. Because God only knows what she would have done if she'd been in charge of him when it happened."

"But why tie it in with a presidential race?"

"Because people expect acts of terrorism to be random. If Matthew had simply disappeared, then even though everyone thinks I'm dead, that still might have led inquiries in a direction I didn't want them to go. But if it was seen as a random act of terrorism . . ."

"Yeah, yeah, I get it," said Wolverine impatiently. "Funny how I get the feeling that you're not telling me everything."

"I am! I swear!"

"Swear all you want. Bottom line is that this can all get sorted out later."

He clambered forward, popped a claw, and sliced a strip of cloth from Haze's sleeve. He used it to tie a tight gag around Haze's mouth and then cut another piece to bind his hands even more tightly behind him. Haze gulped as the branch on which he was perched wavered beneath him. He wasn't at all convinced that his support wasn't going to snap and send him crashing to the ground below. Unfortunately for him, Wolverine didn't seem the least bit interested in hanging around and assuaging his concerns.

"Maybe—*maybe*—I'll bring your son back here before we take off," said Wolverine. "If I do, you damned well better cooperate every step of the way. If you don't . . . well, I think you better understand that it won't bother me one bit to have a kid see his father cut to pieces in front of him. Kids are resilient. They bounce back from stuff like that. Get it?" His mouth bound, his eyes wide with fear, all Haze could manage was a brief nod. "Good," said Wolverine.

Moments later, he vanished from view, descending quickly and quietly to the ground. Haze didn't want to think about how Wolverine was going to overcome the DNA encoding in the booby traps, if for no other reason than that he was concerned he might vomit with the gag still in his mouth.

28

MATTHEW HAYES WANDERED AROUND THE ISLAND, calling, "Hello! Hello, is anybody there? Help!"

He looked frightened and helpless, and when he spoke, his voice was quavering. "Hello?" he called again. "I . . . I could use some help here!"

He turned a corner and jumped back, startled. Kaz was standing there facing him, hands on his hips. He looked annoyed.

"What the hell do you think you're doing?" he said.

Matthew hesitated and then, his tone and voice sounding very different from how they had a moment earlier, said, "Figured I would try to draw him out."

"You 'figured.' You know what, Quince? Stop figuring."

Quince, clearly annoyed, allowed his body to shift back to his normal appearance. "I haven't been able to raise Brawn. Haze, neither."

"Yeah. I know," said Kaz. "Can't say I'm too thrilled about that."

"Think it was Wolverine?"

"Of course it was Wolverine, you idiot." Kaz considered a moment and then said, "Head back to the lair. Stake it out. If you see any sign of Wolverine coming, you call me."

"You want us to split up? Isn't that asking for trouble?"

"Brawn and Haze stayed together; didn't seem to do them a whole lot of good. What're you, afraid of Wolverine?"

"I took the runt once already. I'm perfectly happy to finish the job."

"Good. Then finish it."

Kaz put out his fist, and Quince thumped his knuckles against them. "Let's get it done."

Quince turned away from Kaz and started toward the lair. He hesitated, turned, and looked over his shoulder, but Kaz had already vanished back into the forest.

Kaz made his way quickly through the forest, listening for any sign of one of the booby traps going off. Certainly, that was the easiest, fastest way to track down Wolverine. No matter how skilled he was, he still wasn't going to be able to elude infrared beams or motion detectors. Wolverine was many things, but a ghost wasn't one of them. As long as he had physical presence, he was certain to detonate any one of dozens of traps strewn throughout the island.

He had a motion detector on his wrist similar to what Haze had possessed, and he was paying strict attention to it now. If Wolverine twitched so much as a muscle, Kaz would be able to find him.

Then he picked up something moving just twenty meters away. He froze, keeping a wary eye on the target's movement. He watched as the target approached a section of the woods that Kaz knew for a fact was rigged for traps. To be specific, a web of laser beams that would cross-cut any unauthorized individual into small quivering chunks of meat.

The target entered the perimeter. Kaz waited for the booby traps to go off.

Nothing.

No response at all.

The obvious conclusion was that it was one of his own people, against whom naturally the booby traps took no action. If he had to guess that it was someone on his own, he would have thought that it was Brawn. Haze tended to stay put and wait for unwary individuals to come to him so that he could spring a surprise attack.

"Brawn, come in," said Kaz through his comm link. No response. This was starting to bother the hell out of him. What if Brawn was hurt somehow? He could have had a dust-up with Wolverine and wound up on the wrong side of the altercation. Kaz was a big believer in not leaving a man behind, and even though Brawn was clearly still up and around, there was something about it that just didn't sit right with him.

Quickly, as noiselessly as he could, Kaz made his way through the forest, zeroing in on the man he believed to be Brawn. He kept a wary eye out for any other signs of movement on his motion detector, but nothing was showing itself. If Wolverine was still in the area, then he wasn't budging. Perhaps he was dead. There was a cheerful thought. If Brawn had managed to dispose of Wolverine, that was going to make their lives a hell of a lot simpler.

He moved faster and faster through the woods, while Brawn maintained his slow, steady, slightly lurching pace. Kaz was becoming more convinced by the minute that Brawn was hurt. Tossing aside caution, he ran at full speed, vaulting distances with the accelerated strength in his legs. Within minutes, he'd drawn close enough that he actually could see Brawn in the near distance. Brawn was staggering, and then he stopped moving, leaning against a tree to brace himself.

"Brawn!" he called. No response. Brawn didn't turn to face him or even acknowledge that he had shouted his name.

He gathered his strength and leaped the intervening distance between himself and Brawn. Brawn hadn't budged since Kaz had first called to him. He was leaning against the tree as if it were the only thing that was keeping him propped up. Kaz landed five feet behind him.

There was blood soaking through the back of

Brawn's shirt. His trousers were likewise stained dark. "Brawn, for God's sake!" he said.

Brawn turned to face him. His face was barely recognizable as his own. It was dark and bruised, as if every capillary beneath the skin had ruptured. The skin around his mouth was hanging loosely, and his eyes . . .

His eyes were not his own.

It took Kaz's shocked mind seconds to process what he was witnessing, but that was all the time that was required.

"Brawn" suddenly moved with unnatural speed, all feigning of weakness tossed aside. Telltale claws snapped out of the backs of his hands, and he thrust forward. Kaz barely moved back in time; had he been a half-second slower, he would have been disemboweled.

"You sick bastard," snarled Kaz. "You skinned him. *You skinned him!*"

Wolverine, hiding within the skin of Eli Brohn, didn't respond except to attack once more.

Kaz realized he was about to vomit. He yanked out his gun and fired in one smooth movement, utilizing his damping power at the same time to try to counter Wolverine's natural agility. His first shot hit home, tearing a hole in Brawn's skin, but Wolverine ducked beneath the second blast and jammed his claws into Kaz's shoulder. The gun fell from Kaz's numb finger.

Kaz leaped skyward, trying to get away. He arced through the air, and suddenly something struck him hard in the forehead. He realized belatedly that Wolverine had picked up a rock and thrown it with deadly accuracy. It clipped him in mid-flight and sent him spiraling to the ground.

He took just enough time to see that Wolverine was coming right after him. It was a sick sight to behold. Wolverine must have figured out that the DNA of the Dragon Corps members prevented the booby traps from firing. So he killed Brawn and created a "suit" for himself out of Brawn's skin.

Kaz scrambled backward, trying to get his wits about him. His elbow bumped against something. He looked down and saw a laser cannon, one of the booby traps that wasn't functioning because of Wolverine's successful masquerade as Brawn.

What Wolverine didn't know was that they came with manual overrides.

Kaz yanked the laser cannon from its mooring, flipped the override switch, and fired.

Wolverine barely managed to get out of the way in time. The laser cannon sliced across his upper thigh, and Wolverine staggered, his healing factor short-circuited through Kaz's influence. Even as Wolverine rolled to one side, he sliced through one of the towering trees and sent it crashing down toward Kaz.

Kaz rolled back and retreated, firing blindly with the laser. He kept running, and suddenly there was the snap of a snare. Kaz looked down and saw that he'd tripped something, some sort of wire.

He barely had time to register that piece of information before bullets cut through the air.

The impact of the bullets hammering his body lifted him off his feet. He had no idea where he'd been hit; all he knew was that he was being pounded. He hit the ground some feet away, still desperately clutching the laser cannon. He staggered to his feet.

He saw a form moving through the woods toward him, and he swung the laser cannon up and fired blindly. The laser cannon struck home, nailing the approaching figure, slicing crossways across his torso. His entire right arm came clean off, and he screamed.

The scream was not Wolverine's voice.

Kaz lowered the laser cannon, his own pain forgotten.

The figure staggered forward, and it was not Wolverine. Instead, Quince stumbled forward, clutching at the gaping hole where his arm had been. His body was trying to repair itself but wasn't succeeding. His mouth was moving, trying to speak, but not managing any words.

"You idiot! I told you to get back to the lair!"

"Heard . . . shooting . . . wanted to . . . to help . . ."

Out of the corner of his eye, Kaz spotted movement. He twisted fast, opened fire, but it moved too quickly.

Kaz backpedaled, trying to stay one step ahead of his pursuer, and suddenly the ground went out from under him. He had just barely enough time to realize that his pursuit of Wolverine had brought him full circle, and he was going over the same cliff that Wolverine had tumbled off earlier.

"This isn't over!" he had enough time to shout before tumbling backward off the cliff.

"I kind of think it is," Wolverine called after him as Kaz fell away.

Quince lay on the ground, moaning. He looked up, uncomprehending, as what appeared to be Brawn stood over him, looking down at him. "Eli . . . help me . . ." he whispered.

"Eli can't help you."

He heard the familiar voice coming out of Brawn's mouth. He tried to focus on the man standing over him. "Wolverine . . . ?"

"Stay here. You're hurt pretty bad."

"I . . . I don't understand . . ."

"There's nothing for you to understand."

He looked at the gaping wound that even his malleable body wasn't able to repair. "Am . . . I going to die?"

"Maybe."

Wolverine started to walk past him, and Quince grabbed his leg. Wolverine looked down, ready to hack off the other arm, but Quince said, "If I die . . . find my parents. Tell my dad . . . I'm sorry . . . and tell my mom . . . it was all . . . Dad's fault . . ."

His head slumped to one side. Wolverine stared down at him and said, "Yeah, I'll get right on that," but

Quince was in no position to hear him—or anything—again.

Logan gave no more thought to the individuals who had been pursuing him. He made his way quickly across the island and soon had zeroed in on the building that had to be the lair.

The skin of the late Brawn was beginning to stiffen all around him. He wasn't sure how much longer it was going to last. Furthermore, he didn't think bursting in on young Matthew Hayes looking like a walking corpse would help him to earn the kid's trust.

Still, he needed to keep the imposture up for a little while longer, just to make certain that he had navigated his way beyond the various booby traps that doubtless still remained to pick him off.

Upon finding the flat, saucer-shaped structure that served as the Dragon's Lair, Logan saw no reason to hesitate. He went straight up to what appeared to be the main entrance and shoved open the door. He braced himself, waiting for some sort of response to his entering the house. There was none.

He made his way quickly through the house from one room to the next. Deciding to be as methodical as possible, he started at the top and worked his way down. He discovered various rooms of interest, including an armory. He disdained to take anything from it, however. He wasn't much for relying on any sort of weaponry other than that which his own body provided.

Of far greater significance was a central surveillance room. Not only were there monitors giving him views of the entire house, but there was also a control console that provided full access to the house's alarm systems. He was impressed to see that there was an array of lasers and such strewn throughout the house, making it no less deadly than the approach to it had been.

He studied the controls carefully, and then, taking his time, he proceeded to shut them down one by one. Within minutes, he had managed to deactivate every trap in the house.

This is too easy . . . way too easy.

He didn't want to be suspicious of the fact that he was finally catching a bit of luck, but he couldn't help it. He kept waiting for something to blow up in his face. It was simply the way things tended to go with him.

Having dispensed with the internal security systems, he started going through the monitors one screen at a time, hoping to catch a glimpse of where Matthew Hayes might be. Sure enough, he finally found him. He was sitting on the floor of a place that was labeled "Safe Room" on the monitor screen. His legs were drawn up, his knees tucked under his chin.

It took only a matter of moments for him to learn the safe room's location within the house itself. He shrugged off the skin of Eli Brohn, leaving the sticky mess in a pile on the floor. Then he found a sink and towels so that he could wipe the blood and gore from his skin. It took him a while to do so, and there was still stickiness in his hair, but it was the best he could do under the circumstances.

He pulled a set of camouflage shirt and pants from a closet and put them on to replace the ruined clothes he'd been wearing. They were big on him, but it was nothing that he couldn't deal with by rolling up the sleeves and cuffs. He didn't bother replacing the boots; he was generally more comfortable barefoot, anyway. Then he padded through the house, down the stairs toward where the safe room was.

He found the large secured door and looked it over. There was a time lock on it, and he had no means of cutting it short. But that didn't necessarily present a problem for him. He studied the door carefully, found the bolts where it was secured, and popped his claws. He placed the points of the adamantium weapons against the hinges and pushed. The claws slid through easily, and Logan began carefully running them along the door's perimeter.

Once he had cut all the way around it, he gripped the outer lock and pulled as hard as he could. The door didn't budge at first, but after long moments, his strength began to overcome the door's resistance. With an ear-splitting shriek of metal, the door came loose, slowly at first but then faster. Logan didn't let up for an instant, and minutes later, the door to the safe room yanked clear with a popping of air.

Logan staggered and almost fell with the door on top of him. But he regained his balance before that could happen and then, with a grunt, set the door to one side. It clanged heavily to the floor, and Logan shook out his arms before peering in.

Matthew Hayes looked up at him, wide-eyed. Then he blinked like an owl that just had a spotlight shone in its face. "Who . . . ?"

"I'm here to get you out."

"Who are you?"

"Name's Logan. Now, come on, there's lots of folks who want to know that you're all right."

"Wh-where's my dad?"

Logan was relieved that he'd had that little chat with Haze (Haze, Hayes, how could he not have seen that one coming?), because otherwise he'd have no idea what the kid was talking about. "Your dad's fine. Come on." He put out a hand to Matthew.

Matthew pulled back. "My dad wouldn't want me going anyplace without him."

"Well, you're going someplace with me. Not giving you a choice here."

He knew that he should be more patient with the kid, but he'd been through too much to trade words with him. He was reasonably sure that he'd disposed of Dragon Corps, but he had no way of knowing for sure. It was always possible that there were additional members that he'd missed. Plus, for all he knew, there was some sort of failsafe activated, and the whole island might be scheduled to blow sky high.

"I don't want to go with you," Matthew said insistently. "I want my dad!"

"I'll bring you to him."

"Bring him here first!"

"Kid, this ain't a negotiation. I know you're scared; I know you dunno what's going on. But you gotta trust me. I'm one of the good guys, and I'm getting you out of here right now."

He reached for Matthew Hayes, this time determined not to take no for an answer.

He snagged the boy by the wrists.

Suddenly, Logan's entire body began to tremble. He looked down just in time to see the air rippling around Matthew's fists, as if a massive amount of power were starting to build up within them.

Uh-oh.

Instantly, he released Matthew's wrists and drew back a fist to try to knock the kid cold. Punching out a boy certainly wasn't Logan's optimal way to proceed, but he wasn't seeing any other choice.

As it happened, he didn't get the opportunity. Twin concussive blasts of force ripped out of Matthew's hands. They slammed squarely into Logan, lifting him off his feet and sending him hurtling across the room, through the far wall, and into the adjoining room.

He staggered to his feet and peered through the holes in the wall. Matthew was standing there, staring at his hands in shock. His gaze shifted to Logan, and he said, with more intensity in his voice, "I want . . . my dad."

"I'll bring you to him."

"Bring him here."

And Logan decided that a good, solid lie wouldn't hurt at this point. Besides, for all he knew, what he was about to say was absolutely true.

"There's a bomb ticking down under this island. We've got maybe twenty minutes tops to get out of here before it goes ka-blam. If I leave you here to go get your dad and then bring him back, that's gonna take up all the spare time we have. None of us gets clear. If I bring you to your dad, then we'll just have enough time for all of us to get off the island. So, long story short: come with me, you and your dad live; be a hard-ass about it, and you and your father both die."

"What about you?" Matthew said defiantly.

Logan shrugged. Then he reached over, picked up a fallen kitchen knife, and drew it across the upper section of his forearm. He winced as it carved a large section of his skin away. Matthew's face twisted in revulsion— and then his eyes widened in astonishment as the skin healed right back up.

"I got what's called a healing factor," said Logan. "Blow me up, rip me up, tear me to shreds, I'll just come right back together again, sooner or later. Sure, if this place blows up, there won't be much left of me. But what is left will grow back. Can't say the same for you. So, it's your call, sonny. No hurry. Take your time. It's only yours and your dad's lives at stake."

Matthew blanched considerably as Logan said that. Logan leaned back against a cabinet and crossed his legs nonchalantly.

"You . . . you better take me right to him," Matthew said.

Logan got to his feet. "You drive a hard bargain, kid."

"Damned straight."

"In all my years, Pamela, I have to say, this is like nothing this reporter has ever seen. Or, to be more precise, like nothing I have ever seen in this country. The country has, quite simply, gone berserk. The president's announcement that he has set aside the results of the election has split Congress down partisan lines, but the reaction from the American people has been almost uniformly negative. Army bases throughout the country are on high alert. All government office buildings have been shut down except for such locations as the Pentagon, where Army units have been scrambled to serve in a protective capacity. Although it had been rumored that the president and vice president have been relocated to a secure location, there are now reports that the president has chosen to send his family to a secure location but is remaining himself at the White House."

"How is the security situation at the White House itself, Stu?"

"I'd have to say it has become a flashpoint for hostility, Pamela. Riot squads have been organized to break up the demonstrations that are currently swelling beyond all capacity. No shots have been fired yet, but many believe it's just a matter of time until—

"Pamela! Pamela, I've just received word that gunfire has been exchanged. National Guardsmen are reportedly firing on the crowd! I'm going to try to get in closer so we can see clearly what's—people are screaming! They're running in every direction now. Shots are being fired overhead. I see—"

"Stu? Stu! Stu, come in! We . . . we seem to have lost contact with Stu Cabot. We will be back on with him as soon as . . . um . . . all right, we have word from our New York feed, we're going live to New York, where masses of people are assembling outside the United Nations, demanding that the UN take over the election as they would any election result being denied by a dictator in a Third World country. Over to you, Graham Murphy . . ."

29

CORPORAL WESTLAKE FELT AS IF HE WERE HAVING an out-of-body experience while still fully conscious and alive.

He didn't see the fury building around him so much as feel it. He didn't think he was developing some sort of empathic ability; it just seemed as if anger were another form of energy, and it was building up all around him, as palpable as the winds of a gathering storm.

Word had spread instantly throughout the crowd about the president's announcement. In this day and age of instantaneous communication, people were hooked into the Internet through their various personal devices and so had witnessed the speech he'd made, a speech that people were decrying as everything from a coup d'etat to the instituting of martial law. Personally, Westlake didn't know how he felt about it. On the one hand, the president had a point: the electoral process had been usurped, and this should be investigated just as any other case of fraud would be. On the other hand, that was precisely the point: if the president believed that the election had been unfairly rigged, then shouldn't he be obliged to seek redress through the legal system? File a suit, request an injunction, something like that? Should he be allowed to usurp the Constitution in order to protect it?

It was one of those times when Westlake was glad he was in the Army. There was something comforting about being able simply to obey orders and not worry about the moral ramifications.

Except . . . even under those circumstances, he still worried about the morality of his orders. He wondered if that made him a bad soldier or a good one.

Either way, he was relieved that he had arrived earlier so that the crowd had had time to accept him. As it was, if he'd shown up out of the blue in his uniform right about now, the crowd might well have turned on him, believing that he had been dispatched to take offensive action against them. Granted, that would have been a ludicrous notion—one soldier against a mob—but then again, mobs weren't noted for their brilliant reasoning capacity.

Since the president's announcement, the crowd had swelled to at least twice its previous size. Westlake had no idea where the hell everyone was coming from, but he knew that this was going to end badly. More troops had shown up on the other side of the fence, but the civilians still vastly outnumbered them. Flashes of incidents that Westlake had only read about in history books came to his mind—incidents typically deemed "massacres" as soldiers had opened fire on unarmed citizens for whatever reason. History had a way of de-personalizing such events. Whenever he'd read about them, it had been through cold, hard facts that detailed in as detached a manner as possible the things that had led up to those first horrible moments of bloodshed. Westlake now realized that such depictions didn't begin to capture the pure, unadulterated emotion that caused such volatile incidents to combust. The fire of human emotions was added to the gasoline of a situation, with the resultant explosion of fury consuming everyone within the vicinity.

Seeing it coming, not knowing how but only that it would, Westlake pulled urgently at Ellen Hayes's elbow. He had managed to stay close to her even as the mob had burgeoned in size. Shouting to make himself heard over the protests and howls of fury, he said to her, "I think we should get you out of here, Ellen!"

She pulled away, looking at him with pure rage. "I'm going to make them remember Matthew!"

"This isn't about Matthew anymore! This is about who's going to do something stupid first and who's going to get hurt afterward!"

"Get away from me!"

"Ellen, for God's sake—!"

And that was when he saw it.

It was some kid. Some jerk kid, wearing a jacket with the American flag on the back. He and a couple of his friends, lighting up a row of firecrackers. Why? Probably because they fancied themselves patriots, they associated patriotism with the Fourth of July, and the Fourth of July with fireworks. Oh . . . and because they were idiots. Idiots who believed they were making a political statement rather than being about to touch off a complete fiasco.

"No!" screamed Westlake, and he tried to shove past Ellen to get to them. But he and Ellen were up on a podium, they were down in the crowd, he wasn't going to be able to get to them, and suddenly he realized with dull horror that he couldn't avert the impending disaster.

He grabbed at Ellen, tried to shelter her with his own body. But he didn't have a good grip on her, and, because she had no idea what was going on, she yanked away from him. He had a grip on her shirtsleeve, but the sleeve tore away in his grasp.

His head snapped back around just as he saw them hurl the firecrackers through the air. "God bless America!" one of them seemed to be shouting; it was hard to tell for sure, because he was a distance away, and there was so much noise all around them.

The firecrackers went off, the noises echoing up and down Pennsylvania Avenue.

The soldiers, their nerves already ratcheted up to the breaking point, instantly leaped to the conclusion that Westlake knew they would reach.

They thought they were under fire.

They fired back.

The explosion of Secret Service agents into his office startled the president, watching out the window of the Oval Office. "Away from the window, sir! Now!"

They hauled him away, and the president barely had time to cry out, "What's happening? What's going—?"

"Shots fired! We have reports of shots fired! Soldiers are returning fire!"

This will end bloody.

The words came back to him.

What have I done? Oh, God, what have I done?

Most of the soldiers aimed high. Even faced with what they believed was an attack, they were still cautious enough of human life to fire warning shots.

Some didn't. Some fired directly into the crowd.

People screamed, stumbling over one another to try to get out of the way.

Westlake looked frantically for Ellen, didn't see her. He'd lost track of her. But he saw something else that horrified him: a burly guy in the crowd yanking out a gun, about to fire on the soldiers.

Westlake didn't hesitate. He pulled out his own

weapon, aimed, and fired in one motion. He struck the man in the leg, who went down, crying out and clutching at his thigh.

But the sound of Westlake's own gun just made things worse. The air was alive with shots being fired, shrieks of terror. Rioters had had no problem with the notion of howling words of protest, cloaked in the First Amendment's protection. But that cloak was now tattered, and most of them couldn't get out of there fast enough.

That was when he saw Ellen. She was on the ground, lying flat. She was trying to get up, but the crush of people around her was preventing her from doing so. The people who had been calling her name earlier, treating her like a goddess, now threatened to trample her in their endeavor to get the hell out of there.

Westlake vaulted off the podium, using his forward momentum to elbow his way through the crowd. He still had his gun out, and when people were slow to get out of his way, he swung it up into their faces and growled, "Move." Unsurprisingly, this worked effectively enough so that within seconds, he had gotten to Ellen's side.

"Come on, get up." He started to pull her upright.

That was when he saw the red stain spreading across the front of her shirt.

He muttered a string of profanities as he hauled her up and holstered his gun. The most effective means of carrying her out of there would have been a fireman's carry, but that would have left her more vulnerable to stray shots.

So he held her close to him, his arms around her waist, hauling her forward as fast as he could. Several times, fleeing people bumped into him, almost knocking him to the ground, but he managed to keep his feet.

He looked around desperately, trying to find a break in the crowd. Every time he managed to do so, it was suddenly filled up with more fleeing people. He wasn't hearing shots fired anymore, which was some small relief. "Ellen," he said, seeing her eyes flickering. "Don't go to sleep. Stay with me now."

"Matthew . . . ?" Her voice was soft, distant.

"Yes. Yes, I'm bringing you to Matthew," he said desperately. "You don't want to be sleeping when you see Matthew, right?"

"No . . . no, of course . . . have to stay awake . . . for Matthew . . ."

She smiled. Amazingly, it seemed to light up her face, as if it could carry both of them away from their dire situation.

Westlake saw an opening and went for it, elbowing his way through when a couple of running individuals crossed his path. He knocked both of them flat and kept going, not even bothering to see if they were okay, probably because he didn't care.

Then he was in the clear. And there, just ahead of him, was a police car, siren spinning, barreling down the street. Taking a risk, not seeing any way around it, Westlake darted directly into the path of the cruiser.

The brakes screeched, and the police car slid to one side as Westlake took a few steps to the right to avoid it. Two cops bounded out of the car, yelling, "Hands in the air!" But Westlake ignored them, instead shouting above them, "Westlake, Anthony, Corporal, out of Fort Randolph! I have a wounded civilian here! Are you going to go John Wayne on me, or are you going to serve and protect?"

One of the cops drew closer and saw the blood covering Ellen's shirt. Instantly, he holstered his own weapon and shouted, "Get in the back of the car! Now!"

Seconds later, the police car was speeding toward the nearest hospital. The cop riding shotgun was handing cloths to Westlake, who had Ellen lying across him in the backseat. He applied pressure to the wound, hoping to stanch the bleeding.

"We were answering a call of shots fired at the White House," said the cop in the passenger seat. "That where you were coming from?"

Westlake nodded.

"What the hell happened?"

Westlake, seeing the cloth becoming more stained with red, pushed it harder. "Democracy in action," he said humorlessly.

The police car sped away into the night.

30

ROBERT HAYES, A.K.A. HAZE, LET OUT A MUFFLED yelp when Wolverine suddenly appeared in the branches next to him.

"Listen carefully," Wolverine said without preamble. "Here's what's gonna be. Your kid is down on the ground, waiting for me to bring you to him. Your pals are all dead. Personally, I'd have no problem right now with cutting you down, letting you fall, and you can join 'em." He untied Haze's gag. "The only thing that's stopping me is that the kid down there still cares about you."

"You care that much about Matthew's feelings?" Haze was openly skeptical. "You didn't strike me as the sentimental type."

"Well, the kid also seems to be able to use his hands to generate concussive force on par with a pile of dynamite."

Haze's jaw dropped. "You mean, I was right?"

"Yeah, Einstein, you were right. Now, with your pals dead, you still have a way out of this fiasco. You can claim that you were dragged into this against your will. That they threatened you into cooperating. Play your cards right, you can come out of this a hero."

"And you'd back me up?"

"Kid's a mutant. Having a father who's a mutant to help him survive in this world maybe isn't the worst thing in the world. But this is a one-time offer, Haze. You try anything—you try to use your power to get away, you try to convince the kid he should concuss me into the middle of next week, you pull anything resembling a double cross—and I will kill you. Dead. In front of your kid, makes no never mind to me."

"And if he tries to kill you in retaliation?"

"I'll take my chances. If it comes to a throwdown between me and your kid, who do you really think is gonna come out on top?"

Haze didn't have to reply. Both he and Wolverine knew the answer.

"So we got a deal?"

Haze nodded.

"Fine. Hold on."

Wolverine reached out and grabbed Haze by the back of the shirt. Then he popped his claws and slashed loose the vines that were keeping Haze in place.

Both Haze and Wolverine fell. Haze let out a panicked screech, but Wolverine didn't appear the least bit concerned. He shifted his grip so that he had one arm around Haze's waist and then simply ricocheted from one sturdy tree trunk to the other. The world spun around Haze, and he was sure that just about any second, they were going to hit the ground with a bone-shattering crash. Instead, Wolverine continued to guide their descent until, with seconds having passed like an eternity, Wolverine and Haze landed on the ground. Wolverine's legs easily withstood the brunt of the landing.

Matthew Hayes was waiting for them. He was standing a few feet away and let out a joyous cry when he saw his father. He ran toward him, arms thrown wide. Haze composed himself, got steady on his feet, and picked up the boy, hugging him tight.

For a half a moment, he glanced toward Wolverine and considered using his power to disappear. There was still the possibility that he might be able to sneak away, to elude Wolverine somehow . . .

Then he saw the intense look on Wolverine's face. It was as if the homicidal little mutant had worked his way directly into Haze's mind and was issuing a warning: *You're thinking about it. I can tell you're thinking about it. Don't. Just toss it aside. Don't even consider it. Because it's not going to go the way you want it to.*

Haze shook it off, but the way Wolverine was staring at him made him certain that he hadn't imagined the thoughts rattling around in his head. He nodded, silently acknowledging what neither had spoken but both knew.

"Matthew," Haze said, taking his son by the shoulders, "it's time to go home."

"Go home? But I thought you said Mom wouldn't understand. And—and she won't, Dad. It happened. You were right: it happened. When that guy"—and he made a distasteful gesture toward Wolverine—"came after me. You should've seen it, Dad. I knocked him on his ass!"

"Did you, now?"

"Lucky shot," Wolverine muttered.

Haze had to smile at that. Despite the gravity of their situation, there was something amusing about Wolverine wanting to cling to his pride while a young boy recounted the first manifestation of his abilities.

"Do you know who this guy is, Matthew?" When Matthew shrugged, Haze continued, "His name's Wolverine. He came to tell me that"—his mind raced—"that your mom misses you very much. That maybe my taking you wasn't the best idea in the world. That it wasn't fair to your mom."

"Are you sure? I mean . . ."

"Yeah. I'm sure, Mattie. And if you think about it long enough, then I bet you'll agree."

"Your dad's taking us back to his airplane now, aren'tcha, Dad?" Wolverine said.

"That's . . . that's right, Wolverine," Haze said, trying

to insert heartiness into his voice that he didn't remotely feel. "We're going there right now. And I'll fly us out of here and back to the States."

"Good idea," said Wolverine, as if the notion were entirely Haze's. "Lots of folks back there are worried about you, kid."

"Yeah, but I bet none of 'em worries about me as much as my dad."

Wolverine said nothing. Haze riffled Matthew's hair approvingly and then said, "Let's go, sport."

He started walking, and Wolverine was immediately at his side. "Need to talk to your dad about something private. Grown-up stuff," said Wolverine to Matthew. "Just go on ahead a few steps, okay?"

"But don't we gotta hurry? The island's gonna blow up. You said . . ."

Haze looked at Wolverine uncomprehendingly and then quickly said, "I . . . managed to override that, Matthew. To turn it off. It's going to be fine. We have time. Just do as he says."

Matthew looked suspicious but did as he was instructed. Wolverine moved in close to Haze and said in a low voice, "Did you do something to the kid?"

"Do something?"

"Don't screw around with me, Haze, I ain't in the mood. Your power—did it affect his mind somehow?"

"No. No, not at all. Not"—he cleared his throat—"not . . . permanently."

"You no-good creep. You got into his head. Made it

so that he wouldn't question the stuff that you didn't want him asking too much about."

"Something like that."

"I oughtta just forget the whole deal and slit your throat."

"Go ahead," said Haze defiantly. "You'd probably be doing my son a favor, and you know it. Go ahead, I said. Do it."

Wolverine glowered at him.

"Dad?" Matthew had stopped walking and was watching them carefully. "Is everything okay?"

"Fine, Matthew. Everything's fine. Right, Wolverine?"

"Terrific," said Wolverine.

The trip went more smoothly than Logan could have hoped. He had been reasonably sure that he had managed to deactivate the booby traps around the island from the central point of the lair, but he couldn't be sure. Traveling in close proximity to people who were DNA-protected from the traps, on the other hand, had further added to the insurance. They made their way through the caves and in short order had clambered into the seaplane that had been left moored and bobbing in the water. It took a few minutes to get the plane sufficiently fueled to make the trip back. Haze did a series of last-minute checks to verify that the plane was ready to go.

The sea was as smooth as glass around them. There was plenty of light, since a full moon was hanging high in the sky. Logan thought about the fact that Election Day was already over back home, and whatever decision the American people had made was a done deal. To some degree, he was arriving too late to make a difference. But it wasn't too late to reunite a boy with his mother and further assuage the American people by making them realize that foreign nationals had not arbitrarily seized a random child in order to control an election. In many respects, the election aspect was secondary, to cover a straightforward kidnapping scheme by a desperate father. He suspected that Americans would be far more comfortable with that scenario.

"Let's get this crate airborne," he said.

Haze, in the pilot's seat, nodded. Matthew had already climbed into the passenger's seat, and Logan insinuated himself into the cramped back. He pulled shut the hatch, and Haze fired up the engines. They coughed for a moment and then caught. Moments later, the propellers were whirring, and the seaplane was picking up speed.

"My dad's the best pilot in the world," said Matthew proudly.

"Let's hope so," said Logan.

The plane picked up speed, bumped once, twice, and then leaped skyward. The engines accelerated as the plane angled steadily upward.

Minutes later, the plane had leveled off. "Care to tell me where we're heading?" Haze said after a long period of silence.

"Been thinking about that," said Logan. "Ideally, I'd like to get us to Fort Randolph, but I'm reasonably sure we don't have enough fuel for that. Besides, this is a seaplane, and they're landlocked. So I figure the best place at this point is back to D.C., where we'll hook back up with Agent Craig and his buddies at BNE. They can get this sorted out."

"I don't want to be arrested."

"Look, Haze. It's what I said before: you're the only one of your little group who's still around. Whatever story you come up with, I'm perfectly happy to back you up. But there's one thing you haven't told me."

"Oh?"

"Was anyone else involved?"

"Anyone else?"

"Don't play games with me, Haze. You know what I'm talking about."

"Watch how you talk to my dad," Matthew warned him. "Or I'll . . ."

"News flash, kid," said Logan. "You try to use your power on me now, you'll wind up blasting the whole plane to pieces. I don't care how good a pilot your dad is, he's not gonna be able to do much flying in a giant piece of scrap metal. Now, answer my question, Haze."

"I just don't see how it's relevant."

"The cagier you are, the more I'm starting to think it *is* relevant. See, this goes beyond the kid. There's the whole matter of that video that was released that showed Mazone as masterminding this thing. That doesn't square at all with your whole story about being motivated to be a caring dad."

"Let's just say that there was a confluence of interests," said Haze.

"Meaning you wanted your kid, and other members of Dragon Corps were interested in other things, so you put it all together into one big master plan."

"Something like that."

"I think it's exactly like that. Thing is, that video that was released—that wasn't Mazone in it at all, was it? It's just too amateur hour for something like that to get out accidentally. That was really Quince masquerading as Mazone, wasn't it?"

Slowly, Haze nodded.

"Which means that someone wanted to set Mazone up to take a fall. Who was it?"

"I don't know."

"Oh, come on."

"I don't," Haze insisted. "Look, that's how Dragon Corps operates. No one person knows everything."

"That's impossible. Somebody has to know the entire picture."

Haze hesitated, clearly unsure of what to say, and Logan's ears suddenly pricked up. "You hear that?" he said abruptly.

Haze tried to hear over the roaring sound of the plane's engine. It wasn't an easy thing to do, because it was a small airplane, and the normal operating noise was considerable. "What am I supposed to be listening for?"

"I could swear there's another—"

Suddenly, the seaplane lurched as something thudded repeatedly into the side. The sound was as if someone were throwing rocks at the plane.

"What the hell?" said Haze.

"Bank left! Hard to the left!" Logan shouted.

Without asking why, Haze did as he was instructed. The plane dove quickly. Matthew's fists were clenched, his face deathly white, but he kept looking with determined confidence at his father.

The plane shuddered yet again, and this time, the windshield shattered. Glass flew everywhere. Haze reflexively threw an arm up in front of Matthew's face to protect him. "Somebody's shooting at us!"

"No kidding," said Logan.

Haze jammed the stick forward, accelerating down, and then he drew it back as hard as he could. The seaplane did a one-eighty, twisting and hurtling back in the direction from which it had come. There was a quick flash of another plane below them, and then Haze whipped the seaplane around so that it dropped behind the plane that had been pursing them.

It was another seaplane, but it had guns mounted on the fuselage.

"It's one of ours!" said Haze.

"You have more than one plane?"

"Well, yeah. At several points around the island."

"And you didn't tell me that?"

"You didn't ask!"

"So, use that cloaking power of yours. Make it so he can't see us."

"Right. Right," said Haze, who seemed so distracted that he'd forgotten he had that ability. Logan could understand why; Haze's first and most obvious concern was the welfare of his son.

The plane ahead of them suddenly swept down and around. Haze banked, trying to avoid it, but the other plane had now angled around and was coming right toward them.

"Cloak us!"

"I am!" Haze shouted.

The machine guns on the oncoming plane's fuselage came alive. Haze desperately tried to swerve to avoid it, but he was less than successful. Black smoke began to billow through the window. The engine nearly choked out, and it was nothing short of a miracle that Haze was able to keep the propellers turning.

Matthew was terrified, trying not to cry, trying to be tough, and not succeeding.

Haze angled the seaplane up as the other plane passed directly beneath them. "They're coming around for another pass," said Logan.

"I know that! And considering our fuel line's been hit, I'm not sure it's going to need it!"

"Why aren't you cloaking us?"

"I am!"

"But—" Then the dime dropped in Logan's head, and he scowled. "Kaz. It has to be. He's blocking your power."

"I thought he was dead!"

"So did I. Apparently, he wasn't smart enough to stay that way. Take us up."

"Up? But—"

"Do it!"

Haze did as he was told. The plane shook violently in protest, clearly far preferring the notion of succumbing to gravity and crashing down into the water. Nevertheless, he managed to prod it higher. As he did so, he yanked oxygen masks out from under the seats, shoving one over to Matthew as he pulled the other one over his own face. It gave them some protection against the smoke that was billowing in through the window.

Logan cut loose from the restraints that belted him in and clambered to the hatch. He yanked on the lever and shoved it open.

He managed to spot the other plane just below and behind them. "Get ready to set her down!" he called out.

"What about Kaz?"

"Leave him to me," said Logan.

And with that, he threw himself out of the plane.

He dropped like a missile toward Kaz's plane and landed squarely on top of the fuselage. The plane veered from the impact. His first priority was protecting the other plane, so Logan swung himself down and around. He popped his claws and sank one into the side of the plane in order to anchor himself to it. With the other, he lashed out at one of the twin sets of machine guns that were mounted on the underside of the fuselage. He sliced through the front of it, disabling it.

The plane banked sharply, trying to throw Logan off. Rather than fight it, he went with the motion. As a result, he dropped onto the machine gun on the other side. Wrapping his legs around the pontoon, he cut through the second machine gun with his claws, sending pieces of it tumbling into the ocean.

Logan then swung himself around, clambered to the side of the plane, and yanked open the hatch.

There was a gun pointed right at him, and the grim face of Kaz was scowling at him from the pilot's seat. Then the gun went off.

Logan yanked himself back. The bullet barely missed, and he couldn't help but think that he'd been incredibly lucky just then. He felt as if he were moving with the speed of glue. Kaz's power was working its spell on him, depleting both his natural agility and his healing capability. Fortunately, his claws were not part of his power, or he'd be totally helpless. Even so, it was becoming an increasing strain for him to hold on.

Kaz fired a second time and a third. Then he suddenly pitched the airplane to the side. Logan grabbed desperately at the hatch door. It swung wide, sending his back banging up against the plane. He was now at the wrong angle for Kaz to be able to shoot him. He was also at the wrong angle to get into the plane. And with every passing second, he could feel his strength ebbing, being suppressed.

He saw only one option, and he couldn't say that he liked it much. But it was the only thing that occurred to him.

Using everything he had left, Logan swung on the hanging hatch door and hurled himself forward. He skidded down the length of the fuselage, jammed one of his claws into the front, and swung his free arm down and around and straight through the windshield. He was operating completely blind, unable to see where Kaz was, functioning on pure guesswork.

He heard a scream and felt his claws bury into something.

Anchored by the embedded claw, he yanked himself down and drove his upper body in through the windshield.

Kaz, in the pilot's seat, was sitting there with his mouth hanging open and blood trickling from it. Wolverine's claws were buried deep in his chest and had penetrated the backside of the seat. Logan yanked out his claws and insinuated himself through the window. Kaz's gun was still in his hand, but his arm was hanging limply. It seemed unlikely he had the strength to raise it, much less aim and fire.

Wasting no time, Logan clambered into the copilot seat, flipped some switches, and took over command of the plane. Kaz sat there listlessly, staring at him. Logan cast a glance in Kaz's direction. The bullet wounds he'd sustained earlier had been hastily bandaged. Logan was having trouble believing that Kaz was still functioning. It really was remarkable. With all the damage he'd already sustained, he'd still found enough juice to grab another plane and make a run at taking down Logan. That's what it had really come down to: Logan versus Kaz. The fact that Kaz likely would have wound up killing Haze and his son didn't even enter into it.

"Ease up on the throttle," Kaz said, the words burbling in his throat.

"You're giving advice now?" said Logan as he struggled to get the plane under control.

Kaz seemed as if he was attempting to shrug. "No point . . . not. It's over."

Logan eased up on the throttle, and the plane leveled off. Seconds later, he was bringing it in for a landing on the smooth ocean surface. He saw that Haze was bringing his own plane in, and even though it was crippled, he still clearly had it under control.

As Logan killed the engine, he turned to Kaz. Strangely, Kaz was smiling, as if he found the entire situation immensely funny.

"Why?" Logan said. "Why did you do all this? It wasn't about the boy . . ."

Slowly, Kaz shook his head. "Needed to. Needed president out. Four more years . . . he'll destroy everything . . ."

"Bull," said Logan. "If you really wanted him out of the way, you could have just taken him out. You didn't need something so involved."

"That's not . . . the way he works . . ."

"The way who works?"

"The Dragon." He coughed, blood spurting down his shirt. "Who else runs Dragon Corps 'cept for . . . Dragon? President . . . is one of . . . of them. One of the idiot humans. Dragon . . . is one of us . . ."

"He's a mutant?"

Kaz slowly shook his head, even though doing so required great effort. "More than that. Much more. He's forever."

"Who is he?"

Kaz laughed at that, although it was a sick and ugly sound. "Kidding . . . right? How stupid are you . . . not to know . . . ?"

"Who—?"

"Do me a favor . . . dump me at sea . . . let the legend grow . . ."

"Kaz!" He shook him angrily. "Who the hell is—?"

The only response he received was an all-too-familiar rattling from Kaz's throat. Kaz's head slumped back, his eyes staring at nothing—a nothing that Logan had come to know well in his years.

He was tempted to ignore Kaz's last request and haul his corpse back home. But to what purpose? A dead body begged questions and answered none. Furthermore, the plane wasn't all that big, and fuel was always an issue. Why pack on dead weight, so to speak, that would consume more fuel?

So it was that by the time Haze's crippled plane expended its last gasp by floating alongside Kaz's plane, Kaz's body was well on its way toward the bottom of the ocean. Seeing the empty pilot's seat, Haze exchanged a silent glance with Logan that spoke volumes.

Matthew peered in and said, "Where's the guy who was flying it?"

"He bailed out," Logan said. "Dunno where he went."

Matthew nodded. That was perfectly satisfactory as far as he was concerned.

Minutes later, the plane was heading skyward toward Washington, D.C.

31

CORPORAL WESTLAKE KNEW HE WASN'T ACCOM-
plishing a damned thing sitting in the hospital waiting
room. But he couldn't bring himself to leave. As absurd
as it sounded, he felt as if he would be abandoning
Ellen.

A television set was mounted in a corner of the
room, tuned to CNN. Westlake shook his head as he
watched fires burning in cities around the country. Soldiers were in the streets doing everything they could to
try to keep the lid on, but there was only so much they
could do. Westlake had reported in to General Doyle,
asking if he should return to Fort Randolph. Doyle
had told him to stay put; everything was too insane at
the moment for Doyle to arrange transport back to the
base. "One soldier isn't going to make that much of a
difference," Doyle had told him.

Most aggravating of all, the doctors wouldn't even

give Westlake an update on Ellen's condition. Since he wasn't a family member, doctor-patient confidentiality prevented them from doing so, or at least that's what they told him. So he sat there, feeling like a soul in limbo.

Hell, maybe he was. Maybe he'd actually been killed during the riot and was going to wind up spending eternity right here in this damned waiting room.

"Hello, Corporal."

Westlake looked up and was startled to see Agent Craig standing there, leaning against the door frame. Craig had a sheaf of papers under his arm. Westlake stood, his shoulders straight and stiff. Craig's face was stern.

"Didn't exactly come right back after voting, did you?"

"Apparently, whether I'd have voted or not didn't make a difference."

Craig nodded in acknowledgment of that fact. "You'll be happy to know that Ellen Hayes is going to make it. She's in stable condition."

"She is?" Relief swept through him, but then he said cautiously, "How do you know? They wouldn't tell me. Doctor-patient confidentiality."

"Yeah, you'd be amazed how the threat of a complete tax audit can persuade a doctor to bend that whole confidentiality thing. Come with me."

"Where?"

"To a press conference. Y Street Convention Center. President-elect Sanders is letting the American people know exactly what he thinks of the president's actions."

"So?"

"So this." He handed Westlake the sheaf of paper. "Check out the highlighted section."

Westlake did so, and his eyes widened. "Are you sure about this?"

"Why so stunned? It was your idea, coordinating what people were saying with what set you off."

"Yeah, but . . ."

"I've already informed your commanding officer. He's cleared your accompanying me. He's loaned you out, as it were. Let's go."

It had been described as a press conference, but it was far from that. A mass of Steve Sanders supporters waved signs, pledging fealty and shouting furious imprecations against the president of the United States. The press had turned out, and there were cameras everywhere. Only Sanders's remarkable charisma was preventing the entire thing from spilling over into complete chaos. Secret Service men were arrayed around him, eyeing the crowd cautiously.

Sanders thudded the podium with his fist for emphasis. "The president believes that the American people are idiots! That they are willing to accept this usurping of their voice in what is alleged to be their best interests!

Apparently, the president believes that he knows better what is best for you than you yourselves do! Do you accept that?"

As could have been expected, a thunderous roar of "No!" erupted from the crowd.

"Neither do I! Yet the president has the National Guard, the Army, whomever he can get his hands on that he hasn't wound up sending off to fight pointless wars, now combating their fellow Americans in the streets of the capital and cities across the country. This may well be the darkest time in the history of these United States that anyone can remember!"

More applause, more approval. Sanders felt as if he were being carried toward the ceiling on waves of adulation.

He was about to continue speaking when he saw a squad of dark-suited men, accompanied by a soldier, cutting through the crowd like an icebreaker through an ice field. People were looking at them angrily, shouting epithets, as they were carefully yet firmly pushed aside by the men. Sanders recognized the soldier and one of the men next to him, the foremost, from the memorial service for the Hayes boy.

"Senator Sanders, Agent Craig. We'd like to speak with you for a moment."

The Secret Service closed ranks around him. One of them, clearly in charge, said sharply, "We're going to have to ask you to step back, Agent Craig."

"This is BNE business."

"And this is the president-elect, and I'm asking you to stay back."

"According to your boss, he's not the president-elect," countered Craig, "because the election has just been set aside. We have jurisdiction here."

"Gentlemen, gentlemen, please," said Sanders, his voice booming through the room. "None of this is necessary. You are welcome to say whatever you have to say in front of the American people! I have nothing to hide!"

And then, to Sanders's shock, the soldier standing next to Craig turned bright red. The soldier looked down at his hands but didn't seem all that surprised. The soldier's face was grim as he and Craig drew closer, and there were startled reactions from anyone close enough to see the shift in the soldier's hue.

"Corporal Westlake, Senator. We've met before," he said, his skin tone shifting back to its normal color. "I'm a mutant."

He was close enough to a microphone that his voice carried, and the matter-of-fact way in which he said it startled the assemblage. There were some boos, some hisses, but Westlake turned to the crowd with a look of grim determination.

"Yes. That's right. I'm a mutant. It's something that I've spent a good deal of my life being ashamed about, even though I never had any control over it. The Army would happily accept my resignation over it. People have tap-danced on my face because of it. Beating the crap out of someone simply because of what he is, that's something for Americans to take pride in, isn't it?"

There were some more boos, a few shouts of "Go to hell, mutie!" but otherwise the crowd had quieted, which was nothing short of miraculous.

"Corporal Westlake here," said Craig, "has a very interesting ability. His skin changes color whenever someone tells a lie. You just saw it a few moments ago when you said that you had nothing to hide, Senator. Curiously enough, at the wake for young Matthew Hayes, you shouted"—glanced at a sheaf of paper even though he likely had the phrase memorized—"'What's happening? Who is that? I don't know what's going on!' And when you did so, Corporal Westlake here did his impression of a burn victim."

"Are you insinuating," said Sanders, "that I'm some-how involved with the kidnapping of that boy?"

"Are you?" said Westlake. He took a step closer, his gaze fixed on him. "Go ahead and deny it."

"For what purpose? So you can turn red and thus accuse me of something?" said Sanders. "That you can turn different colors we can clearly see. But we've no word save that of this government agent—this flunkie of the White House—that it's a response to anything someone else says. It could easily be a matter of will-power. You turn colors when you want to."

"Interesting theory," said Craig. "But I notice that you're still not commenting on your involvement with the kidnapping of Matthew Hayes."

"I had nothing to do with that."

Instantly, Westlake's skin went red.

Sanders did not let his smile slip so much as an inch, despite the startled gasps from some members of the crowd and a sudden chorus of questions being hurled at him by the assembled press. "It's just as I said. We've no indication that this mutant is doing anything besides changing the color of his skin. There's no proof that it's responsive to anything other than his desires."

"We have every reason to trust the reliability of Corporal Westlake's powers," said Craig. "We'd appreciate it if you came with us—"

Boos and angry roars began to echo in the convention center. Westlake looked nonplussed by the reaction, while Agent Craig was unflappable. He acted as if he weren't outnumbered a hundred to one.

"There is no level to which the president will not stoop!" declared Sanders. "Trying to fob off responsibility for this—this debacle—on the people's choice for your next commander in chief? What do you intend to do, Agent Craig? Waterboard me? Lock me up in a room for days on end with no food, no water, because I'm categorized as a suspected terrorist and thus have no rights? That's how things work with you, isn't it?"

"Senator . . ." began Craig.

Sanders cut him off. "That's President-elect Sanders,

Agent Craig. That is the title that the American people have given me, despite everything that your president has endeavored to—"

"Aw, shut up!"

Astoundingly, the voice carried above the assemblage. No one was able to determine immediately where it was coming from, but Sanders recognized it immediately. It was obvious from the reactions of Craig and Westlake that they did as well.

Swaggering, confident, a head shorter than anyone near him, but walking as if he could take down anyone who got in his way, Wolverine shoved his way up the middle aisle. He seemed to have appeared out of nowhere. He called out, "Mazone was set up! The same shape shifter who passed himself off as Matthew Hayes faked being Mazone. And that put you in the driver's seat. You're the only one who benefited from all this."

"And why should anyone believe you?" said Sanders.

"They don't have to. They can believe one of the guys who was behind it . . . Matthew Hayes's father. He's right here."

"Right where? Are you out of your mi—?"

And suddenly, Matthew Hayes and his father, Robert Hayes, appeared out of thin air. Matthew blinked furiously in the glare of the news cameras that had all turned on him. No one could hear anyone say anything, because everyone was shouting at the same time. Matthew cowered against his father, who held him tight and looked protective and determined to keep the others away from his son.

"Go away!" shouted Matthew.

"Senator, you're coming with us!" Craig said, and Sanders yanked away, fury in his face.

The Secret Service moved toward Craig and toward Matthew Hayes. Matthew looked more and more terrified, and the wheels were completely coming off the Sanders bandwagon . . .

And that was when the earthquake hit.

To just about anybody else there, it must have felt like an earthquake. Logan, however, knew all too well what had just happened.

This was stupid . . . this was stupid. It was a showboat stunt . . . it was stupid.

They had arrived in a Washington, D.C. that seemed to be the middle of a war zone. Logan had contacted the only man he could trust in this situation, and that was General Doyle. Doyle brought Logan up to speed immediately and told him where Westlake and Craig most likely were at that point. As it happened, the three of them hadn't been all that far from the convention center. Leaving the seaplane bobbing in the Potomac, they had made their way over there and had entered unseen, courtesy of Haze's abilities. It had seemed their timing had been perfect.

What Logan had not counted on was Matthew Hayes flipping out. And he should have. He should have seen it coming. But he didn't, and because of that, everything went to hell.

With the crowd pressing in from all sides, with everything that he'd been through, it was perfectly understandable that Matthew reacted the way that he did. And what he did was bring his hands together, interlace his fingers, and, in pure self-defense, unleash his concussive power.

The air transformed into something very tangible, and it blew apart the crowd, blasted chairs, sent cameramen sprawling every which way, and, most significant, smashed a hole in the far side of the building.

"Get him under control!" Logan shouted at Haze.

Haze grabbed his son, fixed a look on him, and started speaking to him softly, so softly that Logan couldn't hear anything he was saying. Matthew's eyes glazed over, and a passive smile flickered across his face.

Craig's people were moving in from all directions, and Westlake was now at Logan's side, gaping in astonishment at Matthew Hayes. "Is . . . is that really him?"

"Yeah. Sanders. Where's Sanders?"

He could see by the furious look on Agent Craig's face that Craig didn't know the answer to that any more than he did. In the pandemonium, the sheer insanity of everything that was going on, Sanders had slipped out.

"I'll find him," Logan said tersely to Craig. He turned to Haze and warned him, "Don't even think of running.

You do, and I'll find you." And before Craig could say or do anything else, Logan was off.

Despite everything that was happening, despite the screaming and shouts of confusion and people running every which way, Logan was on the scent. He shoved people out of the way, leaped over others, and anyone who even thought about challenging this arrogant runt who was getting physical with them took one look at the expression on his face and gave him plenty of room.

Logan barreled through the convention center. For a moment, the scent seemed to lead him outside, but then he caught a faint whiff that led off in another direction. Up. A flight of stairs to the upper offices had been laid open by the blast, and Logan now could determine that Sanders had headed there. Logan charged up the steps, taking two and three at a time. His claws were out; he was tossing aside caution. If Sanders was going to try to ambush him on the way up, let him. Logan was utterly confident in his ability to cut his way through anything that Sanders would throw at him.

He hit the upper floor, but the scent continued upward. The roof. He was making for a rooftop escape. Logan could just see it: a helicopter swooping down and whisking him away.

He burst through the rooftop access door, claws bared, and—anticipating an attack—leaped into a forward roll and came up ready for anything.

Sanders was at the far side of the roof, calmly smoking a cigarette. He was wistfully gazing up at the night sky. He turned his attention toward Logan and smiled wanly. "That's a very dramatic pose. Kudos."

"To you as well," Logan said cautiously, slowly advancing. "Giving the slip to the Secret Service. Not an easy job."

"Oh, I imagine they'll be along soon enough." He took a slow drag on the cigarette and blew the air out. "The stars are lovely, you know. I never get tired of looking at them. Not ever. And considering how long I've been looking at them, that's saying something."

"Yeah? How long's that?"

"Longer than I care to think. Longer than you'd care to know. I see you keep moving toward me. Do so if it pleases you. It's of little relevance to me." He half smiled. "What do you imagine is going to happen here, Wolverine? Do you think I'm going to be dragged in front of the American people? Subjected to endless investigation? Wind up in jail or get tried for treason? Or maybe you think I'm hoping that I'll be able to explain everything away and thus hold on to the office of president." He let out more smoke. "That's not how it works. That's not how I work. No point in it when time is on my side."

"You're wrong. Your time's running out."

"No, it's not. My time never runs out. You have no idea what you're dealing with."

"Y'know, I've lost track of the number of guys I've killed who've said that very thing."

"Heh. Touché," said Sanders. "But you still don't understand, Wolverine. For me, it's less about the power itself than how I go about acquiring it. Having power— that got boring for me quite some time ago. I'm all about the means now. Otherwise, it's too easy. People will welcome me into their hearts and minds willingly time after time. History's proven that."

"No one's going to welcome you into anything, Sanders."

"Of course they will. They'll forget. They always forget. Within another twenty years, the majority of high-schoolers will have only the vaguest idea who Adolf Hitler was. Not one in fifty today could tell you that World War One was triggered by the assassination of Archduke Ferdinand. If you say, 'Oh, the humanity!' it prompts laughter rather than recalling hundreds of people dying horribly in an explosion. One generation's calamity is another's trivia question. There's no need for me to hang about and make a fuss today, when tomorrow beckons. And for a dragon . . . there's always more tomorrows. Be seeing you."

Logan lunged toward him, covering the distance between them in barely two seconds. But that was more than enough time for Sanders to step off the edge of the roof.

"Freeze!"

The rooftop was suddenly alive with Secret Service agents. They were swarming toward Logan like a wave of insects. Logan ignored them, getting to the edge and peering over, looking for some sign of Sanders's body.

There was nothing. No . . . not quite nothing . . .

Then the agents were all over him, grabbing him, shoving him down, putting guns to his head, cuffing him. Logan offered no resistance. There seemed no point to it. These guys were just trying to do their jobs. Why should he bust the cuffs and cut them to ribbons? There'd be plenty of time to sort things out later.

Everything they were shouting at him was reduced to a sort of general, distant buzzing. Logan was busily processing what he'd seen. It was odd—he hadn't quite "seen" it but instead more perceived it vaguely, like something out of the corner of his eye. A separate patch of shadow against the darkness that had wavered for a moment and then dissipated. And the words echoed in his mind . . .

There's no need for me to hang about and make a fuss today, when tomorrow beckons.

32

LOGAN SAT IN THE SMALL ROOM AT BNE HEAD-quarters with his feet propped up on the desk, his hands behind his head. The chair was tilted back slightly, and his eyes were closed. He didn't bother to open them when someone entered the room. There was no need.

"Am I supposed to pretend you're asleep? How are we working this?"

Logan lazily opened his eyes. "Any way you want to, General."

General Doyle was carrying a briefcase tucked under his arm. He dropped it on the table and remained standing. Even if he'd been wearing jeans and a T-shirt, everything about his deportment would have screamed that he was military.

"My God, Logan . . ."

"I found the kid."

"Yes, you found the kid. But my God . . ."

"What am I being charged with?"

"Nothing."

"Huh. And after they spent six hours asking me what I did with Sanders, I figured sure they'd at least want to take a swing at—I dunno—treason. Or maybe they just got sick of my saying, 'He jumped off the roof and vanished.'"

"The fact that you passed three different polygraph tests with that stupid story probably didn't help."

"Prob'ly not. Then again, I have a feeling you might have had something to do with getting me kicked."

"Actually, it came from higher up."

Logan raised an eyebrow. "Yeah?"

"Yeah."

The door opened again, and several Secret Service men walked in. Logan found it amusing the way they scanned the room as if an assassin might somehow be hiding in a corner or under a table.

"Clear," said one of them.

A few moments passed, and then the president of the United States walked in.

Logan didn't think much of the guy but nevertheless got to his feet and tilted his head in greeting.

"Appreciate the gesture, Logan," said the president. He glanced around and said, "Gentlemen, could we have the room, please?"

The nearest agent clearly wasn't happy about that. "Sir, from a security standpoint, that wouldn't be the wisest—"

"If Logan wanted to kill me, do you seriously think you could stop him?" asked the president with a touch of amusement.

Logan smiled his most winning smile. Even that didn't look especially pleasant.

Clearly against their better judgment, but in tacit acknowledgment of the truth of the president's words, they cleared out. Moments later, Logan was facing the leader of the free world.

"I wanted to say thank you," said the president. "For finding the boy."

"He with his mom?"

"Yes."

"And his dad?"

"In custody. He stated that you could verify his story. That he had his son's best interests at heart."

"He did. Doesn't mean I wouldn't lock him up for the next century. He was in this up to his ass. You don't just claim good dadship and walk away from that."

"The boy's a mutant."

"Yeah," said Logan. "Like his father. Still don't think the father's the best one to look to as a role model."

"Role models are hard to come by." He looked questioningly at Logan. "Do you think I did the right thing?"

"Why should you care what I think? I'm not even a citizen."

"I know. Still . . ." His voice trailed off.

Logan shrugged. "I think you did what you thought you had to do."

"And . . ."

"And I think it showed a complete distrust of the system you swore to defend. I think you were compelled more by your ego than by a need to defend the Constitution."

The president stood there, frozen-faced. "They say it takes a good deal of courage to speak truth to power."

"Mr. President, with all due respect, you rely on an entire system of government to protect you and to get things done for you. I rely on me. So who's really the one with power?"

A long silence.

"We done?" said Logan.

"Yes," the president said tonelessly. "Yes, I think we are. I think it's time for you to go back to your world . . . and for me to go back to mine."

"Wouldn't trade it for anything," said Logan.

He remained standing, thoughtful, long after the president had left.

The photographers and news crews had left.

The various government officials also had long departed.

The only ones left in the living room of the Hayes house were Ellen Hayes herself and Corporal Tony Westlake. Several live-in health-care workers were in the house, courtesy of the U.S. government. They were attending to Matthew, dealing with any signs of posttraumatic stress disorder, and they were also taking care of Ellen, who—although she was well enough to be released from the hospital—wouldn't be back at full strength for weeks.

At that moment, though, Ellen and Westlake were alone in the room.

She was sitting in her overstuffed easy chair, looking distant. Westlake sat on the couch adjacent to her, concern on his face.

"I'm going to be heading back to Fort Randolph," he said to her gently. "But I just want you to know, if you need anything, anything at all . . ."

"I . . ." She was quiet for a long moment. "What should I do about Matthew?"

"About him? What do you mean?"

"He's a . . ." She stopped, gulped, and looked at Westlake. "He's one of you. How am I supposed to . . . it's all too much . . . Bob alive, and my son is . . . I don't know what he is, and . . ."

"It's going to be okay."

"You can't say that. You can't know that. How can you even believe that?"

"Because I truly believe that God doesn't give us any more than we can handle."

She laughed bitterly at that. "What a nice philosophy."

"I really think that."

"Can you stay?"

Westlake blinked in confusion. "Stay?"

"Here. With me. With us. I mean, just for a while. Just as a friend, you understand. I . . . it's too much . . ."

"Look, Ellen . . ." He took her hand in his. "Don't think I haven't thought about that."

"You saved my life. I know I can depend on you."

"You can depend on yourself. You're stronger than you know. No, really, you are," he said when she tried to look away. "I have faith in you. And I will come and visit. And over the long term . . . who knows? And if you need more help . . ." He reached into his shirt pocket and produced a business card. She took it and looked at it in confusion.

"School for Gifted Youngsters?" she said.

He nodded. "It's for, well, kids like Matthew, frankly. If you think that's what's best for him, it's a resource you can draw on. It's your . . . consider it a fallback position."

"I don't know," she said. "I don't know what to do."

"Yeah, you do. In your heart, you know exactly what to do."

She considered and then said, with a hopeful look on her face, as if she were praying she were answering a final exam question correctly, "Hug my son?"

He smiled and nodded.

He helped her to her feet then. She could walk just fine, but she was still slow getting up, and she winced a bit from the strain on her chest. She hugged Westlake then and kissed him on the cheek. She headed up the stairs. Westlake watched her go, picked up his hat, and headed out the door.

To his lack of surprise, Logan was leaning against an Army Jeep at curbside.

"Figured you'd be here," said Westlake.

Logan shrugged. "Everybody's gotta be somewhere. So . . . offer's still open."

"Offer?"

"You'd make a hell of an X-Man."

"Ohhhh, yeah," said Westlake. "That's a large part of what your involvement was all about, wasn't it?"

"Yup. So?"

"So," Westlake said, "my opinion hasn't changed. I still think sequestering yourselves—ghettoizing yourselves—isn't going to help the cause of mutants one bit. You've got to be out there mingling with the public, being part of the mainstream. I mean, look at everything that just happened. Here we are, you and me, high-profile mutants who helped solve a national catastrophe. A new election has been rescheduled for next month. Mazone, cleared of all charges, will be back in place. And . . ."

"And what?" said Logan. He reached into the back of the Jeep and pulled out a selection of newspapers. "You think that the fact that you and I helped solve everything makes a difference? Check the headlines. Read the stories."

Westlake started sifting through the newspapers. He saw what Logan was talking about. Every single story focused on "evil mutants" or, even better, "evil terrorist mutants" having been responsible. Neither Westlake nor Logan factored heavily into any of the reportage. Evil mutants had been behind the kidnapping. Sanders, still a wanted man, was an evil mutant at large. Evil mutants were still in hiding, threatening American interests.

"What's that tell you?" said Logan.

And Westlake, to Logan's surprise and also to his own, laughed.

"Tells me that there's a lot more work to do. But I'm a mutant in the Army, and if I decide to live my life in the service of my country or eventually try something else, I'm still not going to hide away. I'm not going to be driven underground just because of people's prejudices. I'm going to let everyone know that we're here, we're near, and we're staying. And I know you disagree."

"I do," said Logan as he climbed into the driver's side. Westlake got into the passenger's seat next to him. "I disagree. On the other hand, I kind of agree."

He turned the ignition, and the engine roared to life.

"Do you?" said Westlake.

"Yup."

"So if you kind of agree with me, then that makes me kind of right."

"Mebbe."

"What does that make you?"

Logan looked at him with an utter deadpan and said, "The best there is."

He gunned the engine, and the Jeep rolled away while, upstairs, Ellen Hayes held her son close to her and faced an uncertain future.

About the Author

Peter David is the *New York Times* bestselling author of more than sixty books, including numerous *Star Trek* novels, such as *Imzadi*, *A Rock and a Hard Place*, *Before Dishonor*, and the incredibly popular *New Frontier* series. He is also the author of the bestselling movie novelizations for *Spider-Man*, *Spider-Man 2*, *Spider-Man 3*, *The Hulk*, *Fantastic Four*, and *Iron Man*, and has written dozens of other books including his acclaimed original fantasy novels *Sir Apropos of Nothing*, *The Woad to Wuin*, *Tong Lashing*, and *Tigerheart*.

David is also well known for his comic book work, particularly his award-winning run on *The Hulk*, and has written for just about every famous comic book super hero.

He lives in New York with his wife and daughters.